"Very sensual and exciting. Renaud is male intensified, and Aleysia is just the woman to match him. If you like a sexy true-love story, I highly recommend this one."
—*Fresh Fiction*

"A passionate historical tale . . . breathtaking! When I see the name Julia Templeton on the cover of a historical novel, I know within the pages is an extraordinary read. *The Bargain* was that and more; it consumed me for hours! I had to know what was next for these wonderfully dynamic characters. I savored this book and know without a doubt I will read it time and again."
—*Romance Junkies*

"Julia Templeton will blow you away with her latest super-hot erotic historical *The Bargain*. The Norman conquest is the ideal backdrop for this tale of loyalty, love, and courage. Perfectly balanced with enough eroticism to keep your attention, strong dynamic characters, and a fascinating historical period, *The Bargain* is one of the best buys of the month."
—*A Romance Review*

"A heated historical . . . Fans of late eleventh-century romances with torrid love scenes will enjoy the star-crossed tale."
—*Midwest Book Review*

"Four stars! Templeton weaves a sensual spell over readers in this erotic romance set during the time of the Norman conquest of England. She does a fantastic job of slowly developing the love story between Aleysia and Renaud, making their affair and the steamy sex scenes even more exciting."
—*Romantic Times*

RETURN TO ME

"Templeton takes us on a journey of the heart . . . and she gives us a love story we will never forget! I am looking forward to taking Mrs. Templeton's next voyage, wherever that may lead."
—*Night Owl Romance*

"Templeton has taken a chance here—and it works. I was glad I encountered these characters, and I look forward to Templeton's next work in the hope that she will continue to defy the predictable and ordinary."
—*All About Romance*

"An exciting tale."
—*Midwest Book Review*

SINJIN

JULIA TEMPLETON

APHRODISIA
KENSINGTON BOOKS
http://www.kensingtonbooks.com

APHRODISIA BOOKS are published by

Kensington Publishing Corp.
119 West 40th Street
New York, NY 10018

All Kensington Titles, Imprints, and Distributed Lines are available at special quantity discounts for bulk purchases for sales promotions, premiums, fund-raising, and educational or institutional use.

Special book excerpts or customized printings can also be created to fit specific needs. For details, write or phone the office of the Kensington special sales manager: Kensington Publishing Corp., 119 West 40th Street, New York, NY 10018, attn: Special Sales Department, Phone: 1-800-221-2647.

Aphrodisia and the A logo Reg. U.S. Pat. & TM Off.

ISBN-13: 978-0-7582-3815-3
ISBN-10: 0-7582-3815-0

First Kensington Trade Paperback Printing: October 2009

10 9 8 7 6 5 4 3 2

Printed in the United States of America

To my wonderful agent, Jim McCarthy.

1

London, England

Sinjin and his brothers had barely crossed the threshold into Madame Darion's Pleasure Palace, when they were welcomed by a bevy of whores in the large, smoke-filled room. Men of all ages lounged on gaudy red velvet settees and worn chairs, accompanied by alluring women who willingly offered what their wives or mistresses would not.

"Sinjin, you are everything a man should be."

Sinjin looked up from the pair of immense breasts belonging to Paris, a French whore who had straddled him mere seconds before.

Paris rotated her hips in a way that had Sinjin clenching his teeth. "And you are everything a woman should be, my dear." He lightly bit the slope of one luscious creamy-white globe.

Her rouged lips curved in a coy smile. "I imagine you say that to all your women, my lord."

"All my women?" He placed a hand over his heart, doing his best to look hurt. "Paris, you wound me."

"Everyone knows your reputation, my lord. What is the

nickname for you and your brothers—the Rakehells of Rochester? You are a wicked one, Sin."

He mentally groaned at the mention of the nickname that had been whispered throughout ballrooms and brothels from Rochester to London of late. True, he and his brothers had a fierce appetite for women, but to label them all as rakehells was a bit extreme. "You should not be listening to idle gossip, Paris."

"Do you mean to tell me the rumors aren't true?" She actually sounded disappointed.

"Not a word," he replied.

Her lips quirked. "Somehow I doubt that."

Sensing that someone watched him, he glanced to the right to find a full-lipped brunette dressed in a daring gown made of cream lace staring at him with a wanton smile. Tall and long-legged, she sat on a settee in a most arousing way, showing him in one glance what she had to offer.

Paris's fingers brushed through his hair, her nails digging into his scalp. Ignoring the brunette for the time being, he leaned in and kissed Paris, his tongue brushing against the seam of her lips, seeking entry.

She tasted of mint and brandy, but her technique left little to be desired—too little tongue and too much teeth.

"What's your pleasure, my lord?" she asked before kissing a trail to the sensitive curve of his ear.

Blood coursed through his veins, straight to his cock. "I am up for anything."

Her brows lifted as she looked down between them where his cock swelled against the fabric of his pants. "Yes, you most certainly are."

Paris's slender fingers slid down his chest and abdomen, past the band of his pants, to caress his cock from root to tip.

Setting his drink on a nearby table before he toppled it, he kissed Paris again, becoming ever aware of the brunette who watched them intently. Did he have enough money for a ménage à trios? he wondered, mentally calculating the money he had in his coat pocket. If all else failed, he could always send Jeffries back to the townhouse for more.

"Perhaps you can buy me for the entire night, my lord," Paris whispered against his lips, her hand gripping him tighter. "I will make it worth your while, I promise."

"I think we can do without the formality, love. Call me Sinjin."

"I'd rather call you Sin—because that's what you are—Sinful." She bit his lower lip and sucked on it. "I want every inch of your long, thick cock imbedded deep inside my hot, creamy walls."

Aroused by her sensual words, Sinjin could not keep the smile from his lips. "I am more than happy to oblige."

She lifted her skirts a little, and taking one of his hands within her own, guided him to her slick folds. "Do you feel what you do to me?"

"You're hot, sweet Paris."

"I'm on fire, Sin. Shall we venture up to my room?"

He was ready to ask if the brunette could join them when his brother Victor appeared out of nowhere, a concerned expression on his face. "Mother is here."

Sinjin shook his head, hoping he had misunderstood. "Pardon?"

Victor glanced nervously over his shoulder before turning back to Sinjin. "Mother is here, as we speak."

Sinjin laughed, but Victor did not share his amusement.

"I am not joking, Sinjin. Mother *is* here. Jeffries said she has been circling the block for the past five minutes." He brushed a hand through his dark curls, a habit he'd had since a boy, especially whenever he was anxious. "Where the hell is Rory? We've got to find him and get out of here."

Sinjin's heart slammed against his chest. Dear God, he *wasn't* kidding. Jeffries, their trusted valet and faithful servant, would never jest about something as serious as their mother staking out a whorehouse in Covent Garden in the dead of night. "What in God's name is Mother doing in London?"

"Looking for her sons, I imagine," Victor said absently. "We must get Rory and leave by the back way, posthaste."

Sinjin turned to Paris. "Show us the way out."

Paris frowned. "You cannot stay?"

"Not tonight, but I shall return, and when I do, I will make it up to you."

"Promise?" she asked, her lower lip jutting out.

"Of course," he said, having no such inclination. If their mother was in London, it meant his time in the fair city had come to an end.

"There he is," Victor said, relief in his voice as he located their youngest sibling. No surprise, Rory had a redhead up against the wall—his lower body moving in a suggestive motion. The whore's arms were wound tight about his broad shoulders, her fingers messing his too-long hair.

Victor tapped him on the shoulder, and Rory turned abruptly, looking none too happy about being interrupted. "Jesus Christ, Vic! Do you mind?" He glanced at Sinjin. "Bloody hell, you both look like you've seen a ghost."

"Even worse, I'm afraid," Victor said, grabbing Rory's jacket off the back of a chair and handing it to him. "Mother is here."

The color drained from Rory's cheeks as his gaze skipped to something, or rather someone, just beyond Sinjin's shoulder.

Sinjin's gut rolled, and the hair on the back of his neck stood on end. His worst fear was realized when his mother's voice rang out loud and clear from behind him. "You boys will be the death of me, I swear it!"

"What in heaven's name did I ever do to deserve such grief?" Betsy Rayborne placed an age-spotted hand over her heart. "I have been a good mother to the three of you, and what do I get in return—rumors of scandalous behavior, that's what. Do you know you have even acquired a nickname?" She shook her head in disgust. "The Rakehells of Rochester! How utterly humiliating!"

Sitting between his brothers on the only couch in their mother's opulent hotel suite, Sinjin remained silent. A difficult feat when Betsy kept berating him for his brothers' steady slide into a life of debauchery.

"I cannot count the number of times I have heard that deplorable nickname in the past few weeks. And you are in London, for God's sake! Why does all of Rochester know what you have been up to in London?"

"Mother, perhaps you should sit down," Victor said, concern marring his brow.

Betsy ignored the request and leveled him with a look that made him flinch.

"I could have perished from embarrassment last week when Lady Walbery said she had heard the three of you were servicing everyone from a certain duke's own sister to the lowest of servants." Her gaze shifted to Rory. "How many times have I told you not to dawdle with the help, darling? One time is all that is needed for you to regret your actions. Lord knows how many bastards you have scattered throughout England already. I do not desire a constant reminder of your insatiable lust running around one of my estates."

"Mother, they are mere rumors," Rory said, only to receive a ferocious scowl for his trouble.

"I dragged you and your brothers out of a filthy, dirty whore-house this evening. Please do not speak to me as you would to one of your many witless mistresses."

Rory swallowed hard.

None of them had a mistress at the moment, witless or otherwise, but Sinjin was not about to argue with her.

"And what kind of an example are you setting for your brothers, Sinjin?" she asked in a high-pitched voice that had him recalling a time from his youth when he had drank his father's vodka and refilled the bottle with water. His mother had seen to it, by way of a paddle she had nicknamed "the truth seeker," to give him his due. He had been unable to sit for a solid week.

"I am sorry for any distress I have caused, Mother."

He might have saved his breath, for she did not even hear his apology. "I honestly believed you invited Victor and Rory to London to convince them what mature, well-respected men of good breeding could accomplish with their lives. I had been so proud to hear how active you have been on the family's behalf."

He did not have the heart to tell her the only reason his brothers had traded the city of Rochester for London was because Rory's previous mistress had turned to stalking him whenever he'd leave the estate. "Mother, I am—"

"Instead, you encourage your siblings to live a hedonistic lifestyle I find absolutely appalling."

He glanced at the clock. They were nearing the quarter-of-an-hour mark and she did not look at all ready to stop her tirade.

She cleared her throat loudly and focused her attention on Victor. "When I heard rumors you had become involved with a London actress, I defended you to the end, telling all my friends how preposterous the very idea was, that you, my quiet, studious son, would never consider an actress as a love interest.

However, I have recently learned how very little I know about all of my sons." She pulled a kerchief from her sleeve and dabbed at an imaginary tear. "How could you not see through her lies, Vicky?"

When Victor opened his mouth to defend his actions, Sinjin elbowed him, and his brother wisely pressed his lips together.

"And what of you, Rory? True, you are handsome to be sure, as are all of my boys," she said with a smile that did not begin to reach her eyes, "but sometimes looks can be a curse. One day there will be a woman who comes into your life—and God willing, she will bring you to your knees."

Rory took a sudden interest in his boots.

"Looks fade with time, my dear boy. All you have is what is here." She pressed a hand to her heart. "This is what makes you the man you are. And start using *this* for a change," she said, tapping a firm finger to his forehead.

She paced the floor before them, arms crossed over her chest. "I always hoped you would each find the love of your lives one day. Indeed, I had hoped it would happen long before now, especially for you, Sinjin." She took a deep, steadying breath.

Sinjin straightened his shoulders, wary of her next words.

"You are over thirty now, Sinjin, and Victor and Rory, you are not far behind." She sighed dramatically. "I am not getting any younger, nor are the three of you. And that is why I have decided you shall all marry this summer."

Rory came off the couch like it had caught fire. "You mean *Sinjin* will marry, correct?"

Their mother's brows lifted nearly to her hairline. "*Sit* down, Rory."

Rory sat down, albeit slowly.

Sinjin felt Rory staring at him, no doubt hoping big brother would come to the rescue.

7

When Sinjin could once again catch his breath, he sat forward. "Mother, since I am the eldest, I assume you are specifically speaking to me?"

Betsy's lips split into a mischievous smile. "No, my dearest. By the end of this summer, *all* three of you will be married and well on your way to making your father and me the happiest of parents—and, God willing, grandparents."

Rory ran a trembling hand down his face. "Sinjin, for Christ's sake, do something," he muttered under his breath.

Taking his life in his hands, Sinjin stood. "It is rather ambitious of you to marry all of us off, wouldn't you say, Mother?"

She arched a brow. "You question my capabilities, dear?"

Oh God.

"Not at all, Mother. You are capable of anything you set your mind to." He chose his next words carefully, knowing full well they could be his last. "But would it not cause suspicion if all three of us became engaged at the same time?"

"Exactly!" Rory exclaimed. "The *ton* would think we were on the brink of ruin."

Betsy shrugged. "Or they would assume your parents have grown weary of your childish behavior—and finally gave you all an ultimatum."

Sinjin tried another tactic. "The end of summer is less than four months away, Mother. Most courtships last that long and oftentimes stretch longer. Then comes the wedding itself. Therefore, perhaps you could give this little venture a bit more time."

"Do not think for a moment I will relent on this matter." She pursed her lips in a way that made Sinjin nervous. "I am tired of waiting for the three of you to settle down, so I have no choice but to put your feet to the fire, so to speak. Hear me and hear me well, my dears. Each of you *will* marry, and you shall do so by summer's end."

"Sinjin is right, Mother. This seems all rather ambitious," Victor said, a slight edge to his voice.

"Ambitious? Yes, perhaps it is," she said, picking an imaginary string from her skirts. "However, I am extremely motivated."

Feeling the invisible noose growing tighter about his neck, Sinjin asked, "Father knows of this?"

Betsy nodded. "Not only does he know . . . he encourages the plan. In fact, it was your father who came up with the ingenious idea to throw a party at Claymoore Hall to find potential brides for each of you."

Rory brushed his hands through his hair. "And what if we refuse?"

Betsy smiled genuinely for the first time all evening. "You will lose everything."

2

Katelyn Davenport watched the passing landscape out the carriage window, relieved to be away from the stuffy mansion that had been her prison these past three weeks. Not even the gray clouds overhead could dampen her spirits.

"I am sorry to take you away from your betrothed, Katelyn. Was Lord Balliford terribly disappointed you left Rose Alley?" Marilyn asked, twirling a lock of dark hair around her finger.

Katelyn forced a smile. Only ten months apart in age, the two shared everything. However, for the first time in her life, she struggled with keeping the truth to herself in order to ease Marilyn's fears about her upcoming marriage. "I dare say, Ronald is so busy with his ledgers and looking after the crops, he will scarcely know I have left."

"How very dreadful," Marilyn murmured, patting Katelyn's knee. "How come you did not mention this in your letters? Here you had me believing you were happy."

Unable to stand the sympathy in her sister's steady blue gaze, Katelyn looked out the window again, catching a glimpse of her reflection as she did so. Dark circles framed her green eyes, and her auburn hair made her pale skin seem even more so.

"Katelyn, what is it?"

Katelyn glanced at her sister. "I did not mention my unhappiness because I did not want you spending your time worrying about me."

"I am your sister. I will always worry about you." Marilyn pressed her lips together. "What is life at Rose Alley really like?"

More horrible than you could possibly imagine. "The only time I see Ronald is at dinner, which I suppose can be a godsend."

"Why is that?"

"He hands out few compliments and always finds something wrong in my appearance."

"Such as?"

Katelyn shrugged. "Such as . . . the neckline of my gown is far too low to be considered ladylike, or I am not sitting up straight enough. He says I am too thin, and yet when I put more than one lump of sugar in my tea, he warns me that I do not want to grow fat."

"He is one to talk! Has he looked into a mirror?" Marilyn shook her head. "I am so sorry, Kate."

"At least his sister keeps me company, or else I would die from boredom."

"Ah, yes, Meredith, who plays the constant chaperone. How old is she?"

"I would say forty . . . or perhaps a bit older."

Marilyn winced. "Why did she never marry?"

"I asked her that question, and she quickly changed the subject. All I know is that Meredith saves me from having to say much at all when we are with Ronald." *And I am so relieved that is the case.* "They are as close as siblings can be, and from what I gather, they count very much on each other's opinion."

"Tell me—having spent the past month in Lord Balliford's company, can you envision yourself bound to him for the rest of your life?" Marilyn asked, watching Kate closely.

Katelyn's throat tightened. "If it had not been for Father leaving us destitute, I would not."

"Then don't marry him."

"I have no choice."

"Everyone has a choice, Kate."

"Not in this case. Mother would have my head if I broke the engagement."

"Then perhaps Mother should marry Lord Balliford instead of you."

Katelyn laughed. "If only."

"Well, I for one could not imagine making love to an old man. Indeed, I would flat-out refuse, regardless of what Mother says."

Katelyn's stomach twisted, and she felt nauseated at the very thought of sharing Ronald's bed. "Lord Balliford is six and forty, which is far from ancient. Sally Rappaport married Lord Hammond last year, and he is just shy of his seventieth birthday."

"At least she shall be a widow soon."

Katelyn respected the way her sister spoke her mind without thought of consequence. She, herself, could never be so forthcoming. In fact, she always thought about what she was going to say before the words left her mouth, a habit formed after years of standing up to her mother, and paying for her "willfulness" by way of a mouthful of soap or a sharp slap across the face.

Marilyn sat forward, her eyes narrowing. "Tell me you do not cringe when you think about having sex with that man, Kate."

"I dread my wedding night, Marilyn. More than I've ever dreaded anything in all my life."

A smile touched Marilyn's lips. "Then break it off with him, Kate," she said, taking Kate's hands within her own. "Do it now before it is too late."

"Ronald has already paid off Father's debts in full and given Mother a generous allowance—one that will keep her in the style of which she has grown accustomed."

"How do you know this?"

"Ronald told me himself the day I arrived at Rose Alley, and he reminds me whenever he pleases, which seems to be daily."

"What a gentleman," Marilyn said flatly. "You will not marry him just so our mother can wear pretty gowns and keep her place in society."

"But we would be on the streets if not for Lord Balliford, Marilyn."

"Aunt Lillith would take us in. She has said as much, and on several occasions. Mother just refuses to accept her help."

"Mother does not wish to leave London. She detests Bath."

"Aunt Lillith would allow us to stay with her at her London townhouse."

Katelyn knew her mother would never relent. "Mother will not accept such charity. Her pride would not allow it."

"No, she would rather make you miserable by marrying you off to a man you despise, and all so *she* will be happy. It matters not at all that you do not wish to marry."

How many nights had Katelyn lain awake thinking the very same thing, her fury and resentment toward her mother growing stronger by the day.

"Now I know why Mother shipped me off to Bath the day before she told you about your engagement to Lord Balliford."

"She knew you would protest the marriage."

Marilyn nodded. "Exactly, and she knew you would do as

she asked, without thought of yourself. When I received your letter telling me the news of your engagement, I felt sick at heart knowing you were sent away with Lord Balliford before we had the opportunity to speak. That is the only reason I agreed to attend this event at Claymoore Hall on the condition you acted as my chaperone until Aunt Lillith could come."

"I am so grateful you asked me."

"I knew Mother had a previous engagement in London, so she could not attend."

Katelyn wondered if Marilyn knew that their mother had been sighted with a twenty-one-year-old tradesman's son. Apparently, they had started a heated affair when she'd been visiting a good friend and the young man had come around with a delivery.

Marilyn squeezed Katelyn's hands within her own. "We have seven days until Aunt Lillith arrives, and in that time we must come up with a plan to break off your engagement to Lord Balliford."

Katelyn stared into her sister's blue eyes, and for the first time in weeks felt a glimmer of hope.

"If I break the engagement, rumors will circulate, which could possibly destroy any chance of you finding a man to marry. Our family could be ruined. What would others—"

"Will you stop worrying about what other people will do or say? Forget them and forget Mother. Lord knows she has forgotten about your happiness. Has she asked you even once how you feel about marrying Lord Balliford?"

"Never."

"Exactly, Kate. Because she doesn't care."

Katelyn swallowed past the lump lodged in her throat. "I will think on it, but for now I want only to enjoy myself these next two weeks while we're in the country."

"Fair enough," Marilyn replied, glancing out the window, a pleased smile curving her lips.

"Tell me more about this party. Your letter said very little."

Marilyn's eyes lit up. "Well, it is rumored that Lord and Lady Rochester are quite determined to find wives for all three of their sons."

"All three at once?" Katelyn replied, grateful the subject had been changed.

"Yes, all three," Marilyn said, brows lifted high.

"How very ambitious."

"Finding wives should not be too difficult. After all, they are called the *Rakehells of Rochester*—each wickedly beautiful and with a scandalous reputation to match. You should hear some of the stories."

Katelyn laughed under her breath. "The poor things. They must be positively horrified to know their days of licentious behavior are coming to an abrupt end."

Marilyn grinned. "I sincerely doubt they will stop their mischievous ways because of marriage."

"I wonder if they are truly as handsome as rumored," Katelyn said absently. "After all, one person's beautiful and another person's beautiful can be very different indeed."

Marilyn sat forward in the seat. "Well, they are all said to be tall, broad-shouldered, and have dark hair and lovely light-colored eyes. The youngest brother has been called a walking Greek god."

"A Greek god, no less!"

"Yes, he is said to have bedded every single woman in Rochester between the ages of sixteen and forty—both single and married women, mind you."

Katelyn frowned. "Sixteen and forty! I find that hard to believe."

"Perhaps, but it does make one curious, does it not?" Marilyn said with a wicked laugh. "I am anxious to see if the rumors are true. Who knows, perhaps one of the brothers will steal your heart, and then you will be forced to end this farce of an engagement with Lord Balliford."

"I would not count on it," Katelyn said, wondering if playing chaperone, especially in a house full of beautiful young men, all of whom were seeking wives, had been a wise decision. Would she leave feeling bitter and jealous, or relieved to be engaged to a mature man who, although strict and boringly proper, would give her a stable life?

3

The cacophony of noise coming from the parlor made Sinjin yearn to turn on his heel, return to his chamber, and not surface until the end of what would doubtless be a fortnight of horrific proportions.

Since arriving at their country manor the day before, he had been moody and on edge.

"Shoot me now," Victor said, slugging back a shot of their father's finest whiskey.

Sinjin glanced at Victor, who, wearing a new navy suit, had been uncommonly pale since the first prospective bride had stepped foot in Claymoore Hall at nine this morning. Since then, one carriage after another had unloaded giggling young women and their chaperones at the manor's main entrance.

Clapping his brother on the back, Sinjin said, "Come, Victor. It is only marriage, after all. You look as though you're attending a hanging, for God's sake."

"I think I would prefer a hanging right about now," Victor said, looking like he meant it.

As though on cue, the double doors to the parlor opened and a footman cleared his throat, ready to announce their entry, but Sinjin shook his head. The servant's eyes widened and he quickly shut the door with a loud bang.

"I think I might prefer death," Rory said, loosening his extravagantly tied cravat. "Jesus Christ, this thing is so bloody tight it's nearly strangling me. Oh, and speaking of . . . do you know what I dreamt last night?"

Sinjin fought to keep from smiling at his brother's dramatic pause.

"No, but do tell," Victor prompted.

"I dreamt I was shackled to a bed and allowed only food and water. And my wife, who, mind you, had no face, held a vicious-looking knife and stared maliciously at my cock. I need not tell you what she intended."

"No face?" Victor said, ignoring the last, most dramatic part of the dream. "At least you didn't see her face. Imagine if you had. It would ruin the suspense."

Rory narrowed his eyes. "What do you think it means, though?"

"I don't know what your dream means," Victor said, sounding irritated, "but I do know I could use another shot of whiskey. Where the bloody hell is Jeffries?"

"I've had four drinks already. It was get pissed or lose my mind," Rory said, yanking at a glove. "Christ, I hate these blasted things! Haven't worn them in years, but Mother insisted."

"We're to do everything by the book," Victor added, running his hands through his unruly hair. "Do you think it's too late to enlist in Her Majesty's Royal Navy?"

Rory snorted. "You, in the navy?"

Victor looked like he'd been socked in the face. "What the hell is that supposed to mean?"

Rory's lips quirked. "You hate confrontation. You always have. I just cannot imagine you—"

"And what, you're an expert because you have met a hundred different husbands on the dueling field? Why is it you must always fuck married women, Rory?" Victor asked, his voice dripping with sarcasm. "Have you not recognized the danger in such a pastime?"

Rory puffed out his chest. "I could beat any man with pistol or sword. Can you say the same?"

Victor rolled his eyes. "What an accomplishment."

Sinjin stepped between them. "We can stand and quarrel amongst ourselves all night, or we can open that door, walk into that room, and God willing, find women who are tolerable, so we can make our parents happy. Who knows, if I find a woman first, then perhaps Mother will not push so hard for the two of you to find brides."

Rory instantly brightened, his quarrel with Victor forgotten. "Do you think that might be the case?"

Victor glanced at Sinjin, his brows furrowed. "Mother never changes her mind. It is a nice thought, and I appreciate you putting yourself on the chopping block, but I think it will be to no avail. Mother is quite determined."

"There is always a first time for everything," Rory said, straightening his jacket.

Sinjin cleared his throat loudly, and as expected, the footman opened the door with great aplomb. To Sinjin's surprise, a good five dozen women looked back at them with wide smiles. One woman even burst into a fit of giggles until her chaperone elbowed her.

Sinjin's gut clenched with a sinking feeling as he looked around the long parlor of young ladies. There had been a reason his mistresses had not been of the peerage.

"Hello, my dears!" Betsy said as she came toward them, maternal pride shining in her brilliant blue eyes. She had certainly dressed for the occasion, wearing a new dress of yellow silk, complete with matching turban that covered her graying hair.

"Where is Father when we need him?" Rory asked absently.

Sinjin caught Victor's sideways glance. He had not told either of his brothers he had spoken to their mother about their father's absence. Every time he had brought up the subject, she had avoided it, but last night she had finally broke down and told Sinjin that his father was very ill. So ill he could not make the journey from their home in Rochester to Claymoore Hall. At that moment, Sinjin had realized exactly why their mother had given them the ultimatum to marry. Gerard Rayborne, tenth earl of Rochester, needed peace of mind before meeting his maker.

Though Sinjin did not like the idea of being forced into marriage, he was determined to find a bride so his father could die knowing his bloodline would continue. Plus, he'd had many years to sow his wild oats, and had had his fair share of lovers and experiences—not that he planned on remaining faithful after marriage.

God willing, his future wife was standing in this very room.

"Will you look at her," Rory said, bringing Sinjin up short. He followed his brother's gaze to two young women standing at the far end of the long parlor, standing in profile to him, looking out the open window, toward the garden. Just then a cool breeze tossed the silky auburn curls of the slightly taller woman.

Intrigued, Sinjin took another step into the room. The young lady wore a lovely green silk gown, the low bodice displaying nice, full breasts, slightly hidden by a lace modesty piece. She was slender but also had a bit of curve, which he liked as well. The blood in his veins warmed, swooping low into his groin.

Rory might have had the right idea. Earlier that afternoon, Sinjin had walked in on his little brother fucking the upstairs maid. He'd tossed the girl's skirts up and bent her over a chair. The blonde had been quite vocal, moaning and groaning, especially when she caught sight of Sinjin, who quickly backed out of the room.

"She's mine," Rory said, moving swiftly past him.

Sinjin grabbed his wrist. "Not this time, little brother."

Rory jerked his hand free. "That's not fair, Sin. I saw her first."

"For Christ's sake, you two—we are no longer children." Victor shook his head in disgust and pushed by both of them. "Let the lady decide which one of you she prefers. Who knows, she might surprise you both and want me." He flashed a cocky smile and, thankfully, walked off in the opposite direction of the lovely redhead.

Sinjin was thankful he was tall, giving him an advantage in a room full of people, the majority of whom happened to be of the fairer sex.

At least his mother had seen to it to invite a few other males to the party. It would have been exceedingly awkward otherwise.

Crossing the parlor, he straightened his cravat while keeping an eye on the beauty by the window. He smiled cordially as he passed through the crowd. He did not want to appear rude to those who wished to talk to him, but he had every intention of meeting the auburn-haired Venus before Rory swooped in and swept her off her feet.

One look at his brother and most women forgot how to speak.

Unfortunately for Sinjin, the woman in question had not so much as glanced in his direction, completely occupied with the goings-on outside, as was the brunette at her side.

21

His heart accelerated when she brushed a curl out of her face, her graceful fingers lingering on her slender throat. He mentally groaned. Already he yearned to kiss a trail down that long, elegant neck. Hell, he wanted more than that. He wanted her flat on her back beneath him.

Desire rushed through his body as he continued to stare. She had a lovely profile—full, luscious lips, high cheekbones, and a small, dainty nose.

He wondered what color her eyes would be. Maybe blue, perhaps brown, or green like her gown? Whatever the color, he had the feeling her eyes would be extraordinary—that *she* would be extraordinary.

She must have sensed his stare, because she abruptly turned and looked directly at him.

His heart literally skipped a beat. She *was* stunningly beautiful. Perfect in every way.

Perhaps marriage wouldn't be so horrible after all.

She seemed genuinely surprised by his attention. Indeed, with brow lifted high, she even went so far as to glance to her right, only to find no one there. He could see her hesitation as she met his gaze again.

He grinned, pleased to find a rose amongst weeds.

She flashed a quick smile, displaying perfectly straight white teeth and the slightest hint of dimples.

As he continued toward her, she looked somewhat startled, and took a step closer to her companion, whispering something in her ear.

The other woman turned to look at him and smiled coyly, showing large dimples. Such a brilliant smile. He looked from one woman to the other and saw a slight resemblance. Perhaps they were sisters?

He was within a dozen steps away from the lovely duo

when someone reached out and stopped his progress. Mrs. Livingston, a wealthy American widow, beamed up at him. "Sinjin, dear, I would like you to meet my daughter, Suzanne."

Suzanne was not unattractive, nor was she a beauty, but she had expressive eyes, which roamed over every inch of Sinjin's body. Rumor had it the young American had fallen in love with one of the slaves on her father's impressive Virginia plantation. The man in question had disappeared and her mother had whisked Suzanne away, intent on finding a wealthy, titled husband in order to stop the gossipmongers.

The young American would be a fun companion, but the last thing he needed was to worry about his wife fucking someone else.

No, that would not do at all.

At the first break in conversation, Sinjin excused himself and breathed a sigh of relief to see Rory was occupied with a group of young women.

Grateful for the diversion that gave him the upper hand over his brother, Sinjin reached the beautiful sisters and bowed. "Good afternoon, ladies."

They curtsied. "Good afternoon, my lord."

"I am Sinjin Rayborne, but my friends call me Mawbry."

"I am Marilyn," the brunette said, who nodded to her companion. "And this is my sister, Katelyn. We are the daughters of the late Lord Melton."

He bowed. "Marilyn and Katelyn, let me be the first to welcome you to Claymoore Hall."

"Thank you, Lord Mawbry," they said in unison, and laughed gaily, the sound making him grin.

"Have you traveled far today?"

"From Sussex," Marilyn replied. "I enjoy traveling. I read most the way, or talked with Katelyn."

"And you, Katelyn? How did you find the journey?" His heart did a little flip in his chest as he stared into her brilliant green eyes, which matched the color of her gown perfectly.

"The journey was uneventful, thank you. Though I confess I did not travel as far as my sister."

He very much liked the sensual quality of her voice.

"Pray, why did you not travel as far as your sister?" he asked, curious.

She brushed her teeth along her full lower lip. Sinful thoughts raced through his mind at all the wicked things she could do with that lovely, full-lipped mouth.

"I have been visiting my fiancé at his home just outside of London."

His heart dropped to his feet. "Fiancé," he said, disappointment making his voice harsher than intended.

"Yes, my lord. I just recently became engaged."

"Her betrothed does not deserve her," Marilyn muttered under her breath, just loud enough for the three of them to hear.

"Marilyn," Katelyn said in a warning tone.

Sinjin straightened his spine, all ears. When she did not elaborate, he said, "It sounds as though your sister does not approve of your betrothed, Lady Katelyn."

Katelyn opened her mouth, when her sister cut her off.

"It is not that I don't like Lord Balliford. I just believe Katelyn should marry someone more suitable."

"Lord Balliford is plenty suitable, Marilyn," Katelyn said, anxiously glancing over her shoulder to be sure no one else had heard the exchange.

Lord Balliford? Where had he heard that name before, and why in the hell would Katelyn marry someone her sister so openly despised?

Katelyn looked down at her slippers and his gaze followed.

Ironically, the answer came to him when he glanced at her worn shoes. Now that he actually looked a bit closer, her gown fit a bit too snug on her large breasts and was a good inch too short.

Marilyn's clothing was in similar condition.

Their family had obviously fallen upon difficult times.

And suddenly it came to him where he had heard Lord Balliford's name. It had been over a card game with his good friend William, a wealthy merchant who kept up on all the local gossip. He'd said a bachelor, an earl, if memory served, with a quick temper and absolutely no personality had just paid a good sum for the hand of a beautiful young woman whose father had bankrupted them. Though the lady's father had been a viscount, he had squandered away his entire fortune on drink and gambling, leaving his daughters to atone for their father's sins.

Sinjin had thought the situation sad at the time, then forgot about it. Now that he faced this beautiful creature, knowing she had been sold to the highest bidder in order to save her family, he felt a rush of anger and deep sadness that he had missed the opportunity to marry her. And now, a somber, disagreeable man would have the privilege of taking this amazing woman to bed each night.

Damn, if only his mother hadn't made her ultimatum months ago.

"Do you know Lord Balliford?" Katelyn asked, shifting on her feet.

"Not personally. I have only just recently heard of him."

Rory approached, two glasses of champagne in each hand. Sinjin sent him a look that said to go away, but when did his little brother ever listen?

"Good afternoon, ladies," he said, interrupting them. Sinjin watched Katelyn's reaction to his sibling.

"Since my brother is lacking manners, I thought I would

offer you lovely ladies a refreshing glass of champagne," Rory said, an easy smile on his lips.

Sinjin refrained from pushing him out of the way.

"Thank you very much," Marilyn said, taking the glass he offered. Her gaze shifted slowly over Rory.

To Sinjin's surprise and relief, Katelyn did not seem to be as intrigued by Rory as her sister was. "Thank you for the champagne," Katelyn murmured, glancing past them to a group of women who kept moving closer.

Rory flashed Sinjin a cocky smile. "Sin, aren't you going to introduce me to these lovely ladies?"

"Of course. Ladies, let me introduce my brother, Rory. Rory, I'd like you to meet Lady Marilyn and Lady Katelyn."

Rory lifted Katelyn's hand slowly to his lips. "A pleasure to meet you."

4

Katelyn felt immense relief when Sinjin's brother joined them, and not because she found Rory more appealing than his brother—but rather she found Sinjin much *too* appealing.

Indeed, Sinjin was, as were all the Rayborne brothers, handsome to be sure, but not as handsome as his youngest sibling, whose beauty was downright staggering as to be uncomfortable. She could not imagine being married to someone so much more beautiful than herself.

In fact, she liked that Sinjin had a rugged masculinity about him that his brother lacked. Perhaps it was the thin, white scar above his right brow that made him less intimidating than Rory's perfect beauty, and Sinjin's blue eyes were positively lovely, framed by thick, long lashes. And she loved his deep, rich voice, not at all like Ronald's nasally tone that grated on her nerves.

Since Sinjin had approached them, Katelyn had wondered what it would be like to marry a man like the young viscount. A man whose bed she would love to share, to discover everything that could happen between two people . . . instead of dreading her wifely duties, something that haunted her since her engagement to Lord Balliford.

She envied the woman who would one day be Sinjin's bride, and wondered who in this room would win his heart.

Taking a sip of champagne, Katelyn's gaze fell on the eldest Rayborne brother again, glad he had turned his attention to Marilyn so she could stare without being obvious. She liked the way his long, dark hair curled at his collar, how wide his shoulders were, and how lean and narrow his waist. He was the opposite of Ronald in every way. Her betrothed's paunch extended far beyond the waistband of his pants. She knew that on several occasions he wore a girdle, since she could make out the bulky garment beneath his waistcoat and jacket.

She shuddered at the thought of seeing her fiancé naked. However, seeing Sinjin Rayborne naked would be an absolute delight. Her gaze shifted from Sinjin's hard abdomen to the material that cupped his prominent sex. She and Marilyn had studied a good deal of health books their Aunt Lillith had collected. Those books had always made her feel strange and eager to discover what happened between a man and a woman behind closed doors. Indeed, she had touched herself under the covers or in the bath, amazed at the way her body responded. What if a man touched her in such a way? A man like Sinjin Rayborne, for instance.

Marilyn cleared her throat and Katelyn looked up with a start. Her sister smiled at her above the rim of her champagne glass. How did she always seem to know what Katelyn was thinking?

Good Lord, who else in the room had witnessed her bold gaze?

Katelyn noticed how the women around them watched the brothers with an almost greedy look in their eyes. It was a bit sobering to realize that three women in this room could very well be engaged to the brothers by the end of the fortnight. Lucky, lucky girls.

She felt so cheated, so angered that she herself would not be in the running. All her life she had hoped she could pick her own mate, fall in love, and build a family and a future together.

But those were the dreams of a young girl who fancied herself married to a man who adored her. Not a man who preferred spending time in his study, or with his sister, and at every given opportunity told her what she was doing wrong.

Marilyn cleared her throat and Katelyn glanced up. "I'll be right back." Katelyn headed for the nearest doorway, receiving glares from the women she passed. They were no doubt furious that two of the Rayborne brothers had approached her and Marilyn immediately. She had never expected such attention. Strangely, she felt no excitement or anticipation—just bitter disappointment that she was already spoken for.

And that is why she must clear her thoughts, steady her nerves, and return to the parlor and help her sister land a Rayborne brother for her husband. Despite what Marilyn said, Katelyn knew it was silly to hope for something that could never be. Her mother would never relent when it came to Katelyn marrying Lord Balliford and allow her to marry someone else.

Her sister deserved to be happy, and she would do what she must to make sure that happened. If not, Marilyn would end up like Katelyn, married to an old man whom she had nothing in common with, and facing a lifetime of loveless matrimony.

Crossing into the hallway, she heard women's voices approaching, so she slipped into the first room to her right.

It appeared to be a study, with dark paneling and lots of tomes stuffed into tall bookcases. The drapes had been pulled and she welcomed the darkness, the only light slipping in through a small gap in the curtains and from the embers burning in the grate. She walked toward the fireplace and stared down at the charred coals.

She had seen Sinjin's gaze fall in the vicinity of her faded silk shoes and the short hem of her old gown. Her embarrassment had been intense, but thankfully when she looked into his eyes, she did not see pity or judgment. Just kindness . . . and something else she had not expected.

Desire.

Lord help her, but Katelyn desired Sinjin Rayborne with a desperation that frightened her. Never had she expected to experience such an immediate attraction to another person. She felt exhilarated and horribly frustrated about her circumstance.

The door opened, and Katelyn brushed trembling hands down her face. "Marilyn, I'll be out in a moment. I just need to catch my breath."

"What is wrong, Katelyn?"

Katelyn gasped. It was Sinjin Rayborne, and instead of leaving, he came closer. So close she could feel the heat of his body. She took a quick step back, ran into the mantel, and nearly knocked a picture off the ledge before righting it. He made her so nervous!

And good lord he smelled lovely—a mixture of sandalwood, fine brandy, and a masculine scent that was all his own.

"Why did you run away, Katelyn?"

"I didn't run."

"Yes, you did." He stood before her now, his presence all-consuming. His dark suit must have cost more than her yearly allowance—the fine material in such stark contrast to her faded gown.

"I run from my circumstance, not from you," she managed, looking at him, mesmerized once again by his beauty. He was everything a man should be—everything she had hoped her intended *would* be.

He reached up and lifted her chin with gentle fingers, his thumb brushing over her bottom lip.

His touch was sheer heaven.

"Sweet Kate," he said, a second before his lips claimed hers.

Somehow her arms encircled his neck and her breasts pressed flush against his wide chest. She couldn't get close enough, wanting to feel every inch of his hard body against her own—a delicious feeling she would relive every moment of every day for the rest of her life.

The kiss grew deeper, his hand holding the back of her head like she would flee. She had no such inclination. Indeed, nothing, and no one, could pull her away from this man at this moment.

Heat flooded her veins, coursing through her body. Now this is what it felt like to be desired and to desire in return. A white-hot need had her insides twisted in a tight knot. "I want you," she whispered against his lips.

He pulled away slightly.

Oh dear God . . . had she said the words aloud? She opened her eyes to find herself looking into intense blue eyes. His hands bracketed her face. "What did you say, sweet Kate?"

"Nothing," she blurted.

The sides of his mouth curved in a knowing smile, and she wondered if he would be so cruel as to laugh at her. She could not stand it if he did, and nearly told him as much when his lips brushed against hers again. "Don't ever be afraid to tell me your true feelings."

How different he was from Ronald, whom she was terrified to speak to for fear of him reprimanding her. Always, she had to be on guard with her intended.

"I want you, too, Kate. Most desperately."

His words thrilled her, making her think of long nights in his arms, discovering each other's bodies, making love until the early morning hours.

His hand moved to her breast and she did nothing to stop him. She yearned for his touch, ached for what he could show her. Long fingers plucked at a sensitive nipple, the sensation heating her blood, making the flesh between her legs pulse and ache.

She released a shocked gasp when she felt air against her naked backside. He had lifted her skirts, his fingers brushing along her inner thigh, then higher to the entrance of her sex. She swallowed hard as he cupped her there.

"You're already wet for me." He sounded pleased.

He slid a long finger inside her sheath, her inner walls squeezing him tight. Her breath caught—the feeling so wonderful, she groaned.

She kissed his neck as his thumb brushed her sensitive button again and again. He knew just how to touch her to make her heart race and her body sing, sensations she had always wondered about but doubted she would ever feel, especially after learning of her engagement to Lord Balliford.

A knock sounded and Sinjin moved quickly, bracing his foot against the door. He brought a finger to his lips, and desire pooled in her belly when she remembered where that finger had been mere seconds before.

Her gaze shifted over him slowly, taking in every single detail. She could not help the smile that came to her lips. How lovely he was, his hair slightly mussed from where she'd slid her fingers through the silky tresses. Handsome, powerful . . . and dangerous.

Never in a million years would she have envisioned such a scenario when she had left Rose Alley yesterday afternoon. She had expected a week of unchaperoned splendor with her sister until their aunt arrived, but never had she imagined that one of the Rayborne brothers would want her.

"The damn door is locked," she heard someone say on the other side.

She held her breath when the door handle turned, but thankfully, whoever it was, gave up seconds later, their footsteps fading down the hallway.

Thank God it hadn't been Marilyn. Her sister would have taken one look at Katelyn and known what had transpired.

Sinjin locked the door and turned to her, a wicked smile on his handsome face. "Now, where were we?"

Sinjin took Katelyn by the hand and led her toward the settee. He kissed her softly, savoring the taste of her sweet lips against his own. How tentative she was. So uncertain, so untried. He wondered if she had ever been kissed before. The way her heart pounded made him believe this could be her first time.

Oh, the things he could teach her.

She pulled away abruptly, looked at the settee, then back at him. "What do you intend, my lord?"

This was no light skirt he could tumble and then leave without consequence, nor did he want to. Katelyn Davenport was a lady, and should be treated as such.

A lady who is also engaged to another man.

He pushed the unwanted thought far from his mind.

Katelyn pressed her full lips together and he was reminded she had asked him a question.

He reached out and toyed with the curl resting against her collarbone. "What do I intend?" His finger slid from her hair, and he drew a line down to the slope of one lovely breast. "Why, I intend to kiss you, Kate."

She swallowed hard, then looked toward the door. "And what else, my lord?"

His lips quirked. "Do you not trust me?"

Her gaze returned to his. "Should I trust you, Lord Mawbry?"

He couldn't help but laugh at her serious expression. One second she said she wanted him, the next she looked ready to bolt.

She frowned and took a step back, nearly upending a side table in her haste. "I am engaged to another man," she blurted, steadying the table with a trembling hand.

The smile died on his lips instantly. "You need not remind me that you are spoken for."

He took a step toward her, and she immediately took another step back. Coming up against the settee, she let out a startled gasp as he kissed her.

One hand rested on her hip, the other brushed the hair from her lovely face. How delicate she appeared. Her every feature fragile in its beauty.

And that bastard Balliford would look into that beautiful face every day of his miserable life.

Some men had all the luck.

Sinjin wanted to tell her not to marry Balliford, and yet he could not very well ask her to marry him already. He was not a man to beg, and honestly, even after his mother's ultimatum, he felt that marrying was merely a contract, and a nuisance at best, but it would change very little of how he lived his life. He would take a wife . . . and go about his life as he always had. Indeed, his wife might prefer to live at one of his estates while he spent his time at another. He would still have his other women, take them to bed when he wanted, and when he grew weary of them, that was that.

And yet what would happen if he had a wife like Katelyn at home waiting for him? Would he get caught up in the excitement of having a lovely young woman as his bride, or would he quickly grow tired of her and move on?

Irritated with the path his thoughts had taken, he deepened the kiss and was pleased when she kissed him back. Quite exuberantly, too. Her right breast pressed hard against his bicep. He shifted slightly, jerked the modesty piece aside, and with little urging, brought the pert globe up enough to where a pale rose nipple appeared over the bodice of her gown.

He kissed a path down her neck and toward the nub that had tightened and extended. He tasted the delicate bud, and instantly Katelyn moaned, her fingers digging into his shoulders.

Using his teeth with caution, he sucked and laved her nipples slowly. He pulled her skirts up, feeling the smooth, creamy skin of her thighs against his fingers. She was perfection, every inch of her a lover's dream. Already he could feel the heat of her sex against his fingers. Soon, he vowed, he would be buried deep inside her honeyed walls, and together they would experience paradise.

"Oh dear God," she sighed against his shoulder. "That feels lovely."

He smiled inwardly, thrilled by her response.

5

Katelyn's entire body hummed with desire. Never could she have imagined that the act of making love could be so wonderful. Her body had come to life under Sinjin's touch, and as she looked down at him, watching him lick and nibble at her breasts, she felt a wave of pleasure wash over her, sending a sharp ache straight to the juncture of her thighs.

Sinjin urged her back onto the settee, following her down. He pressed fully against her, and her pulse stuttered when she felt the length of his arousal.

Her thighs fell open, and she instinctively lifted her hips. Sinjin's cock throbbed against her hot mound. All it would take was to unbutton his pants and slide home. She wouldn't deny him, not for a second. His hand slid beneath her skirts, splaying against her thigh, so close to the heat of her sex.

The musky scent of her essence penetrated his senses, and he couldn't resist. He slid his head beneath her skirts and inhaled deeply before he tasted her.

Katelyn's breath left her in a rush. Dear God, she could not believe he would do something so—so wicked and yet so utterly delicious.

He licked her again, and she arched her back, all thoughts evaporating as his hands cupped her buttocks and lifted her to his lips.

His tongue danced over her flesh, swirling around her swollen button, flicking back and forth, over and over again.

Her insides twisted and her heart pounded harder and harder as she climbed toward a pinnacle she had experienced only by her own hand.

As her fingers wove through his hair, she urged him to continue, with little moans and contented sighs.

Her cheeks turned hot as he lifted her skirts to her waist. How scandalously she was behaving, especially given the fact she was engaged and had only met Sinjin not thirty minutes ago.

Wicked, wicked woman.

She dared to look down to watch him as he pleasured her, and he chose that moment to look up. His wickedly beautiful eyes met hers. She watched with bated breath as his long tongue stroked her, the tip flicking against her nub, making her bite her lip. He sucked her delicate pearl and she cried out as sensation upon sensation rocked her entire body.

She closed her eyes and savored the feelings rushing through her, knowing that this could very well be the first and last time with this man.

Her sex throbbed and pulsed as he continued to tease her, her heart pounding harder and faster with each flick of his tongue. Her thighs clamped against him, her nails digging into his shoulders as she finally reached climax.

Sinjin watched Katelyn as she came—her expression one of wonder and desire, her moans and sighs making his cock impossibly hard.

Excitement and exhilaration rippled along her spine as Sinjin continued his oral play.

There was a reason the sinfully handsome lord had gained the reputation as a rake, and from where she lay, she could see he deserved it. Rightfully so. He was a master.

Sinjin slid a finger inside Katelyn's heat. He grit his teeth. God, she was so tight. He pumped his finger inside her, and she gripped him like a glove.

His cock strained against the material of his pants, begging to be buried deep inside her. He had never before had a virgin, and he ached to sample her.

His thumb brushed her sweet nub, and within seconds she cried out again, her inner muscles tightening around his finger, coating his hand with her juices.

Once the tremors passed, he removed his finger and kissed her belly, moving upward.

Katelyn was shocked when he kissed her, and when she tasted herself on his lips, she nearly pulled away.

Then she felt the solid ridge of his cock against her sex and she forgot about everything else. He moved his hips against her, and instantly her insides tightened. Her legs fell open farther, and she arched her hips against him.

He had not unbuttoned his pants, nor did it appear he was going to. In all honesty, she wouldn't have stopped him if he had. But as he continued to kiss her, he also continued to move his lower body, and the wonderful sensations of climax she had experienced minutes before began all over again.

As the minutes ticked by without any sign of Katelyn, Marilyn started to grow more uneasy. Her sister could certainly hold her own with most anyone . . . but Sinjin Rayborne wasn't just anyone.

He was an impossibly handsome man, and Katelyn was most assuredly smitten with him. Marilyn had seen the look of desire in her sister's eyes the instant Sinjin had approached them.

And the feeling was mutual. From the second he had joined them, Sinjin had eyes only for Katelyn. Indeed, many of the women in the room had sent her sister scathing looks as she passed by, but she did not seem to notice. She had been too occupied with her own thoughts, and Marilyn would almost guarantee those thoughts focused on Lord Balliford and her impending marriage. Perhaps Sinjin could talk some sense into Katelyn and convince her to call off her engagement.

What concerned Marilyn more than her sister's fragile state of mind was the fact that Sinjin had disappeared moments after Katelyn had excused herself, and neither one had surfaced since. And his family was starting to take notice. Rory kept watching the doorway the two had exited, while managing to hold his own in a conversation with a young lady who had joined them seconds after Sinjin's departure.

Marilyn didn't bother to excuse herself, as she had been absent from the conversation for the past few minutes anyway.

Slipping into the hallway, Marilyn noticed a white-haired chaperone turning the door handle to the first door on the right. Apparently, the door had been locked.

Marilyn had a feeling she had found her sister—and chances were, Sinjin Rayborne, too.

The chaperone appeared miffed, her brows furrowing. "What the devil?" she muttered to herself, trying the door again, to no avail. After several more failed attempts to enter the room, she finally gave an exasperated sigh and found immediate success with the door across the hallway.

Marilyn stepped up to the door and leaned close, hoping to

hear her sister's voice from within, but she was instead met with silence.

Her stomach tightened. She glanced over her shoulder, and finding the hallway clear, knocked lightly on the door.

No answer came. In fact, she couldn't hear anything but the myriad of voices coming from the parlor.

She knocked again, and this time she heard hurried footsteps, a pause, then the door swung open and Sinjin Rayborne appeared, looking slightly . . . rumpled from when she'd last seen him.

Oh dear.

His hair was mussed, his cravat not so intricately tied, and even more disconcerting was the fact he was being very careful not to open the door all the way. Her gaze slid to where his erection strained the material of his pants.

Her stomach twisted in a knot. Perhaps Katelyn had gone to their room instead? There was only one way to find out.

"Forgive me—I thought my sister might have come this way. I did not mean to disturb you and your comp—"

"Your sister is here."

Schooling her features, Marilyn lifted her chin. "Might I have a word with her?"

"Of course." He stepped back and motioned for her to enter.

One look at Katelyn and Marilyn knew the two had shared more than conversation. Indeed, Katelyn's entire neck was flushed, the modesty piece askew, and her coiffure had been severely compromised, with a few strands hanging free that had not been before.

The discrepancy would be noted immediately upon returning to the party, which would not do.

"Perhaps we should take a stroll about the gardens before returning to the parlor," Katelyn said, her voice sounding huskier than usual.

Marilyn nodded. "An excellent idea."

Sinjin brushed a hand through his hair and righted his cravat, checking his efforts in the mirror by the door. "I'll return to the parlor." His gaze skipped to Katelyn. "I look forward to the days ahead, Lady Katelyn."

Katelyn grinned like a schoolgirl. "As do I."

He slipped out of the room, and Marilyn counted to ten twice before she turned to Katelyn. "Tell me you didn't have sex with him."

Katelyn opened her mouth, then closed it as quickly.

"Oh dear God." Marilyn crossed her arms. "I know I encouraged you to enjoy yourself, but you really must be careful, Kate. You only just met the man."

"It is not what you think."

"Then please assure me that I am wrong, for you both look extremely rumpled and flushed. I just hope his valet catches him on the way back into the parlor, or speculation will be at a fever pitch."

"We merely kissed."

Marilyn frowned. "We are talking about Sinjin Rayborne, notorious rakehell and scoundrel. You did more than kiss, dear sister. I can see it in your eyes."

Katelyn's lips curved. "Oh, Marilyn, it was lovely. I cannot possibly put the experience into words."

Marilyn's heart missed a beat. "I fear I am going to regret this question, but pray, what *exactly* was lovely? Please be specific."

Truthfully, she had never seen Katelyn look so elated. Her cheeks were flushed a lovely shade of pink, her green eyes glowed from within, and her grin was so wide she looked positively giddy. "Never had I imagined being with a man intimately would be so—so wonderful."

Who knows, perhaps one of the brothers will steal your heart,

41

and then you will be forced to end this farce of an engagement with Lord Balliford. Marilyn's words from earlier today came back to haunt her.

Good gracious, what had she done? True, she had wanted Katelyn to find a way out of her impending marriage . . . and had hoped that one of the Rayborne brothers would perhaps take notice of her, but she had not anticipated this scenario at all.

No wonder the brothers had such wicked reputations. To corner an innocent lady in a room within minutes of a first meeting was surely something for the record books. Marilyn would have to be on her toes from here on out. Her sister's virtue depended on it.

"But you weren't alone for more than ten minutes. I am lacking in experience, to be sure, but—" She couldn't even say the words, for she knew that a lot could happen in a matter of minutes, and apparently it had from the expression on Katelyn's face.

Marilyn ran a hand down her face.

"You think me wicked?" Katelyn asked, her voice clearly distressed. "You do, don't you?"

Shaking her head, Marilyn managed a reassuring smile. "No, I do not think you are wicked. I am merely surprised, that is all. I just believe that it will be in your best interest to play slightly hard to get."

Katelyn straightened. "I did not make love to him, Marilyn."

Marilyn regretted being so stern when she could see Katelyn's good mood diminish and guilt start to take over.

"I am so glad you enjoyed yourself. You should, and I think tonight is only the beginning of what can be an incredible fortnight."

Katelyn's lips curved into a mischievous grin. "I think you are right."

Katelyn glanced at the clock on the bedside table and sighed. Marilyn had been snoring for hours. If only she were so lucky. She could not calm her thoughts for even an instant. After the intense interlude in the study with Sinjin, she had been too excited at what the future had in store for her.

Her body had been brought to life, and she wanted to experience the sins of the flesh with Sinjin Rayborne. Her body still hummed from where he'd touched her . . . and tasted her.

She smiled to herself, remembering the thrill of watching him pleasure her, the heat in his eyes as he'd looked up at her while his tongue danced over her sensitive pearl.

Even now her skin tingled in anticipation.

She glanced at her sister's back. Marilyn had not stirred for hours now and was sleeping deeply, her soft snores filling the room.

Katelyn's hand crept beneath the covers and she cupped her own breast, testing the weight in her hand, her thumb brushing over a sensitive nipple.

The peak instantly pebbled against her palm. Katelyn licked her lips and pulled lightly, tugging the same way Sinjin had.

Her heart picked up speed as liquid heat warmed her veins.

She closed her eyes, remembering the feel of Sinjin's hard sex scorching her belly and thigh as he moved against her. She wondered what it would feel like to have that solid length buried deep inside her, bringing her to the brink of ecstasy and beyond.

She peeked over at her sister, grateful to hear her steady snores.

Katelyn's hand slid down her belly and over the curls that

guarded her womanhood, her fingers brushing over the tiny pearl. She cupped her hips, seeking more contact, more friction.

Marilyn shifted slightly, and Katelyn's breath caught in her throat. She couldn't move, but when Marilyn sighed, her breathing continuing to be even, Katelyn once again continued to explore.

She imagined Sinjin's hands on her, focused on his face, his body.

The first stirrings of climax made her stomach tighten, and she lifted her hips off the mattress, pressing harder with her fingers.

Her flesh pulsed against her hand, throbbing hard, and she bit her lip, savoring the wonderful sensations rolling through her.

When the tremors passed, her hands fell from her body. She pulled her chemise back down and rolled onto her side. How wanton she had become in such a short time. Days ago, she would have never envisioned herself doing the wicked things she had done with Sinjin Rayborne in a dark study. But she had, and if all went well, she was determined she would experience everything between a man and woman with the renowned rake.

But you're engaged to be married, and perhaps tomorrow Sinjin will realize the folly in pursuing you. Her better judgment told her that she was a fool to think she had a chance at becoming the future Lady of Mawbry, and yet her heart said something altogether different.

6

"Yoo-hoo, Lord Mawbry, over here."

Sinjin rolled his eyes and counted to ten twice before stepping out from behind a tree to find Suzanne Livingston grinning at him with a smile that made him anxious to find another guest.

His mother's grand idea of playing hide-and-seek was ending up an exercise in extreme patience, as it seemed all the women refused to stay hidden, and instead went out of their way to be found.

Ironically, the only woman he wanted to "seek" was nowhere in the vicinity. Indeed, he had not seen Katelyn all morning, which had proved exceedingly depressing as he'd been unable to think of little else since their tête-à-tête in the study last night.

Sinjin managed a smile for Suzanne as he tapped her on the shoulder. She giggled and snorted a few times, before making her way back to the rest of the party.

Where the hell did his brothers get off to? He had seen both Rory and Victor earlier in the game, but now either they had bowed out or were doing a little hiding of their own. He hardly blamed them.

He honestly felt badly for his brothers. Had he taken the initiative and married before his mother's ultimatum, then the outcome for Rory and Victor might have been very different. They, too, could have spent the remainder of their twenties, and perhaps part of their thirties, sowing their wild oats. As it was, they would be husbands, and possibly fathers-to-be, before the end of the year.

"My lord, over here!"

Sinjin bit back a sigh. Never had he thought he would find being in the company of women so taxing. "There you are, Lady Clara."

Lady Clara fluttered her lashes. "You have found me, my lord." She brushed against him, deliberately pressing her breast against his bicep. She wasn't stupid. Lady Clara's most impressive attributes were her enormous breasts. She was quite comely, too, with a riot of brown hair and wide amber eyes, though she paled in comparison to Katelyn Davenport.

Every woman paled in comparison to Katelyn.

"Indeed, I have, Lady Clara, and I fear I must keep searching for the others."

She pouted, her lower lip jutting out in a most unbecoming way. "Very well, my lord, though I do hope one day very soon to have you all to myself." With an exaggerated sigh, she sauntered off in the direction of the manor grounds, where a picnic luncheon awaited all the guests.

He wondered what his mother had been thinking in suggesting such a game. After all, the danger in playing hide-and-seek without chaperones was being accused of indecent behavior. Granted, Sinjin was normally not one to take advantage of an innocent young lady.

He hadn't been particularly worried about bad behavior last night, though, had he?

He was still surprised how far he had gone with a virgin, not to mention a woman betrothed to another man. But he had not been able to help himself—nor, did it appear, could she.

He heard two women talking and almost walked past a copse of trees when he recognized the voices of Lady Katelyn and Lady Marilyn.

To his surprise, his heart actually skipped a beat as he approached the duo.

Leaning against a tree, Lady Katelyn had her hands behind her back, while Marilyn sat on a nearby rock. She laughed at something Katelyn said, but the smile slid from her lips when she caught sight of Sinjin.

Katelyn followed her sister's gaze. Her eyes widened and she glanced at her sister.

"Lord Mawbry, what a surprise," Marilyn said, standing. She brushed her skirts out, then looked at Katelyn.

"Good afternoon, ladies. You have done an impressive job at staying hidden, especially considering the majority of our guests have already been found."

"Was it our laughter that gave us away?" Marilyn asked, a whimsical smile on her lips.

"Indeed, it was." He was slightly unnerved that Katelyn had said nothing so far. "And how are you this afternoon, Lady Katelyn?"

Her throat convulsed as she swallowed hard. "I'm very well, my lord."

"You look beautiful." He said the words before he could stop himself. And she did look lovely—the pale yellow walking dress showing off her slender figure, cupping her firm, full breasts.

"You know, I think I shall take a look at the creek. I'll be just over here," Marilyn said, pointing in the distance.

Katelyn opened her mouth as though to stop her sister, but Marilyn just kept on walking.

Sinjin waited until Marilyn was out of sight to approach Katelyn. "I've been looking for you all afternoon."

"We slept in."

He nodded, unused to such awkwardness with a woman. Always he had been confident, and yet now he felt like a greenhorn with his first crush.

"How did you sleep?"

"Fine," she replied, her gaze shifting to his lips. "And you, my lord?"

"I tossed and turned all night."

Her lips curved slightly.

"I'm assuming you suffered from a similar fate?" he asked, and now that he was closer he could see the slightest hint of dark circles beneath her brilliant green eyes.

"I confess it took me a while to finally fall asleep."

"When I fell asleep . . . do you know whom I dreamt of?"

"Who?"

He stopped a few feet from her, then pulled her to him. "You."

"I dreamt of you, too," she said breathlessly, lifting her face to his.

Relief washed over Sinjin. For a minute he had wondered if she'd had second thoughts.

He kissed her softly, savoring the feel of her arms sliding around his neck. She fit so perfectly to him, as though she had been made just for him.

His tongue slid over hers, and she moaned low in her throat as he cupped her bottom and pressed his cock against her belly.

A bell rang in the distance, his mother's signal that the game had ended and lunch was ready to be served.

He put Katelyn at arm's length. Her eyes opened slowly, and he smiled as he looked at her kiss-swollen lips. "I don't want to leave you, but we must return."

"I'm coming your way," Marilyn said, and only then did Katelyn step away.

"I want to see you."

She nodded, and he could not help but kiss her again. Nearby he heard women giggle, and Katelyn heard them, too, because she scanned the trees.

The group passed by and Sinjin followed behind the women, who all let out a delighted, yet startled yelp when he snuck upon them.

Katelyn and Marilyn walked in silence until they descended the hill that lead to Claymoore Hall.

The three-story Elizabethan manor with its multitude of glass windows was immense and in such contrast to the small home where she had spent the majority of her life, that Katelyn couldn't help but envy the woman who would one day be the lady of such an estate.

"It's lovely," Marilyn said, as though reading her thoughts. "Such incredible architecture."

Katelyn nodded in agreement.

"Lady Rochester has truly outdone herself," Marilyn said, motioning to where servants dressed in gray and white attire scurried about, serving their guests who lounged beneath the towering oaks in the meadow.

"Indeed, she has. I did not realize so many people were in attendance," Katelyn said absently.

Many of the guests lounged on multicolored blankets, and chairs had been set out for older chaperones.

She immediately searched for Sinjin and found him sitting beside a beautiful blonde she had not noticed last night. The woman had all the graces of the aristocracy, and even from a distance, Katelyn could tell her dress was expensive.

A new arrival? Who was she, Katelyn wondered, jealousy pulsing through every nerve.

"There is the middle brother," Marilyn said, motioning toward a tall figure standing near a table that threatened collapse with the veritable mountain of dishes piled upon it.

As though sensing their perusal, he turned to them and nodded. "He's lovely, isn't he?" Marilyn said, and Katelyn couldn't help but grin. Perhaps her sister was not immune to the Rayborne brothers' charm, after all.

He walked toward them, a devilish smile on his lips. His eyes were larger than Sinjin's, but the same color blue. His face was just as angular, but his chin was squarer, his lips a touch fuller, and his hair wavier than his sibling's.

"I wondered when I would finally meet the lovely Davenport sisters," he said, lifting Marilyn's hand in his own and kissing it, before doing the same with Katelyn. "My brothers have been talking about you nonstop."

Katelyn and Marilyn shared a smile.

"I am Victor."

"Nice to meet you," Katelyn and Marilyn murmured simultaneously.

"Would you do me the honor of joining me for lunch?"

"Of course," Marilyn said, and Katelyn smiled, sliding her hand around the elbow he offered.

"Sinjin tells me your aunt will be joining us shortly."

"Yes, this weekend."

"Well, then we shall have to have as much fun as we can before she arrives," he said with a wink, and Marilyn laughed under her breath.

They took a seat on the grass nearest the fountain, where Neptune rose from a chariot out of the water.

"Who is she?" Marilyn asked, motioning toward Lady Celeste and Sinjin.

Victor followed her gaze. "Lady Celeste is the daughter of a duke. Apparently she's spent the past five years in a convent just outside of Paris. She's fluent in three languages, and her dowry is downright obscene."

"Impressive," Marilyn said, glancing at Katelyn.

Katelyn's heart nearly fell to her feet. How could she possibly compete with a beautiful duke's daughter? True, she understood that Sinjin desired her, but would he consider marrying her over someone of Lady Celeste's station?

They waited silently as a servant poured them each a cup of tea, and Katelyn took the opportunity to watch Sinjin and Celeste without being too obvious. How at ease they looked in each other's company, the very picture of pre-wedded bliss.

"I am sure your parents would be elated if you, or one of your brothers, were to marry Lady Celeste. Perhaps you should fight for her attention?" Marilyn murmured, and Victor lifted a brow.

"Lady Marilyn, I am but a second son. My brother is the prize."

Katelyn looked down at her cup. She wasn't stupid. She realized what a catch Celeste was, and she was sadly mistaken if she thought Sinjin would choose her, an engaged woman, with little or no money, over a duke's daughter.

Marilyn and Victor chatted incessantly, while Katelyn spent the next hour in misery, watching Sinjin as he listened attentively to everything Celeste had to say. To her great dismay, he had not so much as glanced in her direction.

A crack of thunder pierced the quiet, and a few of the ladies squealed loudly.

Lady Rochester stood and clapped her hands together. "Ladies and gentlemen, let us return to the manor before our situation becomes even more dire. We shall see you all in the dining room this evening. Until then, take cover!"

Sinjin stood and escorted the willowy Lady Celeste and her chaperone straight past Katelyn. To her chagrin, the other woman was even lovelier up close.

Victor stood and extended his arm to Katelyn. She slipped her hand around his elbow, trying not to lose faith that Sinjin wanted her. He patted her hand in silent commiseration.

Marilyn caught her gaze and smiled softly, but Katelyn could see the sympathy in her eyes.

7

Katelyn slid farther into the luxuriously warm bath. For as long as she could remember, she always enjoyed taking long baths, but these past weeks Ronald had told her time and time again that taking a bath more than once a week was a waste of water and the use of his servants' good time.

Thankfully, Ronald was not here now. He would be horrified by her scandalous behavior.

She smiled inwardly.

Marilyn had left her fifteen minutes ago, saying she wanted to take Victor up on a game of chess before dinner. The two had certainly created a bond, and Katelyn hoped her sister was well on her way to landing a Rayborne brother.

If only she were so lucky.

She tried not to think about Sinjin and Lady Celeste, but it was nearly impossible. He had been so enraptured with the duke's daughter, it was as though the moment alone in the woods had not happened.

No doubt the pairing would be the topic of discussion at dinner this evening.

Yet another reason she should stay in her room and use a headache as an excuse as to why she had missed the festivities.

The door opened and closed behind her. "Surely you did not beat Victor in chess already?"

The footsteps came closer to the privacy screen, and Katelyn went very still. Those footfalls were heavier than her sister's would be. She sat up a little. "Marilyn?"

"I'm afraid not."

Her breath left her in a rush. "Sinjin."

"What a lovely sight."

She caught his reflection in the long, oval mirror. His hands were planted firmly on his narrow hips, and to her dismay, he looked even more handsome than before. Damn him!

Ignoring the excitement that rushed through her, she slid down, her chin hitting the water. "My lord, what are you doing here?"

"Please, we have shared too many intimacies to allow such formality between us. I insist you call me Sinjin," he said, approaching the tub, his eyes scanning the water.

There were suds, but not enough to hide everything.

She crossed her arms over her breasts.

The side of his mouth curved in a smile, as though amused by her modesty.

"Sinjin, please, if someone were to discover—"

"Everyone in the house, save for a handful of servants, are downstairs . . . where you should be as well. Are you not coming to dinner?"

"I wanted to savor the bath."

He reached down, his fingers dipping into the water. "It is getting cool."

She felt anything but cool. In fact, she felt positively flushed.

A dark brow lifted. "Tell me the truth—were you intentionally ignoring me, Katelyn?"

"Not at all," she said, a touch too quickly. And how dare he ask her such a question when he so obviously had been ignoring her. Unable to meet his quizzical gaze, she glanced away. "I thought you would be occupied with a certain duke's daughter."

She clamped her mouth shut. Now why had she said that?

He pulled a chair up to the side of the bath and leaned forward, his elbows resting on his knees. "Are you jealous, Katelyn?" His voice was silky soft.

"Why should I, of all people, be jealous? I am as good as married."

Any humor left his face and he sighed heavily. "I need not be reminded."

"No, but perhaps I do."

"Why, you are not yet married."

"No, I am not . . . but soon we will *both* be married, will we not? After all, isn't this party about finding you and your brothers brides?"

He was on his haunches beside her seconds later, a long hand gliding through the water, just inches from her right breast. "That was my mother's intention all along." His fingers brushed over her nipple, and it was all she could do not to arch against him. "Who knows what the future holds." He rolled a nipple between thumb and forefinger, the sensation delicious. "But I suppose it would not be wise for either of us to spend too much time in each other's company, since you constantly remind me that you are to marry."

Is that why he had so clearly ignored her earlier today—because he didn't want anyone to speculate on their relationship?

She glanced at his hand and then into his eyes. The blue orbs sparkled with mischief and something else she dare not explore.

"Tell me, what would your betrothed say, if he knew I was watching you bathe . . . running my fingers through the water, touching your breast?" he asked, weighing her breast in his hand before a fingertip circled around her rigid nipple.

Need and desire pulsed through her, and she yearned to pull his hand down between her thighs, to the throbbing that had started the second he touched her.

Without even being aware of it, she leaned closer and he smiled softly. He had a sexuality that couldn't be denied... one that drew her to him like a bee to honey.

He pulled on her nipple, his fingertips squeezing lightly, and then a touch harder. Surprisingly, she didn't feel pain, but instead an intense pleasure that made her hunger for more.

With her body on fire, and a thousand different thoughts rushing through her head, she finally closed her eyes and allowed herself only to feel and not think of the consequences.

Her thighs relaxed and fell open; then his hand was there, sliding between her legs. She sighed as the tips of his fingers circled around her tiny nub, teasing the sensitive flesh before sliding over her slit. He parted her inner lips and eased his finger inside.

She groaned with pleasure and knew she approached dangerous territory—the point of no return. Her mother had always warned her to guard her maidenhead, a woman's greatest treasure meant for her husband. Indeed, Ronald would expect her maidenhead to remain intact, his to take come their wedding night.

And yet, despite the warning bells clanging in her head, she could not say the simple word *no*. How could she, when her body was screaming for him to continue?

"So tight," he whispered, sounding pleased.

Her channel squeezed his long finger, adjusting to the intrusion as his thumb brushed over her sensitive nub again and again.

Sinjin wanted Katelyn with a desperation that frightened him. How passionate she was, and each time they were together, he wanted her even more.

She lifted her hips against his hand, and sighed loudly when his other hand plucked at a nipple. Sinjin swallowed a moan as her head fell back on the tub's edge and her breathing quickened.

Katelyn opened her legs wider, and a deep moan emanated from Sinjin, a sound so deliciously primal, she longed to hear it again.

He leaned forward and kissed her, and she opened to him, savoring the taste of him as his tongue swept inside her mouth.

Adding another finger inside her sheath, he very slowly started to simulate the act of making love.

Katelyn wished it was his manhood inside her, and not his fingers. In fact, she nearly told him as much but stopped herself short of doing so. What would he think of her if she said the words? Certainly the virginal, virtuous Lady Celeste would never be so scandalous.

His lips left hers and he slowly kissed a trail down her neck to the pulse beating wildly at her throat. She reached up, her fingers weaving through his silky dark hair, the band that had held it back dropping off into the bath water.

Sinjin smiled, excited by her reaction. Her nails brushed against his scalp and he moaned, urging her on.

Once again, he kissed a path downward, to her collarbone; then he kissed her breasts, taking special care to lavish attention on one, then the other.

As climax claimed her body, her snug sheath gripped his fingers. She held tight to his arm, her hand curling around his bicep. "Sinjin . . ." She said his name on a sigh and his cock swelled harder against his belly.

He'd had to stroke himself to climax last night, and would have to do the same tonight. Indeed, he would have an erection until he came inside her tight sheath.

After the tremors stopped, his fingers slid from her body and her hips followed. She could feel her cheeks burn, but she didn't care. Let him know the need she felt pulsing through her.

He looked deliciously ruffled from where she had brushed her hands through his hair. How she wished they had the luxury to get to know each other, to spend long hours talking and making love.

As she stared at him, white-hot need rushed through her entire body. He could lift her from this bath right now and do whatever he pleased, however he pleased, and she would not deny him.

Wicked, wicked woman, she thought as he stood and raked his hands through his hair, tying it back with the band that he fished out of the tub.

A knock at the door had her heart jumping to her throat. He handed her the robe draped over the privacy screen, and went to the door.

"It's Victor," came the voice from the hallway, and Sinjin sighed with relief.

"What is it?" he asked, opening the door a fraction.

"Mother is looking for you," Katelyn heard Victor say through the crack. "We are getting ready to sit down to dinner. Do not linger, Sin. She already has Jeffries scouring the ground floor for you."

"I'll be there shortly. Tell her I spilled a drink on my shirt and I needed to change." It wasn't entirely a lie, as his shirt front was wet from her bath water.

"Oh, and check a mirror, will you? You look a bit rough," he said with a wink, and Sinjin shut the door behind him.

Katelyn stepped from the tub, and before she had a chance to reach for her wrap, he stood there, his gaze searing into her.

She noted the obvious bulge in his pants and swallowed hard.

He crossed the room, pulled her into his arms, and kissed her. "I would give anything to stay with you," he whispered. "Please reconsider coming down to dinner. I want to see you before I go to bed."

There was no way she could face anyone right now. Plus, she needed the time to compose herself and her emotions. Perhaps she would write a letter to her mother, expressing her thoughts and trepidation about marrying Ronald. Maybe, just maybe, her mother would understand and let her off the hook, and honestly, she had no desire to see Lady Celeste at the moment. "I shall see you tomorrow."

He smiled softly. "I shall tell your sister you have decided to stay in for the night. Sweet dreams, Kate. Until tomorrow."

"Until tomorrow."

Katelyn slept surprisingly well given the fact a thousand thoughts had been racing through her mind from the time Sinjin had left her chamber last night.

Despite the fact she had behaved scandalously with Sinjin, she would not regret her actions in the least. In fact, she could hardly wait to see him again, and would enjoy herself, and nothing and no one could stop her.

"Oh my God, Katelyn, you must come with me at once," Marilyn said, storming into the room, her eyes wide, her face flushed with excitement.

"But I'm not ready yet."

"This can't wait." Marilyn motioned for her to follow. "Come now, before it is too late."

"Too late?" Intrigued, Katelyn followed.

Marilyn took her by the hand and they rushed down the hallway. "We must be very quiet."

"What is it?"

"You shall see. Now, be silent," she said as they approached the end of the hall. Marilyn stopped and nodded toward the last doorway, which happened to be slightly ajar. "Go ahead and look."

Katelyn frowned but stepped closer to the door and looked inside.

Her breath left her in a rush seeing the tall, dark-haired man standing at the foot of the bed, no shirt, and his pants bunched about his knees. He stood between two slender thighs that were spread wide.

Feminine gasps and groans filled the room, along with the slap of flesh against flesh.

The man turned just a little, enough for Katelyn to recognize the youngest Rayborne brother, Rory.

The woman moaned as his thrusts quickened.

Katelyn wondered just who the woman was, and didn't have long to wonder when the blonde she had sat next to at tea yesterday morning reached up to pull Rory's head down to kiss her nipples. It was Lady Anna . . . who had acted so demure and innocent.

Rory stopped thrusting while he played homage to Anna's breasts. Katelyn remembered the way Sinjin had touched her last night; her stomach tightened and heat rushed through her body, settling low in her groin.

Marilyn edged in beside Katelyn, angling to see.

Katelyn swallowed a gasp when another man came into view. He was kneeling on the bed.

"Oh, my God." Marilyn mouthed the words, biting her lower lip.

Rory pulled out, then flipped the woman onto her stomach.

Whomever had joined them remained a mystery, his face hidden by the canopy. However, whoever he was, he had an impressive build, a nice wide chest, a narrow waist.

He unbuttoned his pants and slid them down, revealing a long, thick cock sprouting from a nest of dark hair.

The man's abdomen was thick with muscle, reminding her of Sinjin's chiseled stomach.

Lady Anna gave a sigh of appreciation, and to Katelyn's shock, the woman took his length into her mouth. Obviously she had experience, as she licked and sucked vigorously.

The man's hand moved to her head, his fingers weaving through her hair.

The man wore a ring, and to her dismay, she realized she had seen that ring before. Had it been Sinjin? With heart racing, she searched her memory.

Lady Anna's fingers fisted the blankets beneath her, and she arched her back as Rory slid inside her once again, settling into a steady rhythm, his large hands gripping Anna's hips tight.

Anna became more aggressive as she licked and sucked her other lover. The man played with her breasts, his fingers tweaking her nipples.

The man who had joined the other two leaned down and kissed Anna's head. Marilyn gasped beside her.

Victor.

Relief rushed through Katelyn. Thank God it wasn't Sinjin. Then again, perhaps the eldest Rayborne brother would make an appearance at any second. Good grief, the men certainly had earned the reputation they had acquired.

Seconds later, Rory pulled out of Anna, and fluid shot from his shaft onto her back. As he struggled to catch his breath, he rubbed her between her legs and she moaned.

Victor followed shortly behind, and Anna licked and swallowed his seed.

Marilyn tugged at Katelyn's dress, and that's when she heard someone coming up the stairs, not far from where they stood.

It was Lady Anna's chaperone, an old woman with a leathery face who would not take kindly to finding her charge in such a compromising position.

Katelyn stepped away from the door, pulling Marilyn with her. They started toward the stairs.

"Good morning," Katelyn said, loud enough for the occupants of the room to hear.

The chaperone's brows furrowed as she glanced from Katelyn to Marilyn, and tried to see over their shoulders into Anna's chamber. Katelyn moved closer to Marilyn. "Good morning. How are you today?"

"We are very well, thank you," Marilyn said. "You are Lady Anna's chaperone, correct?"

"Yes, I am Mrs. Steinway." She moved to the right, trying to pass.

"You are from Sussex, are you not?" Katelyn asked, blocking her.

"No, Wessex." Mrs. Steinway glanced past them—her frown deepening as she noticed the partially opened door. "Will you please excuse me?"

"Of course," Katelyn said, moving out of the woman's way.

They lingered on the stairs, ready for the commotion, but Mrs. Steinway entered the room and closed the door behind her. No screams could be heard.

"Come on." Marilyn grabbed Katelyn's hand and rushed back to their chamber.

Inside the room, Marilyn walked straight to the far window, threw it open, and looked out.

"What are you doing?" Katelyn asked.

"Looking for Rory and Victor. I thought perhaps they would be on the ledge outside Lady Anna's window."

62

"They must be hiding away in Anna's bedchamber. Certainly they would not risk leaving by way of the window. Too many people could see them in broad daylight. To do so is sheer folly."

Marilyn laughed under her breath. "I would not have believed it had I not seen it with my own eyes."

"I know!" Katelyn's heart still raced from what she had witnessed. She had never before seen two people making love, let alone three, and it had been exhilarating.

"How utterly scandalous. I dare say I shall never be able to look at Rory or Victor in the same way." Marilyn shook her head. "And Lady Anna. Who would have thought?"

"Indeed." Katelyn fished through her jewelry and found simple diamond earrings. "What if they saw us, Marilyn?"

"They did not see us, Katelyn," Marilyn said with a laugh. "They were far too occupied to pay us any mind."

"Yes, but they heard us."

"We wanted them to hear us." Marilyn shrugged. "We should not be the ones who are embarrassed. We weren't in a room in the morning light, making love to two men."

No, but Katelyn had been intimate with Sinjin Rayborne, and she was engaged to another man. "Do you think Rory or Victor will end up marrying Lady Anna?"

"Absolutely not," Marilyn said, as though the very idea was preposterous.

"Why?"

"Katelyn, she was making love to both Rory and his brother. Why would any man marry such a woman?"

Why indeed?

8

Sinjin was entranced.

He desired Katelyn Davenport with everything he possessed, and by damn, he would have her, despite the obvious dilemma that she was already spoken for.

Last night, when he had entered her bedroom, he'd had no intention of touching her . . . and yet, seeing her in that bath, tiny tendrils of hair framing her face, he could think of little else but possessing her.

And now she sat down the table from him, speaking in low tones to her sister. She had not looked at him once since he'd entered the room, making him wonder if she was still angry about the attention he had shown Lady Celeste yesterday.

He hated to admit it, but Katelyn's jealousy excited him, and made him realize the attraction truly was reciprocated.

Little did she realize he had flirted with Lady Celeste in order to keep the other females from whispering about Katelyn. She had been concerned about the gossipmongers from their first meeting, and now they would no longer speculate about Katelyn being the focus of his attention.

Rory entered the room, bringing Sinjin's attention back to the present. His little brother strolled toward the bulging sideboard. He'd always had a ravenous appetite, but it did not show on his lithe form, compliments of a rigorous regimen of fencing and boxing.

The majority of the women at the table turned to watch Rory, many giggling and blushing. Sinjin nearly rolled his eyes. God had truly blessed his youngest sibling with looks and grace. Unfortunately, Rory knew full well the power of his looks and used it as a weapon at will. Hopefully with time, and the love of a good woman, that would change.

Finished piling his plate with an assortment of meats, pastries, and eggs, Rory flashed a smile at the long table of women and walked toward Sinjin. An effeminate footman rushed forward to pull out his chair.

"Thank you," Rory said, charming grin still in place, as he took a seat and allowed the man to place a napkin on his lap. He even went so far as to wink at the servant, who flushed at the attention.

"I wondered when you would surface."

"Whatever do you mean?" Rory said, looking uncertain on what to eat first.

"Where have you been all morning?"

"Well, if you must know, I just had the good graces of escaping Lady Anna's bedchamber seconds before her chaperone came to check on her. Thank goodness for the Davenport sisters."

Sinjin flinched. "The Davenport sisters? What do you mean?"

Rory leaned forward. "Relax, brother. Katelyn and Marilyn merely waylaid Anna's chaperone. If not for them, I would have found myself in a very sticky situation, as would Victor."

He lifted his brows. "You *and* Victor? Having a ménage in our parents' home is quite daring, even for you."

"Well, we could hardly deny Lady Anna's invitation. It was too enticing, and I must say, she did not disappoint." He buttered a piece of toast. "I look forward to another go at it. Feel free to join us if you'd like. I'm quite certain she'd entertain all of us, if only we ask."

The invitation held no appeal. "How did Katelyn and Marilyn discover you?"

"I've been asking myself that question, too, and I suppose in our haste we forgot to latch the door and it came open."

The knowledge that Katelyn had watched his brothers fuck Lady Anna irritated Sinjin to no end, which was absurd. It's not like she had participated . . . but still. What had she been thinking about while watching? Had she wished she were Lady Anna? A thousand equally frustrating questions raced through his mind.

Victor walked into the dining room minutes later, his color high and his smile wide. Little wonder.

He didn't bother with food but sat down beside Sinjin, waving off the overexuberant footman. "Good morning, dear brothers."

"Do not pretend that you are just now seeing Rory," Sinjin said, taking a sip of tea.

Victor glared at Rory. "Bloody hell, can you keep anything to yourself?"

Rory shrugged. "He did ask, and I thought I would tell him before Katelyn does."

"We do not know for certain that it was Katelyn or Marilyn," Victor said, motioning for a servant to fill the empty cup before him with tea.

Sinjin sat up straighter and glanced at Rory. "I thought you said it was both?"

"I got a quick glimpse from the corner of my eye," Rory said, stabbing at the ham on his plate. "I wasn't sure it was her until I heard her voice."

"It is one thing to act the libertine in your own house, but what if it had been Mother or another of our guests who had caught you in the act? I guarantee you that any of our younger female guests would shout the news from the rooftops, and both, or in this case, one of you, would be engaged."

Both brothers winced.

"Point taken," Victor said, glancing down the table at the Davenport sisters. Katelyn did not look their way, but Marilyn waved, an amused smile on her face, before turning to her sister. "I think it's safe to say they *both* saw us." Victor had the good grace to look sheepish.

Rory's lips quirked. "Indeed, they saw a lot more than intended, if I do say so myself."

The side of Victor's mouth lifted.

"Watch out, Sinjin. Lady Katelyn might just prefer one of us now that she has seen the complete package." Rory wiggled his brows.

Sinjin resisted the urge to knock his brother's perfect teeth right out of his head. That, or a crooked nose might just set his ego back a bit. "As your elder brother, I would ask that you please behave like the gentleman you are from here on out. And for all our sakes, make sure you lock the door next time."

"Understood," Victor said, appearing genuinely sorry for his participation.

Sinjin glanced at Katelyn. She refused to look at him. In fact, she whispered something to her sister and then headed out of the dining room.

"I'll talk to you two later. Remember, we'll have guests arriving throughout the day for tonight's ball. Please make sure you are on hand to welcome them." He wiped his mouth with the napkin and set it on his empty plate.

"Thank God, the cavalry is arriving," Rory murmured under his breath. "Maybe then Mother won't be breathing down our necks all the time."

Many of their friends and acquaintances had been invited to the ball tonight—a positive for all of them, enabling more time to focus on individual pursuits.

"Where are you going?" Rory asked.

Victor glanced at the end of the table, namely, the empty seat Katelyn had just vacated. He didn't say a word, but instead took a sip of his tea.

"Please behave from here on out," Sinjin said, before leaving his brothers. He entered the hallway and started for the staircase. Just then he saw the hem of Katelyn's blue skirts as she rounded the corner.

Glad to be out of the stuffy dining room, Katelyn rushed up the stairs. It had felt more than awkward to be in Rory and Victor's company so soon after seeing the two make love to Anna. And the way Sinjin watched her made her believe he *knew* that she had watched his brothers.

Making it up the stairwell, she started down the hallway to her chamber, when she was abruptly pulled into the nearest alcove.

"You've been ignoring me, Katelyn."

"Sinjin, what are you doing?" she asked, her heart pounding hard against her breastbone.

His blue eyes narrowed. "I should be asking you the same thing."

She swallowed hard, and looked past his shoulder before meeting his gaze again. "What do you mean?"

"You would not even look in my direction at breakfast. Not once."

She licked her lips and his cock instantly hardened. He had to get her into his bed or he would lose his mind.

Releasing a breath, she blurted, "Truth be told, I was embarrassed."

"Embarrassed. Why?" There was something strange in his voice, and in the way he watched her. Was he jesting with her? Did he know the truth? Perhaps his brothers had said something to him at breakfast.

She opened her mouth, then hesitated. "I saw your brothers this morning . . . in a most compromising position."

He lifted a dark brow. "Whatever can you mean?"

"They did not mention anything to you just now?" she asked, skeptical. But then again, she had not told Marilyn everything that had transpired between herself and Sinjin.

"I think Rory mentioned hearing you and your sister in the hallway outside Lady Anna's door."

"Oh no," she whispered under her breath. "I saw him—or rather your brothers, making love to Lady Anna."

"Ah, the truth finally emerges."

"Why did you not just tell me you knew?" she asked. But he ignored her question and instead asked her one of his own.

"How did you come upon them making love?"

"The door was open."

"So you were passing by the room, saw them, and out of curiosity, you stopped and watched?"

She swallowed hard. "Not exactly."

"Then what do you mean, *exactly*?"

"My sister had been on her way to breakfast when she saw them from the corner of her eye. She came back to the room to get me."

"So Marilyn forced you to watch?"

Katelyn tilted her head to the side and released an impatient sigh. "No, she did not force me. It is not that I meant to stare, but I had just never seen anything—"

A smile teased the corner of his mouth.

She clamped her lips together, then counted to ten twice. "I admit that it was wrong for me to watch. I know that, but in truth, I couldn't have watched for more than thirty seconds when Marilyn alerted me that someone was coming."

"You did not hear someone coming?"

She shook her head. "No, I did not."

Which meant she had been entranced by what was happening in the bedchamber. She didn't say it, but she didn't have to.

"I'm sorry, Sinjin. I'm so embarrassed."

His eyes instantly softened. "My brothers should be apologizing, not you."

His long, dark hair brushed his wide shoulders, and she yearned to brush her fingers through the silky tresses. During breakfast, she had watched him at the sideboard, her heart thundering a million beats per minute. She had noticed the other women in the room respond to him, their appreciative stares sliding slowly over his impressive backside. Jealousy had rushed through her, but she had pushed it back, reminding herself of the priceless moments she had spent in his company, of all the wicked things they had done . . . of all the wicked things they would do.

Long, elegant fingers brushed her jaw, and she pushed her face into his hand.

Her pulse skittered as his head lowered.

He tasted of mint, and smelled of sandalwood and musk. His arms came around her and she was abruptly pushed up against the wall. There wasn't an inch of his body that wasn't flush with hers, and he flexed his hips, digging his thick, rigid erection against her stomach.

The material of her gown inched up; then his hand was on her thigh—and then at the moist flesh between her legs. "You're so hot for me. So wet."

He made her forget all sense of propriety. Of who she was and where she was. The alcove was only slightly hidden from view. A curious individual could find them easily enough—just as she had seen Anna, Rory, and Victor making love.

Despite the voice in her head that screamed for her to stop, she clung to him, her fingers digging into his strong back.

"Touch me," he whispered against her mouth, and her pulse skittered. She had never before touched a man.

She reached between their bodies and fumbled with the buttons on his pants. Within seconds, his cock sprang free of its confines.

Though she continued to kiss him, she was thoroughly distracted . . . and extremely curious. She pulled away and looked down at the glorious phallus in her hand—at the purple, plum-sized head, the thick base. The texture felt like satin over steel, and unlike anything she'd ever experienced.

His breath came out in a rush, and she glanced up at him to make sure he was all right. His eyes were closed, the long lashes casting shadows upon high cheekbones. A deep-throated moan escaped his lips, and his hand covered hers, fisting around hers, squeezing tight, sliding down the thick length and up again. With each stroke, his hand moved faster, and his breathing grew deeper and more ragged.

Two fingers slipped inside her dripping channel, and the pad of his thumb brushed against her nub—around it, over it, flicking it—and soon she was biting her lip to keep from crying out in ecstasy.

Sinjin was crazy with desire. How ironic that he had just given his brothers grief over their irresponsible behavior in their parents' home, when here he was in the open, where someone could stumble upon them at any time.

Her hips flexed, and her breathing grew labored. Tight inner muscles clenched his fingers, coating them with her slick dew. She rested her forehead against his shoulder and released a sated moan, her breath hot against his chest.

Slender fingers tightened around his cock, and she became

71

more aggressive, her strokes longer, more fluid. He smiled, delighted at her enthusiasm.

Sweat beaded his brow as the seconds ticked by, and only when he heard voices in the distance did he pull away. His cock felt ready to explode.

He had to find release soon. With trembling hands, he pushed the hem of his shirt back into his pants.

"I want you, Kate. I need to be alone with you."

9

Sinjin checked his appearance in the mirror outside the ball-room. He wore a black suit with a gold vest and crisp white shirt that Jeffries had set out for him. He could hardly wait until the end of the party, when he could return to wearing more casual attire.

"Good evening, my darling," Betsy said, coming up from behind Sinjin. He swore she relished her sneak attacks.

"Good evening, Mother." He extended his arm. "May I escort you into dinner?"

"Of course." She slid her hand around his arm. "So what do you think of Lady Celeste?"

"She's lovely," he said with false enthusiasm.

"Did I mention her father is a duke?"

"Indeed, you did mention it . . . several times, if I recall."

She snapped her fan against his bicep. "The man who takes Lady Celeste as a bride is a lucky man, indeed. We are fortunate to have her attend our little soiree."

"Perhaps Victor or Rory would be interested."

"Perhaps they would be, but Lady Celeste is a duke's daughter." She glanced over her shoulder, no doubt looking for Victor and Rory, then back at him. "No disrespect to your brothers, but Lady Celeste's chaperone said she would expect her charge to marry the heir."

"And you did not argue the point?"

"I wanted to, but you made such a connection with Celeste it seemed a moot point."

"It sounds as though you are already planning the wedding."

She touched his jaw with a gloved hand. "Not necessarily. I love you, and I want only the best for you. There are some of the most beautiful women in all of England beyond that door, desperate for the chance to get to know you better. Be the generous host that I know you can be and shower them all with attention."

"I shall certainly try, Mother."

"But be sure to pay Lady Celeste extra special attention."

He forced a smile. "Yes, Mother."

Victor and Rory raced up the steps and Betsy turned. "It's about time you two made an appearance. I just sent Jeffries off to find you."

"Sorry, Mother," Victor murmured, brushing his still-damp hair back with his hands, while Rory flashed a smile as he pulled a pair of rumpled gloves from his jacket pocket.

Betsy shook her head in dismay.

The footman opened the door, and they walked into the crowded ballroom.

All eyes turned to them, and Sinjin was relieved to see the familiar faces of his friends and acquaintances looking back at him. An old childhood friend Everett Johnston actually appeared sympathetic. He understood Sinjin's position, given that his overbearing father was pushing him to marry. Even Sinjin had told Everett to find a bride, and fast, since his father had recently married a nineteen-year-old who already looked heavy with child.

"Mingle, boys," Betsy said, wandering off to do the same.

Sinjin scanned the ballroom for the woman who had bewitched him. Since his mother's lecture, he would be wise to focus his attention on Lady Celeste.

He recalled Katelyn's innocent touch from earlier, the way she had looked at his cock with such wonder and desire. Though she had no idea what she was doing, he certainly could tell that with a little tutoring she would be an incredible lover.

Where the bloody hell was she?

As the musicians began to play, he scanned the dance floor and saw Marilyn dancing with a young man he recognized as an acquaintance of Rory's. Nearby, Katelyn danced with Thomas Lehman, a filthy rich Irishman who had come by his fortune through a wealthy grandfather who had died under mysterious circumstances.

The man had been linked to some of London's most beautiful courtesans, and apparently he was on the make for a new mistress, as he couldn't take his eyes off Katelyn.

Thomas was extremely clever, it was told, going to any lengths to get what he wanted.

"Looks like Lehman is treading on your territory," Victor said, coming up behind Sinjin.

"You say that like I should be concerned."

"I *did* walk in on him fucking my mistress."

Sinjin frowned. "Which mistress?"

"Do you remember Alexandria?"

"The dancer?"

"Yes, incredibly flexible."

"If I recall, he did you a favor. She was too demanding."

Victor's lips quirked. "Perhaps, but I did miss her oral technique." He rubbed the back of his neck. "Tell me what you want me to do. I am at your complete disposal."

"You should be worrying about yourself and your own future. Is there not a single woman here who has caught your fancy?"

"No, and to be honest, Rory and I are depending on you to take the pressure off of us. We have high hopes that once you make a good marriage, mother will be so content, she will renege on her demands."

"Rory's optimism is rubbing off on you, I see," Sinjin said, keeping a watchful eye on the dancers. He was relieved when the dance ended and another, a paunch-bellied man, claimed Katelyn's hand. She seemed much more relaxed with her new companion, and he felt a certain amount of relief knowing she was out of Thomas Lehman's clutches.

Victor nodded. "Now I'll ask for the next dance, and I'll see if Rory can't claim another. One or two will suffice, although honestly, I think Katelyn will not be in short supply of dance partners tonight."

Sinjin sighed, knowing Victor was probably right.

Katelyn glanced at the grandfather clock in the far corner. It was nearly midnight and she had not once danced with Sinjin. It didn't help her increasingly sour mood that he seemed to occupy his time with a certain blond-haired duke's daughter, who was dressed in an amazing gown that showed off her slim body to perfection. Her every movement was grace itself.

"You are sulking, dear sister," Marilyn said, giving her a quick hug. "Tell me what is going on in that head of yours, or need I ask?"

"I was just thinking how very unfair life can be."

Marilyn took a sip of punch. "She cannot possibly compete with you."

"I hate to tell you this, but she is. Sinjin has been with her all night."

"Only because his mother asks it of him."

"How do you know?"

Marilyn shrugged. "Lady Rochester is not stupid. Lady Celeste is the wealthiest woman here and, therefore, a perfect match for her eldest, the heir."

"I thought you were supposed to make me feel better."

"However, her son is infatuated with someone else. You should have seen Sinjin's face when you were dancing with Thomas. I swear he was ready to come out of his skin."

"Truly?"

"Oh, yes. It was delightful to watch."

The words brought some relief. "Why has he not asked me to dance?"

"His mother is watching his every move. You must remember that from the second he met you, Sinjin has focused his attention on you. One of Lady Rochester's best friends inundated me with questions about you and your forthcoming marriage. I reassured her that you were counting the days until you became Lady Balliford."

"Did she look convinced?"

Marilyn nodded. "Yes, very much so."

"I am in hell."

A smile touched Marilyn's lips. "No, you are not. I assure you that you have not seen the last of Sinjin Rayborne. You know that you could always use Thomas to further aggravate Sinjin. Let's face it, men want what other men have."

"And what about you, Marilyn? Are you not the least bit interested in Victor or Rory?"

Marilyn brushed a wayward curl off her cheek. "Now that I have seen both Rory and Victor in a different light, I find it hard to imagine a life with either man as a husband. Such a man could never be true to me."

Just as Sinjin could never be faithful to his wife. She must face the fact that the brothers had gained a reputation that they had truly earned in every sense of the word.

"Look at Lady Anna," Marilyn said, motioning to the blonde who stood amongst a group of young men, all clamoring for her attention. "It is little wonder they are rallying around her like dogs in heat. Her reputation must be well-known because there are no other ladies, even those more beautiful and wealthy, who have such a following."

Katelyn felt a blush rush up her neck as she looked at the other woman, remembering the way she had made love to the two brothers.

How many other women present pretended they were maidens when that was not at all the case?

With a pang, she realized if Sinjin had his way, she, too, would fall into that very same category. However, Katelyn would never make love to two men at the same time.

"Lady Katelyn, could I have the privilege of this dance?"

Katelyn glanced up to find Thomas standing before her, dark blond curls gleaming under the lights of the four enormous chandeliers. He was extremely handsome, and well he knew it, smug, confident smile in place. Within the first five minutes of meeting him, he had talked about himself incessantly, asking nothing of her. She detested talking about herself, but still . . .

She didn't want to leave Marilyn alone, and she was about to decline his invitation to dance when she saw Victor walking toward them. Marilyn grinned widely, and soon Katelyn was led to the dance floor by her escort, Victor and Marilyn directly behind.

As luck would have it, the dance ended up being a waltz. Thomas looked pleased as he took her in his arms, holding her far closer than she was comfortable with. Her heart slammed against her breast when she saw Sinjin walk onto the dance floor with Lady Celeste. The girl's cornflower blue eyes sparkled with delight as she stepped into Sinjin's powerful arms.

Katelyn glanced up as Sinjin and Lady Celeste danced by, and their gazes finally met and held, but only for an instant. There was little expression on his face, and yet she sensed his jealousy. The same jealousy that raged within her.

She smiled inwardly. Maybe Marilyn was right.

Thomas pulled her closer, so close she could feel a certain part of his anatomy pressing against her belly. She tried to distance herself, but the hand at her waist pulled her closer. "Meet me in the garden tonight, Lady Kate?"

She nearly stumbled over her feet. "I fear you mistake me for someone else. I am a chaperone here, sir."

"A chaperone?" he asked, a slight curl to his lip that was downright mocking.

"Indeed, I am engaged to be married."

He shrugged. "A mere inconvenience." His hot breath fanned her throat. "I can bring you pleasure the likes you have never experienced."

Arrogant cad! She didn't know whether to laugh or slap his face. She ultimately dropped her gaze, and he chuckled under his breath.

"I like your spirit." He pulled her tight. "I want us to be the most intimate of friends."

How she yearned to lift her knee and hurt him where it would injure him most.

Not liking the way he baited her, she ignored him and hoped the dance would end soon.

The smile slid from his features, but only for an instant. "We are friends, are we not, Lady Katelyn?"

"Yes, of course we are friends." She deliberately stepped on his foot. "I'm so sorry."

"You can make it up to me later, outside in the garden," he whispered against her ear.

10

Sinjin was ready to rip Thomas's head clean from his body. Not only had the man held Katelyn in a most intimate manner, Sinjin could tell by the look on her face and her high color that he had said something inappropriate. He could only imagine what.

Sinjin danced with Lady Celeste, and his mother positively beamed at him as he waltzed by.

He smiled and returned his attention to Celeste. He had gone out of his way to be kind to the young woman all night, and now he worried that he might be leading her astray. He didn't want to give her false hope. It was odd to be in such a position as he now found himself, and he didn't like it one bit.

He liked even less that he was falling hard for a woman who was engaged to another man. Try as he might to convince himself that he must find another woman because Katelyn was spoken for, Sinjin could not conjure any excitement to do so. The woman he desired was engaged to another, and now as she danced with another man, he felt ready to come out of his skin.

He didn't want anyone else touching her.

What would it be like to go to bed beside such a woman each night, and wake up with her every day? He envisioned living at his rural estate in Somerset, checking the crops and attending to business during the day, and returning to her every night.

Never had he considered a life of such domestic tranquility before. In fact, he spent less than a month each year at his country home because he could not bear to be away from all the trappings of society.

However, now he envisioned a more relaxed existence at his estate. He imagined Kate's belly round with child, and that wedded bliss *could* be a reality.

"My chaperone tells me that there is a hunt tomorrow afternoon. I would like to attend—that is, if you do not mind."

"Why would I mind?"

She lifted a brow. "Some men do not believe women should hunt."

"I think a person must do what pleases them."

"So you approve?"

"I would think that approval would come from your chaperone instead of myself."

It was obvious by her expression that his answer disappointed.

Katelyn and Thomas danced past them, and the Irishman's lips nearly brushed Katelyn's neck. Sinjin straightened his spine.

"My lord, I wish to please you," Celeste said.

Sinjin returned his attention to her. "If you wish to participate in the hunt, then by all means, please do so." He hoped he did not sound as irritated as he felt.

Her lips curved. "Then I shall."

He refrained from rolling his eyes. "I look forward to it."

Victor danced with Marilyn. He winked as he passed Sinjin.

As the last notes of the waltz faded into the high ceiling, Sinjin breathed a sigh of relief. "Thank you so much for the dance, Lady Celeste," he said, taking her by the hand and walking her back to her chaperone.

He handed her off to the woman, who looked extremely pleased. Giving a formal bow, he walked straight for Katelyn, not stopping to talk to anyone else.

Thomas had walked Katelyn to the far side of the room, and she looked around anxiously, probably for her sister, who was busy talking to another guest.

"Mr. Lehman, what a surprise. I was not aware you would be joining us," Sinjin said, keeping his voice cordial.

"Lord Mawbry. I came with a good friend of your younger brother's. I hope you do not mind."

"Not at all," he lied.

Sinjin glanced past him to Katelyn. "May I have the pleasure of the next dance, Lady Katelyn?" Sinjin asked, extending his arm.

She looked genuinely pleased by his request. "Of course, my lord," she said, her fingers slipping around his elbow. How lovely she was . . . her features so fine and delicate, her green eyes brilliant.

"Please excuse us, Mr. Lehman," Sinjin said, and Thomas gave a curt nod as they walked by.

Katelyn smelled incredible—a feminine scent of jasmine with a hint of vanilla. He yearned to bury his face in the soft red curls that had been painstakingly adorned atop her head. A few tendrils fell around her delicate throat.

They said nothing to each other while they walked to the dance floor. Once there, he took his place across from her, ready for the music to begin.

She breathed deeply, her full breasts rising from the tight confines of her low bodice. He noted the diamond necklace she wore. A gift from Balliford, perhaps?

The gown of blue silk clung to her body like a second skin. It was one of the finest gowns she had worn so far, and he wanted to buy her more, to spoil her beyond reason. She deserved only the best, and what a joy it would be to clothe that body, draping those lovely curves in the finest materials money could buy.

The music started and they moved forward, toward each other, and held hands, the steps taking them down the aisle of other dancers. "Have you enjoyed yourself tonight, my lord?"

"I have, thank you. And you?"

She nodded. "Very much."

Was she playing with him? "I was not aware you knew Mr. Lehman."

"I did not know him until tonight."

"From the way you got on, I thought perhaps you were old friends."

"No, we are not."

He breathed deeply through his nose, hoping to regain his composure. It wouldn't serve him to act the jilted lover.

"Lady Celeste is lovely," she blurted, and to his surprise, he saw jealousy in her eyes.

"Indeed, she is."

Sinjin's gaze followed hers. Ironically, Celeste was dancing with Thomas.

She winced. "Oh, you have competition, I am afraid."

"Thomas Lehman is hardly what I would call competition."

"I understand he is quite wealthy. Some women might be enticed, despite the fact he has no title."

Sinjin's lips quirked. "What else have you heard?"

She smiled coyly. "I dare not say what else."

"You forget how far a title goes in high society."

"You need not remind me," Katelyn murmured.

The step brought them together, and she took his hand, as the dance required. "Meet me outside in ten minutes," he said.

"Where?"

"At the east exit you'll find a pathway that leads to a walled-in garden."

"I shall try my best."

Ten minutes later, Sinjin stood in the gardens, waiting for Katelyn to arrive. He took a deep breath of fresh air while listening for the door.

He made sure to stay out of sight of any of the windows on the second and third floors that looked out into the gardens. At a young age he had learned each curve of the stone pathway, and knew by experience the most advantageous positions in which to stay free of prying eyes.

He remembered his first such experience with a scullery maid. She had been twenty-six and he a boy of fourteen when she'd introduced him to the joys of sex. He had never wanted to leave Claymoore Hall after that fateful encounter . . . that was until his father had found him in a compromising position with said servant. The woman had been immediately relieved of her duties, and Sinjin had been heartbroken—until he took up with her replacement shortly thereafter.

A door opened and Katelyn appeared, taking him away from his musings. She looked uncertain as she started down the pathway toward him.

He waited until she was nearly upon him to reach out and grab her hand.

She gasped, "Sinjin, you startled me."

"Sorry, I just wanted to be careful."

She glanced back over her shoulder at the manor. "We cannot be gone long."

"I've wanted to be alone with you all night," he said, pulling her close.

"And I've wanted to be with you." The words thrilled him.

The bodice of her gown was low, making it easy to access her breasts. He cupped the lovely mounds, dropping a kiss on each delectable slope. His thumbs brushed over her nipples and she released a ragged breath.

How he ached to take her beneath him, to claim her maidenhead right here and now. But Katelyn was not a light skirt to be taken at whim.

He pulled her bodice down enough to access her nipples, and he licked each, before taking one into his mouth and sucking lightly.

She released a sigh, her hands threading through his hair, anchoring him there.

Katelyn couldn't believe the incredible sensations rushing throughout her entire body. She felt like there was an invisible thread being pulled taut between her breasts and her woman's flesh. Sinjin must have sensed her need because he moved his leg between her thighs, causing friction to the tiny bud at the top of her sex.

Her moans only served to fuel Sinjin's desire. His cock hardened when she started moving against his thigh, her hot mound nearly burning through his pants.

They had entirely too many clothes on, and if he had his way, he'd have her naked beneath him. He'd never wanted anyone so desperately.

Putting his own needs aside, he focused solely on her pleasure.

The friction against her sensitive sex was so great, combined with the feeling of his lips on her breast, that she cried out as her body pulsed with wave after wave of sensation.

She was completely caught up in the moment when in the

distance she heard a door slam. Katelyn's breath hitched as she registered footsteps coming their way.

Sinjin must have heard, too, because he put a finger to his lips.

Katelyn's breasts were still exposed and she reached up to adjust her bodice. It would be bad enough to be discovered standing in the dark together, but being partially undressed would be even more incriminating.

Sinjin stepped farther into the shadows, bringing Katelyn with him. He could feel the pounding of her heart against his chest, see the concern in her eyes as she watched the pathway.

Thomas Lehman walked past a second later, the embers from his cigar burning bright.

Sinjin straightened. He appeared to be alone. What the hell? Had he followed Katelyn in the hopes of a liaison?

Katelyn glanced over and saw who it was, and her eyes widened.

"Lady Kate, are you out here? Do not hide from me."

Katelyn opened her mouth in disbelief, and Sinjin put a finger to his lips.

A few minutes later, he walked back their way, his gaze scanning the brush.

For God's sake, the man was certainly determined.

After he passed by, Sinjin slid his hands around Katelyn and pulled her close once again.

Once the door opened and shut, he kissed her tenderly. Katelyn savored the sensation of his velvety tongue sliding over hers, the feel of being in his strong arms, of feeling so desired.

"I cannot believe the nerve of that man," she said against his lips.

"Forget him."

The door to the manor opened and closed mere seconds later.

"Jesus Christ, if that's Lehman, I swear I will kill him."

His eyes were so heavy-lidded and dark, and she wished more than anything they could finally consummate their relationship, for she wanted him as badly as he wanted her.

Perhaps more so.

"Katelyn, are you out here?"

"It's my sister," Katelyn said, looking down to be sure her clothes had been set to rights.

Marilyn raced up the pathway and Katelyn stepped out. "Marilyn, what are you doing?"

"Thomas is roaming the house for you and asking where you got off to." She glanced at Sinjin, her brows furrowing. "And your mother is searching for you as well."

Apparently, he had not done a very good job at keeping his attraction to Katelyn a secret. He should have avoided dancing with her, but he could just as soon stop breathing.

"Then I shall put her mind at ease." He kissed Katelyn's cheek, then whispered in her ear, "Until tomorrow."

11

Katelyn gripped the reins of her horse tight within her fist as she watched Lady Celeste ride out to meet Sinjin and his brothers. The woman looked absolutely stunning dressed in a blood-red riding habit that must have cost her father a small fortune. She was beautiful, elegant, and every man stared at her with desire.

Sinjin wore dark brown buckskin pants and a fawn-colored linen shirt. He looked deliciously handsome, and when he glanced in her direction, she could not help the thrill that rushed through her. She still found it hard to believe he had singled her out from all of the women the moment she had arrived at Claymoore Hall.

Lady Celeste said something to Sinjin, and he turned to her, a ready smile on his lips. Katelyn tried to ignore the jealousy rushing through her, but it was difficult, especially because Lady Rochester threw them together at every turn.

"You're far more beautiful than she is," Marilyn said, as though reading Katelyn's thoughts.

"You're only saying that to make me feel better."

"And is it working?"

Katelyn shrugged. "It wouldn't be so horrible if my riding habit wasn't three seasons old."

"Three seasons old it might be, but you look ravishing in it."

The navy blue had faded with time, but the cut was flattering on Katelyn's body—although it fit a bit tight on her breasts. "Thank you."

"There's much to be happy about. It's going to be a delightful day," Marilyn said, lifting her face to the sunshine. "There is no one to tell us what to do. It is just the two of us—at least until Aunt Lillith arrives," she said with a wink. "And we shall never forget this time for as long as we live." She glanced at Katelyn and smiled. "Come, let us get a place in line. I'll be damned if Lady Celeste is going to best me in this hunt."

Those not participating in the hunt lined up on either side of the starting line. Katelyn realized with a pang that this very well could be the last time she was allowed to hunt, for Ronald had made it known to her, as had his sister, that women who participated in such events only did so to draw attention to themselves.

She shook her head. Each day she was away from Ronald, she felt more like her old, carefree self, and she couldn't imagine returning to such a humdrum existence.

"He's looking at you," Marilyn said, grin in place.

Katelyn didn't bother to ask whom Marilyn was talking about. She could feel Sinjin's gaze on her as they approached and took their places in line.

Rory flashed a wolfish smile as they approached.

Dressed much like his brother in buckskin pants and a lightweight shirt, Rory's gaze shifted from Marilyn to Katelyn and back again. She didn't think she could ever look at him or Victor without thinking of the ménage with Lady Anna. The blonde was also riding in the hunt, and when Katelyn glanced at her, the woman smiled coyly. She honestly didn't know what to make of the other woman, she seemed to have so many different sides to her personality.

"I'm delighted you are taking part in the hunt." Rory's gaze slipped to her chest, and Marilyn cleared her throat, which promptly brought his gaze back to where it should be.

Rory's lips quirked. "I am glad you ladies are joining the hunt. Many of the other guests are not so inclined, which I find disappointing."

"Our father insisted we learn to hunt from an early age." Katelyn glanced at Marilyn. "And you should keep in mind the fact that my sister is an excellent shot."

Rory sat up straighter. "Is she? Then it is a good thing we are friends."

Katelyn grinned, feeling more at ease with him.

"Indeed, sir," Marilyn said. "You are fortunate."

Katelyn looked at Sinjin; their gazes caught and held for a moment. He nodded in greeting, and she gave a curt nod in return.

His dark hair was held back with a band, but already a strand had come loose and fell forward. It gave him a rugged, unfinished look, reminding her of a pirate. Oh, yes, she could see him as captain of a ship, and she his willing captive, she thought with an inward smile.

An elaborately dressed footman approached Sinjin, and only then did he look away. The two exchanged words; then seconds later the footman blew the horn.

The horses leapt off the line to the cheers of the women and men who did not participate, and followed the hounds, who barked excitedly.

Although her horse had seemed rather docile at first, now it charged forward, along with the others. Katelyn's heart pounded in time to the horse's gait.

Marilyn darted off to the left with Rory, and Katelyn considered following the same route, but instead stayed with the general pack, always keeping Sinjin in her sights. He finally broke from the back and she followed at a distance. They rode at a steady pace, and the rest of the pack fell away.

When she was sure they were alone, she leaned down low and rushed past him, along the creek. His laughter followed her and she smiled, the blood coursing through her veins.

Sinjin flew past her and she urged her mount faster. He jumped the creek with ease, then turned back to watch her. She made the leap easily, though without as much grace as she would have liked. She yearned to please him, to impress him.

They darted in and out of the trees, and laughter bubbled in her throat. She couldn't remember the last time she had felt so free and alive. What she wouldn't give to experience a lifetime of these moments.

Sinjin slowed in front of her, and she reined her horse in, exhilaration rushing along her spine. Her heart constricted with the raw emotion she felt as she looked into his handsome face, that irresistible smile that promised endless moments of rapture.

His blue eyes stared at her intently. "Come with me?"

Nodding, she followed alongside him, aware that he stared at her, wondering exactly where he was taking her, and what they would do when they got there.

That question was answered a few minutes later when she saw a small cabin on the horizon.

From the moment Sinjin saw Katelyn on the starting line, he had hoped to spend time alone with her, but with his mother watching his every move and Lady Celeste hanging by his side, it was proving more difficult than he had anticipated.

As fate would have it, he had managed a way to extricate

himself from Lady Celeste and the others, and find the woman who had haunted his every waking thought.

He wanted to take Katelyn to a place where they could be themselves and not worry about constantly looking over their shoulders. And that quiet place happened to be the gamesman's cabin, a place his father would go in order to get away when life became a bit too difficult or the pressure of his station became too great.

The small dwelling had been built by his great-grandfather's trusted steward for the very purpose Sinjin's father used it. It was a reminder of where they came from and how hard they had worked to sustain what they had.

He dismounted and turned to help Katelyn, only to find she was already off the horse. The riding habit hugged her slender body, cupping her breasts in a most delightful way and outlining her long legs.

"We can be alone here. No one will disturb us."

She glanced past him to the cabin. "How can you be so certain? What if another couple wishes to use the cabin?"

"We shall lock the door," he said, reaching out and taking hold of her hand.

Excitement rushed through Sinjin as they walked up the steps together.

Just as expected, the key was still hidden on the bottom of the lantern. He unlocked the door and motioned for Katelyn to enter.

From the outside, the cabin appeared plain, but inside, the one-room cabin housed expensive furnishings and an intricately carved four-poster bed that took up the better part of one wall.

Katelyn glanced nervously at the bed.

Sinjin turned the lock.

She lifted a brow. "Should I be afraid?"

"Very."

A smile touched her lips. "I might scream."

"No one would hear you," he said matter-of-factly.

"How do you know?"

"The others will be miles from us by now."

"Then I shall have to take my chances," she said with an exaggerated sigh, taking a step farther into the cabin.

Sinjin lit a candle and pulled the drapes closed, enshrouding the small space in darkness. The flame flickered, sending shadows across the walls.

Katelyn's stomach tightened. "Do you come here often, my lord?"

Did she mean with other women? "No."

"Not even as a boy?" She sounded skeptical and he refrained from laughing.

"My grandfather would not allow anyone here. After he died, my father would come when he and my mother had a disagreement; but for the most part, the cabin remains locked and forgotten."

"It's lovely. I see why your grandfather liked coming here."

"As do I." He was pleased she liked it. Many of his past lovers wouldn't feel the same.

"I dreamt of you again last night," he said before he could stop himself.

She grinned, and her eyes danced. "I dreamt of you, too."

Intrigued, he sat on the edge of the bed. "What did you dream?"

"That's hardly fair. You told me that you dreamt of me first, so you must tell me about your dream first."

"I wouldn't want to frighten you."

She arched her brow. "You do not frighten me."

"Good, I am glad to hear it." He brushed a hand over the blanket. "What of your dream?"

Realizing he was not going to tell her about his dream, she said, "Well, I dreamt that you came to my room, locked the door, and told me to close my eyes."

"And did you do as I asked?"

She licked her lips and his cock bucked against the buttons of his leather pants. "Yes," she said, "I did."

"Come here," he said, not wanting to waste any more time.

She didn't hesitate. She walked toward him, not once dropping her gaze, and stopped inches away.

"Undress for me."

She flinched as though he'd struck her. For a few silent moments, she watched him. He could sense her desire and wariness all at once. "You first."

Enjoying her spirit, he stood and shrugged out of his shirt. Next, he kicked off his boots and socks, before pushing his pants down, following with his drawers.

He straightened, and looked at Katelyn.

Her throat convulsed as her gaze shifted over him.

Blood surged straight to his cock.

Katelyn could scarcely breathe. She had never seen anything so beautiful in all her life as Sinjin's naked body. He was the most striking of statues come to life—gorgeous olive skin over thick muscle and sinew.

Perfection.

A shiver raced through her, straight to the very core of her womanhood.

She shifted on her feet.

He planted his hands on his hips and smiled. "Your turn, my lady."

Katelyn wished she had even an ounce of his confidence.

With trembling hands, she unbuttoned her jacket and tossed it aside.

His gaze shifted to her breasts that were straining against the too-small shirt.

She followed with her blouse, then her boots, skirt, and stockings . . . until all that remained was her chemise. She untied the pink ribbon and the material slipped to her feet in a whisper.

Sinjin's gaze slid over her.

Slowly.

Heat raced to her cheeks, and her heart roared in her ears as he looked at every single inch of her. Rather than be horrified, his intense gaze excited her and made her yearn for what lay ahead.

When his gaze once again met hers, his eyes were slightly darker, heavy-lidded, and there was also something primal about the way he watched her.

He didn't say a word but pulled her against his hard length.

Katelyn shivered. Her reaction had nothing to do with the temperature of the room and everything to do with the man standing before her.

She released a deep breath and he smiled.

"Are you sure about this?"

"You should have asked me that question *before* you told me to take off my clothes."

He laughed and kissed her forehead, reveling in the feel of her warm skin against his. He turned to where her hips nudged the mattress.

Her heart pounded against her chest. This was it. She would no longer be a virgin after this encounter. She would be a woman in every way.

He lifted her chin with his fingers and kissed her softly. His hand drifted down her throat, to a breast, where he cupped the globe, a thumb brushing over an erect nipple.

Katelyn's stomach tensed at the sensations rushing through her body. She rested a hand against his wide chest, her fingers drifting over his rippled belly and finally to his cock, which jutted proudly to his navel.

Her fingers slid over him, and she was amazed at the silky texture over the rigid length, the color of the plum-sized head.

He nudged her back onto the bed and touched her hot sex, inserting his middle finger inside her weeping core. Desire licked at her spine as Sinjin's finger worked in and out of her.

Using his knees, he spread her thighs wide, then slid between them. His long, thick cock probed the entrance of her delicate folds. Lowering his head, he took a nipple into his mouth, his tongue swirling around the erect peak, over and over again.

She arched her hips against his hand, greedy for him to fill her with his solid length.

He readied himself at her moist center and slid inside her liquid heat, inch by inch. He grit his teeth. She was so snug he knew he might spill himself if he didn't take things slow.

Katelyn winced against the pain of the intrusion. She bit her bottom lip as he eased inside.

"Are you okay?"

She nodded.

With a solid thrust of his hips, he was buried deep inside her. The pain began to ease as he began to move slowly, in and out. He kissed a trail from her breasts, up her neck to her lips.

Soon enough, every inch of her body throbbed with promise. His hips continued in a steady rhythm.

As he deepened the kiss, she shifted beneath him, and he moaned deep in his throat.

Sinjin looked into her eyes, the green depths alive with wonder and passion. Wanting to prolong the experience, he slowed his pace, easing the tip of his cock out of her to where the head kissed her opening. She followed him with her hips and he smiled, pleased by her response.

Her nails dug into the skin of his shoulders as he quickened his pace, and she spread her thighs wider, arching against him with each steady thrust.

How much she had learned in such a short time.

Katelyn felt her insides tighten as her body climbed closer and closer toward the ultimate finish.

Sinjin watched her closely as her head fell back on the covers, her mouth open, her lips curving as another pleased groan emanated from her. Hearing her breathing quicken and feeling her nails bite into his shoulders, he knew she was so close.

He thrust a few more times, cupping his hips hard against her, putting pressure on her clit. Instantly, he felt her sheath tighten around him, pulsing as she climaxed, pulling him farther inside.

Only when the final tremor passed through her did he allow himself to let go. It didn't take long, just a few strokes, and he came with a pleased groan.

He kissed her softly, then looked down into her green eyes that were so brilliant, and sparkling with an inner light and fire he recognized well.

"That was wonderful," she breathed on a sigh.

Her words pleased him. "That was just the beginning."

12

The horn sounded, signaling the fox had been slain, and the hunt was over.

Katelyn sat up, the blankets falling to her waist. "We should return."

Sinjin brushed a hand over her slender back and his cock instantly rose to attention. Never had he imagined finding paradise in the arms of a virgin, but he had. It had been sheer bliss, and he fought the urge to beg her to call off her marriage, but he needed to tread lightly, take matters a day at a time.

"I don't want to leave," he said, more content than he'd ever been.

She smiled. "Nor do I, but we must."

He hated the thought of going back to Claymoore Hall, where his mother watched him like a hawk and he was forced to flirt with countless women whom he had no interest in.

The woman he wanted was with him, and no one else held any appeal.

Katelyn kissed him softly, her green eyes alight with an inner glow.

She pulled the covers back, and the red stain on the sheets instantly drew his attention. He had felt her maidenhead when he'd penetrated her, but seeing the evidence was even more powerful. *Mine,* his male pride all but roared.

He had been her first, and God willing, he would be her last. There was no way he could share her. No way he could accept the thought of her being another man's wife.

He nearly voiced his thoughts aloud when she started gathering up her clothes. Her hair had long ago come out of the clip and now hung about her hips in thick waves. He caught a glimpse of her high buttocks as she bent to pick up her chemise.

His cock throbbed against the sheets.

"Come here, Katelyn."

Katelyn heard the husky quality of Sinjin's voice. She looked over her shoulder at him, her gaze sliding to his erection.

Her nipples instantly hardened, and heat shot to her sex. "We must return, Sinjin." Even she sounded unconvinced as she inched toward the bed.

"We will not be long, and have no fear . . . my brothers will cover for us."

"They know we are here?"

"No, but they'll figure things out quickly."

Reaching out, he pulled her back down onto the bed. Katelyn laughed as he drew her close against his hard body. Letting the clothes slide to the floor, she went into his arms.

He shifted them to where she straddled his hips, his huge cock rising up between them.

Uncertain of how to proceed, she was relieved when Sinjin eased her onto her knees and positioned his cock against her slick opening. The plum-sized head probed her sensitive folds, and she came down slowly on him, taking each glorious inch into her body until she was seated fully against him. She gasped, stunned at how he filled her so completely.

Sinjin's hands cupped her breasts, his thumbs brushing over her sensitive nipples. He pinched the tips lightly, pulling them into taut buds. He sat up, kissed her breast, took a nipple into his mouth, and sucked.

His touch was magic.

With one hand resting on his shoulder, the other curling around the headboard, Katelyn rocked against him. His hands slid to her hips, and he urged her into a faster rhythm. Soon she was riding him with wild abandon, the headboard hitting the wall with each bounce.

His blue eyes had turned darker, his thick lashes casting shadows against his high cheekbones. God, he was so beautiful, so amazing, and she knew she would not forget this moment as long as she lived.

Long fingers slid to her mons, brushing over the tiny bundle of nerves at the top of her sex. He teased her nipple with his tongue and teeth, and the multiple sensations pushed her over the edge.

The first shiver of orgasm rippled low in her belly, growing with intensity with each thrust of his cock and lick of his tongue. He cupped his hips, putting pressure on her sensitive nub, and she cried out.

She watched in wonder as he came, the cords of his neck straining as he lifted her off his cock, semen gushing onto her belly. He fell back on the pillows, a loud, satisfied groan filling the cottage.

Katelyn lingered in the woods just beyond Claymoore Hall. Sinjin had left her minutes before to return to the manor before his mother sent a small army to find him.

She would wait a little while before making an appearance. Perhaps she would claim problems with her horse, but she feared that the truth would be all over her face.

"There you are."

With a gasp, Katelyn turned to find her sister walking toward her with horse in tow. "Sorry, I didn't mean to startle you," she said, looking slightly irritated. "Where on earth have you been?"

"Have you been looking for me?" Katelyn asked absently.

"Yes."

"I'm so sorry. How long were you waiting?"

"Quarter of an hour, perhaps half an hour." Marilyn came closer, her head tilted to the side as she studied Katelyn. "Where have you been?"

"With Sinjin."

"Alone?"

"Yes."

Her eyes widened. "Yes? That's all you are going to say?"

Oddly, Katelyn felt a lump form in her throat. She had always wondered what it would feel like to become a woman. She had envisioned it would involve mourning the passing of her maidenhead, and yet, what she had experienced in that cabin with Sinjin had been nothing short of heaven. It had been the single greatest experience of her life, and she knew they had only scratched the surface.

Indeed, how could she possibly go back to such a mundane existence with Lord Balliford now that she knew how wonderful making love could be with someone you desired, someone you cared for?

"Oh my God, you made love to him." Oddly, there was no accusation in Marilyn's voice. No condemnation. Just surprise. "I need not ask you how it was, for you are positively glowing."

Katelyn was off her horse a second later and hugging her sister, her dearest friend. "Am I?"

"Indeed, you are." Marilyn put her at arm's length. "And

you must tell me every detail . . . later. Now we must return to the manor before someone comes looking for us."

"What if others know?"

"How would they know?"

"You knew."

"And I am your sister. For all anyone knows, you were riding with me."

"I saw you ride off with Victor."

"Yes, we had a nice time. In fact, we stopped by the river and had a rock-skipping contest."

"You like him."

Marilyn nodded. "Yes, I like him very much. He is a charming companion."

"He thinks quite highly of you," Katelyn added.

"Then we have a mutual respect for each other." Marilyn winked, then mounted with little effort. Her sister was one of the best riders Katelyn knew of.

Katelyn hesitated. "Marilyn, I am afraid."

"Afraid of what?"

"That I shall have to marry Lord Balliford," Katelyn said, mounting the horse. "That I will wake from this fantasy and realize that it was all too good to be true."

Marilyn rode up alongside her and reached out her hand. "If it comes to pass that you must marry Balliford, then I shall steal you away like a thief in the night and we will never again be seen or heard from." There was no teasing in her voice or in her expression. She meant every word.

"Do you promise?"

"Absolutely. I shall not leave your side from this moment forward . . . unless you ask me to. We are in this together, dear sister."

"What if Mother has her way?"

"Our mother must be very careful, else she will find herself with no children at all." Marilyn dropped her gaze between them, a tight smile on her lips. "We could survive in this world without her, Kate. Lord knows she has lived her life without us."

"I know you're right. It's just difficult when all our lives we've been brought up to obey our parents, to respect them and not question their authority."

"Yes, but there comes a time when we must do what is best for us." Marilyn lifted her chin, released a deep breath, and forced a smile. "I no longer wish to talk about Mother. It only upsets me and ruins my good humor. Come, let us return to the manor and take full advantage of the incredible food the cook will have made up."

"Race you," Katelyn said, digging her knees into her mount's sides.

Marilyn's laughter followed close behind.

The stable master was waiting to take the horses from them the second Katelyn and Marilyn approached the stables.

Inside the manor was quiet, and many of the guests had already retired to their rooms, no doubt for a sojourn before tonight's dinner and entertainment.

Katelyn wondered if she could find a way to be with Sinjin again tonight.

Unfortunately, the cabin was too far away from the manor, and their absence would surely not go unnoticed. She could ask Marilyn to cover for her, but even her loyal sister could only improvise so much.

Marilyn closed the chamber door behind them. "I have suffered in silence long enough. Since you have not been forthcoming in the least, I shall ask you—what was it like?" Marilyn inquired.

"Oh, Marilyn, I cannot possibly explain it."

"Too beautiful for words?"

"I understand now why men enjoy it so."

"You think women do not?"

Katelyn shrugged. "Mother always said it was a chore."

Marilyn looked skeptical.

"It seems like every book I have read, or what whisperings I have heard, always explains making love in a way that hardly describes the act as romantic."

Marilyn grinned. "Well, Lady Anna might be the first to contradict you."

Katelyn laughed under her breath.

A knock sounded at the door, silencing them. "Perhaps that is a servant with tea," Marilyn said, crossing the room.

"That would be lovely."

Marilyn opened the door. "Aunt Lillith, what are you doing here?"

Aunt Lillith's brows furrowed. "You knew I was coming."

Katelyn swallowed her intense disappointment that her time alone with Marilyn, without a chaperone, had come to an abrupt halt. "We thought you'd be arriving this weekend."

Lillith's gaze shifted back and forth between Marilyn and Katelyn. "I was able to come earlier, but I can see neither of you is pleased to see me." She looked wounded.

Katelyn forced a smile she didn't feel. "We are glad to see you, Aunt Lillith. You just surprised us, that is all."

"Do not lie, child. It does not become you."

Aunt Lillith was stunning, and looked a good decade younger than her thirty-eight years. Her complexion was fair and flawless, her golden blond hair was silky soft, and her hazel eyes sparkled brilliantly.

Lillith had never had children of her own, and her body was as lithe and slim as it had always been. To Katelyn, she had always been one of the most beautiful women she had ever known, and not simply by her outward appearance, but by the woman she was and how she carried herself. She had a sterling reputation and was widely regarded as a role model to young ladies of her acquaintance.

Their relationship had always been relaxed . . . more like sisters in many respects. However, she feared at the capacity she would play now that Katelyn had started a sexual relationship with Sinjin.

"We are always happy to see our favorite aunt," Marilyn said, finally snapping out of her shock.

The compliment seemed to appease some of the hurt caused by their less-than-cordial welcome, because Lillith smiled radiantly. "Tell me all about this party and what you have been up to."

Katelyn wondered what her aunt would think if she was truthful about her wish to call off her engagement. Would she have an ally in Lillith, or would she run straight to her mother?

"All the Rayborne brothers are positively gorgeous," Marilyn began.

"If the older two are as handsome as Rory, then I imagine women are fighting amongst themselves in order to win their attention."

"You met Rory?" Katelyn asked.

"Yes, I passed by him on my way in." Lillith's eyes widened and she grinned, exposing deep dimples. "I do not think I have ever seen such a striking man."

"Rory is confident and a bit arrogant, but very likeable," Marilyn said with a smile. "And Victor is very funny."

Lillith's brows lifted nearly to her hairline. "You seem taken with him, Marilyn."

"He is my friend," she said matter-of-factly, and Lillith nodded.

"And what of Sinjin?" Lillith asked.

To Katelyn's horror, she felt a blush rush up her neck to her cheeks.

Marilyn cleared her throat. "Approachable. He is more mature than the other two, is kind and thoughtful, and looks after his brothers quite dotingly."

"And what do you think of him, Katelyn?" Lillith asked.

"It is obvious he loves his brothers very much," Katelyn said. "He's very nice."

"He sounds delightful. Indeed, they all do. I am anxious to meet all of them this evening."

Marilyn met Katelyn's gaze but quickly looked away.

"Will you be sharing a room with us?"

Lillith shook her head. "Lady Rochester has been good enough to find me a room of my own, but it will not be ready until late this afternoon, after another guest leaves."

Thank God for that.

"Do not fret, girls. We shall have a lovely time," Lillith said, sliding an elegant hand over the polished wood of a side table. "You will not even know that I am here."

13

Lillith watched as hot wax dripped from a candle onto the lace tablecloth that covered the opulent table.

Lady Rochester certainly knew how to throw a party. The room was full of England's most sought-after debutantes and wealthy young men of privilege.

It reminded her of her coming-out party, which felt like a lifetime ago.

If only she'd had the opportunity to throw her nieces a proper coming-out ball. Perhaps she could have saved dear, sweet Katelyn from a horrific marriage. Poor, poor girl. She would be absolutely miserable married to the pompous, boring Lord Balliford.

Lillith had tried in vain to talk her sister into another match, but Loraine never would listen to reason. No, she didn't want to interrupt her life by finding a good match for her eldest daughter. She had just leapt at the first man who came along, a friend of her late husband's.

Indeed, Lillith had even dropped by Loraine's rented London hotel suite on her way to Claymoore Hall. Her sister had barely let her in, and when she did, she tried to pass her young lover off as one of the help. Lillith knew better. She had heard the rumors circulating.

Her sister would never learn. She had married William when she was only twenty, and after the birth of Katelyn, took up with lover after lover. Poor William had tried everything to make his young wife happy, but the only thing that made Loraine happy was variety.

It had almost been a relief to Loraine when William died eighteen months ago. However, William had his own vice and left the family with substantial gambling debt. A debt that Lord Balliford had apparently paid off.

And Loraine was blowing through the money, spoiling her young lover with expensive gifts, not caring that she had a thirteen-year-old son in boarding school, who had taken on the title of his father and desperately needed his mother.

Yes, Loraine had all but thrown Katelyn into Balliford's lap, and would soon do the same to Marilyn. That is why Lillith hoped that perhaps one of the Rayborne brothers would be a good match.

A handsome young man took a seat opposite her. She sat up a little straighter. "You must be one of the brothers."

He grinned and her heart missed a beat.

"Yes, I am Sinjin."

"Ah, the oldest."

"Indeed. You must be a new arrival."

"I am. My name is Lady Nordland. My nieces are here."

His eyes widened. "Do you mean Lady Marilyn and Lady Katelyn?"

"Yes."

If possible, his smile brightened even more. "They are delightful young ladies. I am so glad you decided to join them."

"I fear they do not share your sentiment."

"I doubt that."

"I did not plan on arriving until this weekend. I assure you, they were quite taken aback when they opened their chamber door to find me standing there."

"Well, I can certainly understand to a point."

"Point taken," she replied with a smile, already liking the gorgeous viscount.

She glanced farther down the table at Katelyn. Her niece was talking to a tall blonde. "Lord Mawbry, do you know the man speaking with Lady Katelyn?"

Sinjin leaned forward. "Yes, that is Thomas Lehman."

"I do not know the name."

"He is Irish."

"Ah. He must not realize my niece is engaged."

"I think he knows. The question is . . . does he care?"

She nodded, making a mental note to keep an eye on the Irishman's advances.

"Did you grow up near your nieces?"

"Yes, I did. That is, until I married and moved to Bath. Unfortunately, I was only able to see my nieces when I visited." She made sure to leave out that the latter part of her marriage she had spent as much time at her sister's house as she could tolerate. She loved her sister, but sometimes she could be quite controlling. And having a controlling husband had made Lillith less tolerant of such a trait.

"You must have been a child yourself."

She smiled sincerely, enjoying his easy manner. "Not quite a child."

"What can you tell me about your nieces?"

She was delighted by his interest. "Well, although they are sisters, they are very different in personality and temperament. If you've talked with them, you might have noticed this already."

110

He nodded. "Marilyn seems to talk a bit more than her sister."

"Yes, but Katie watches. She might not say much, but she observes. She sees everything."

Sinjin brought the glass of wine to his lips and took a drink.

"Katie has always loved all things feminine. For as long as I can remember, she played with dolls, dressed up like a princess, and rarely got into trouble. She's proficient at playing the piano, singing, and as you could probably tell by this afternoon, she is quite comfortable in the saddle, but so is her sister."

"And Marilyn, is she equally schooled in the arts?"

"Yes, but Mary preferred being outside to her studies. She was forever getting her hands dirty, and she seemed to be fond of climbing trees. Indeed, I swear the maid must have changed her clothes half a dozen times a day, much to my sister's distress."

"I am not at all surprised," a young woman murmured. She sat to Sinjin's right and had been avoiding Lillith all evening.

"Do you know my nieces?" Lillith tried to keep her tone cordial.

The young lady looked at her, all innocence. Lillith had noted the excellent quality of her dress, the expensive jewels, the confident air, like she was better than everyone else at the table. She sniffed. "I do not pretend to know them well."

How Lillith hated arrogance.

"A pity, for they are lovely creatures," Lillith said, flashing the young woman her most winning smile.

Across the table, Sinjin Rayborne did his best to hide a grin by wiping his mouth with his napkin, but Lillith had seen that smirk and had a feeling she had a friend in the handsome lord.

* * *

Rory was bored out of his mind. Dinner was taking an eternity, and he dreaded what was to come. His mother had mentioned allowing the young ladies present to display their many talents by way of singing or playing the pianoforte.

If only he could beg off without anyone noticing, ride to the closest inn, and drink himself into oblivion.

Unfortunately, his mother had made it a point to let him know his presence would be mandatory, so leaving was not an option. Damn, he had never felt so confined in all his life. He feared what his future would hold. Was being married anything like answering to a mother?

God's truth, he had no intention of answering to anyone, married or not.

Throughout dinner, Lady Anna had been trying to get his attention. He knew she would meet with him anytime, anyplace, but he wanted to keep his options open. She was a dangerous one, that, and he was still a bit uneasy about the mysterious open door during their last encounter.

A comely servant walked into the dining room just then and Rory sat up straighter. By God, she had the largest breasts he had ever seen. He glanced down the table to see that nearly every male took notice, each staring wide-eyed at the woman's incredible bosom.

She bent down to speak to one of the chaperones who she must be attending.

Though she was not particularly beautiful, she had incredible attributes, so who cared?

And Victor had taken note of her lovely tits as well, for a dark brow arched. His brother reached for his glass and downed the brandy in one swallow, not once taking his eyes off the servant.

He abruptly glanced at Rory and smiled.

The game was on.

Rory wiped his mouth, intent on getting to her first.

"Please excuse me for a moment," he murmured to no one in particular, and made his way toward the closest exit.

He waited outside in the hallway. His patience was rewarded seconds later when the servant stepped out and quietly shut the door behind her. She turned, her eyes wide when she saw him. She curtsied prettily, her huge breasts bouncing with the slight movement. He could hardly wait until he got her in bed, astride him, those large mounds swinging to and fro.

His cock already bucked in anticipation.

Now that she was closer, he realized she was at least a good decade older than himself, which did not put him off in the least. He found mature women to be some of the best lovers, their enthusiasm and experience often putting their younger counterparts to shame.

Lord she had a gorgeous mouth. It was amazing. Extremely full-lipped and promising delights he could only imagine. She had on a bonnet, but he could see auburn hair poking out from underneath.

"I have not seen you before."

A smile touched her lips. "I arrived yesterday with my mistress." She had the slightest touch of a Scottish accent.

"Who is your mistress?"

"Lady Montrose."

He didn't recognize the name but made a note of it for future use.

His gaze shifted over her, stopping abruptly on her enormous bosoms. How he wanted to rub his face against those luscious mounds—

"Do ye want me, my lord?"

He had not expected such a blunt question, and it intrigued him she would be so bold. Oftentimes servants would not even make eye contact.

"Yes," he said, "I do."

She reached for him, took his hand, and opened the first door they came to, which happened to be a musty closet the servants used for storing extra linens.

She shut the door behind her, enshrouding them in darkness. Rory was about to tell her this would not do when she started unbuttoning his pants. Before he could blink, she had his cock in hand and was kneading him with amazing skill. In fact, if she wasn't careful he would come.

As though reading his thoughts, she stopped abruptly. Her hand slipped between his legs, and she fondled his balls, rubbing them gently in her palm before a finger slid toward his anus.

His eyes widened. Perhaps he should have taken her up to his room.

She licked her finger and slid it knuckle-deep into his ass, past the tight ring of muscle. "Ye like that, don't ye?" she asked, inching upward.

He didn't say a word, only closed his eyes and savored what she was doing to him.

Leaning forward to kiss her, he was shocked when she avoided his mouth and turned her back to him. She lifted her skirts and drew his cock toward her welcoming heat. "We must hurry. My mistress will be retiring very soon and I must be there when she arrives."

He slid the head of his prick into her and bit his lip on a moan as she backed against him, taking him fully inside her welcome heat in one movement. She rolled her hips, and slid up and down his length. He didn't even have to move.

He felt her play with her cunny and he took control, ramming into her over and over again. "Oooh, that's good," she said on a sigh. "Fuck me hard, my lord."

The closet heated up fast, sweat beading on his upper lip.

Her heated sighs urged him on, and when she reached back and cupped his scrotum, he pumped faster, close to orgasm. Normally he always waited for his lover to finish first, but his need was so great—

"Don't ye dare come before I do," she said firmly.

There was an *or else* quality about that warning, so he slowed and thought of anything but fucking.

Within seconds, she was moaning and writhing, her sex squeezing his cock tight as her climax pulled him deeper inside her honeyed walls.

Her fingers squeezed his ass cheeks tight as she ground against him.

He barely had time to withdraw before he came hard all over her back. Bloody hell, she'd been an unexpected surprise.

The entire closet smelled of sex, and he fought to catch his breath. She righted her clothing and turned to him, opening the closet and allowing some light in. He realized with disappointment that he had not seen those massive breasts in all their glory.

"That was just lovely," she said, with a moan for good measure.

"Yes, very enjoyable," he replied, wiping his cock with the hem of his shirt before stuffing it into his pants.

"I must go. Perhaps we can meet again very soon."

He opened his mouth to respond, but she was already out the door. She closed it behind her.

Rory frowned. For as long as he could remember, he had never been the one to leave before his lover. Well, unless a husband or current lover came home unexpectedly.

He raked a hand through his hair. Perhaps he was losing his edge . . .

14

Sinjin stood outside on the verandah with his brothers while their guests mingled inside, many listening to Lady Anna sing and play the pianoforte, while another group of young ladies and men played cards or charades.

Katelyn and Marilyn had both seemed equally disappointed that their aunt had arrived, and he, too, was disappointed. Her presence would make getting together with Katelyn most difficult—but not impossible.

Dinner had been excruciating, with Katelyn sitting beside Thomas. His mother must have done so deliberately, and the man had taken the opportunity to enforce his interest. Sinjin was desperate to get time alone with her—quite a task since her aunt had yet to leave her side.

"Did you see the maid with the huge tits?" Rory asked, a pleased smile on his lips.

"Yes," Victor said, taking a draw on a cigar. "Incredible breasts. I've never see the like. Positively enormous."

Sinjin hadn't even noticed.

"I fucked her in the closet during dinner," Rory said nonchalantly.

Victor choked on the smoke he had just inhaled.

Sinjin shook his head. He had noticed his youngest sibling leave the festivities and return minutes later with a devilish grin on his face. He should have guessed.

"The closet?" Victor's eyes narrowed. "Bloody hell, man, you really know how to treat a lady."

Rory shrugged. "It was her idea. She grabbed my arm and pulled me in. I had no choice in the matter."

Victor's head fell back on his shoulders and he chuckled. "So how was it?"

"Lovely, though I wish it would have lasted a bit longer."

"I bet she's saying the same thing right about now," Victor said with a nod, resting a hip against the stone balustrade. He turned to Sinjin. "Since we're talking about interludes, I noticed you took a while returning from the hunt today, and when you surfaced you were alone."

Sinjin glanced at him. "I took a wrong path."

Rory lifted a dark brow. "Since when do you get lost—"

"Especially when you know this land like the back of your hand." Victor crushed the cigar under his boot and crossed his arms over his chest. "I think there's something you're keeping from us."

Sinjin didn't want to keep anything from his brothers, and it wasn't like him to lie, but he couldn't bring himself to tell them the truth. He felt protective of Katelyn, and what they had shared had been so intensely gratifying and special, he had no desire to share the details with anyone else.

"You're being awfully quiet, Sin," Victor murmured, watching him closely.

Irritated, Sinjin shook his head. "You know I have no reason to withhold information from either of you. Truth be told, I enjoyed the time away from the hunt. I'm growing weary of the constant entertaining, and much like yourselves, I yearn for a bit of free time, and that's what I got."

"All right, then," Victor said with a grin. "I believe you."

It was obvious he didn't, but he didn't push the point either.

"I meant to ask you who the new arrival is—the blonde you talked with during dinner."

"That would be Lady Nordland, aunt of Lady Marilyn and Lady Katelyn."

"Ah, the apple does not fall far from the tree," Rory said, wiggling his brows.

"Do not get any ideas, Rory," Sinjin snapped. "Lady Nordland is a chaperone."

Rory held his hands up. "And chaperones are off-limits. Well, save for the lovely Lady Katelyn."

"Lady Katelyn is spoken for." Sinjin realized too late his voice had come out clipped.

Rory smiled, and Sinjin realized he was messing with him.

"Stick to your big-breasted maids," Victor said with a wink.

"Indeed, I shall."

Victor chewed on a nail. "Isn't Lady Nordland the widow who has been alone for years now?"

"I don't know," Sinjin said.

"She's quite virtuous, I hear," Victor said, a smile teasing his lips.

"I wonder what it would be like to have a woman who is virtuous," Rory said absently, staring out into the dark lawns.

Growing uncomfortable with the conversation, Sinjin looked toward the long parlor windows. He scanned the crowd and found Katelyn, Marilyn, and their aunt sitting in the back of the room, talking amongst themselves.

Sinjin straightened his jacket. "Well, gentleman, I suppose we have dallied long enough."

"Indeed," Victor said with a sigh. "Back to the proverbial lion's den."

Walking into the parlor, Sinjin kept his eye on Katelyn. She was aware of him, he could tell by the way she kept throwing him glances here and there.

He had to get her alone.

Thomas approached the trio and Sinjin took a deep breath. The man was absolutely incorrigible. Lillith engaged the Irishman in conversation, and when Katelyn glanced his way, Sinjin looked at her, then walked toward the nearest exit.

He could only hope she followed.

"Aunt Lillith, is it all right if I go to the room for a little bit? I have a slight headache."

Lillith, who had been speaking to Thomas, turned to her, her brows furrowed. "A headache. Do you have any other symptoms?"

"No, I'm sure it is just all the activity."

She patted Katelyn's knee. "Of course, my dear. Marilyn, perhaps you could see her to the room."

Marilyn, looking relieved to get away from Thomas, nodded. "Of course."

Katelyn headed for a different exit than Sinjin had.

"I bet he's in the study."

"You saw him enter?"

"No, but I'm assuming. From his expression I'm guessing he wants you to follow him, and the most obvious place for him to go to is the room where it all began."

Katelyn nodded. "I won't be long."

"I'll take my time walking to the room. Perhaps I'll read a

chapter of the book Aunt Lillith brought for me. It's quite good."

"You're the best sister a girl could ask for," Katelyn said as they came upon the study.

Marilyn looked both ways. "Now go."

"Thank you, Marilyn." Katelyn kissed her cheek and disappeared into the room.

Sinjin stood before the fireplace, his back to her.

Her heart constricted. All night she had watched him as he talked with other women, laughed, flirted. All night she had waited to be with him again.

"Lock the door."

She did as he asked, her stomach twisting with anticipation.

He turned, his gaze sliding over her slowly. "God how I want you," he said, coming toward her, taking her into his arms, crushing her to him. Relief washed over her in waves.

Reaching up, he cupped her face with both hands and kissed her softly. Her eyes closed and she breathed deeply of his scent. "You don't know how desperately I've wanted to be with you all night."

His words thrilled her. "I've wanted to be with you, too," she said. Her pulse skittered when he pressed a kiss against her forehead. He made her feel so cherished, so desired. "I saw you talking to my aunt at dinner."

"She's a lovely woman. So beautiful."

His thumbs brushed along her cheeks. "Yes, she is."

"It sounds as though you are very close."

"We are very close."

"Your aunt says that you were the perfect child," he said, his tone teasing.

"Well, I was easier to control than my sister, but hardly perfect."

He chuckled. "Yes, Marilyn sounds like she was a bit more

of a handful. From what little I know of your sister, I am not at all surprised."

Katelyn laughed under her breath. "Indeed, Marilyn is more of a handful than I, but a more loyal sister I could never find."

He nodded. "I always yearned to have a sister, but I would not trade my brothers for anything. I still do not know how we will stand to be apart once we all marry."

At the mention of marriage, Katelyn sobered. These past days had been a wonderful dream, and soon that dream would end and she would have to return to a life with Ronald.

An endless life of needlepoint and long, agonizing days and nights.

"You're daydreaming, Katelyn," he whispered against her lips, and she looked into his beautiful blue eyes. His tongue teased her lips and she opened her mouth to accept him.

Her hands moved up and down his strong back. Hard muscle shifted beneath her fingers, and she yanked his shirt out of his pants, desperate for skin-to-skin contact.

He cupped her breasts, using his thumbs to lift the heavy globes up and over the bodice. Bending his head, he sucked and laved one peak, then the other.

Katelyn threaded her fingers through his hair, holding his head there. He lifted her skirts with one hand and cupped her mons. Glancing up at her, he said, "Are you sore?"

"A little, but I don't care. I want you."

His gaze searched hers, and she would never forget the expression for as long as she lived. He looked ravenous, ready to rip off her clothes. "You're already wet for me, Katelyn."

The words excited her, sending a thrill rushing up her spine and heat flowing through her veins.

He fumbled with the buttons on his pants. Impatient, she pushed his hands out of the way and took his hard length in hand, her fingers curling around the thick base.

A moan came from deep in his chest; then he was lifting her, and her back came up against the wall.

His sex probed her entrance; then he eased her down on his rock-hard shaft, inch by delicious inch.

At first, he didn't move a muscle, just groaned, his eyes closed. Then he opened them, and he stared at her as he began to move, his jaw clenched tight.

Sinjin's hands cupped her ass, and he tried to be as gentle as possible. It wasn't easy, especially with her firm breasts bobbing up and down with each thrust, and her soft moans urging him on.

He cupped his hips, staying deeply imbedded inside her heated walls as he sucked on a nipple.

Katelyn felt the stirrings of climax begin low in her belly. As he teased the rigid peaks relentlessly with his tongue, she clung to him and rolled her hips.

He lifted his head and kissed her; then he thrust hard, his hips moving in an even rhythm.

She dug her hands into his hair, her fingers weaving into the silky softness. He ground against her delicate nub, and she cried out as she came, her velvet walls pulsing around his hard length, drawing him deeper into her body.

Sinjin watched as Katelyn's lips opened slightly, the way her chest heaved, her rosy nipples erect and swollen from his kisses, poking over the trimming of her gown. He looked down where he was buried to the hilt within her molten core. He slowly slid out, then in, and knew by her expression she was climbing higher and higher toward orgasm.

He pulled out completely, the head of his cock teasing her tight opening. She followed his rod with her hips and moaned in frustration and he slid inside.

As her insides clenched him tight and throbbed around his hard length, he thrust faster and harder, and came with a satisfied moan.

15

"Shall we go for a walk?" Aunt Lillith asked Katelyn.

They had joined many of the other women for tea out on the verandah, where the guests could enjoy the sunny day.

Katelyn set her cup down and stood. "Of course."

Marilyn stood to join them, but Aunt Lillith shook her head and she sat back down.

Their gazes caught and held for a moment, and Katelyn's pulse quickened. Did Lillith know about Sinjin?

They walked down the steps and onto the pathway in silence, passing by two male guests who rushed to get out of the way. The older of the two stared at Lillith, but she didn't take any notice. She never did.

"Come, let's get off the path, shall we?"

Katelyn nodded, her foreboding growing as they cut across the lawns. Lillith slid her hand around Katelyn's elbow. Birds flew from a tree, nearly startling her out of her skin, but her aunt didn't flinch.

Lillith seemed so . . . intense. Very unlike the Aunt Lillith she knew and loved. "You wished to speak with me?"

Lillith looked over her shoulder, and seeing that they had walked a good distance from the manor, nodded. "I think it might be wise if we leave the party, my dear."

Katelyn nearly tripped. "Whatever for?"

Lillith stopped, and Katelyn was forced to as well. She straightened her shoulders. "Because you are falling in love with Sinjin Rayborne, and you know such a union cannot be since you are already spoken for."

She opened her mouth to deny it, but Lillith cut her off. "Every time you look at him, you glow from within, and I can tell he desires you as well."

She had not realized they had been so obvious.

"I do not know how far your relationship has progressed, and a part of me does not wish to know."

"I could not help myself, Aunt Lillith."

Lillith closed her eyes and took a deep breath. "Oh dear," she whispered, opening her eyes a second later. To Katelyn's relief, she saw no condemnation there, no disappointment—just sadness.

Katelyn dropped her gaze. "I shouldn't have told you. I should have kept it to myself."

Lifting Katelyn's chin with a trembling hand, Lillith smiled softly. "Thank you for telling me the truth. I expected nothing less of you."

She dropped her hand, looked toward the manor, then back at Katelyn. "And I understand why you could not help yourself when it comes to Sinjin. He is very handsome and charming. However, like most beautiful men, he knows his power over women."

"He's not like that, Aunt Lillith, I swear."

"I know men like Sinjin Rayborne and his brothers. Trust me, my dear, I do."

Katelyn wanted to defend Sinjin, but she stopped herself short of doing so. "I thought you and Uncle Winfred were happy."

Her lips quirked. "Everyone thought we were happy because we were such excellent actors. When I first met your uncle, I was a year younger than you are now. So young, and he was everything I desired in a man—charming, handsome, and older, which meant he had experience in the ways of the world, and I found that exciting. I yearned to be taken care of, and I felt this man, who was ten years my senior, could do just that."

"What happened?"

Lillith pressed her lips together. "Well, the infatuation I felt for Winfred during our courtship faded quickly in the face of reality. The charming man who had once treated me like a princess during our courtship changed into a monster the moment the wedding ceremony was over and the ring was on my finger. I endured years of harsh treatment at his hands. His cruelty shaped me into the woman I am today."

"You are well respected, Aunt Lillith."

"Yes, and I have fought hard for that reputation. Winfred chipped away at my soul year after year, but slowly and steadily I am regaining what he stole from me."

Katelyn had no idea her aunt had suffered through a miserable marriage. "I'm sorry, Aunt Lillith."

Lillith took a deep breath. "I do not tell you this now to change how you feel about your uncle, but rather for you to learn from my mistakes."

"I honestly thought you were happy."

Her aunt smiled tightly. "You would be amazed at what people can hide behind a smile." She looked away for a moment, as though she were remembering another time. "Anyway, I did not mean to turn the attention of this conversation toward me, but I wanted to let you know I do understand what you're feeling. But having said that, you have to remember not only that Sinjin Rayborne is a notorious rakehell, but that you are engaged to another man."

The reminder was like a dash of cold water to the face. "I cannot stand Lord Balliford, Aunt Lillith. We have nothing in common, and I swear that we have not but two words to say to each another. When he does talk, it's to tell me how disapproving he is of women doing this or that. A life with such a man would be sheer misery."

Aunt Lillith pressed her lips together. "I am sorry, Katelyn. Truly. I wanted differently for you. I wanted you to have the chance to choose your own mate, but your mother has, for whatever reason, cast her eye on Lord Balliford. I know your mother better than anyone . . . and I honestly fear she will not be moved in this matter."

Fear and disappointment rushed through Katelyn. "I must marry Ronald, then?"

"I do not see a way out of it, Katie. I wish I could help, but your mother is so stubborn. She refuses to listen to reason. You are already married in her mind."

All the hope Katelyn had built up slowly started slipping away. Aunt Lillith had always known what to do. Katelyn's heart constricted. Sinjin would go on to marry another, and she would marry Ronald, and all she would have to sustain her would be the memories of these two glorious weeks.

Sinjin sat on a settee beside his mother, watching as yet another female guest made her way to the pianoforte to display her musical talents.

Even a few of the gentlemen had joined in to sing, one of them the infuriating Mr. Lehman.

Sinjin wished the man would just leave already.

As Miss Suzanne started to play an interesting rendition of "Greensleeves," he looked around the long parlor, searching for Katelyn.

Where on earth was she? He had not seen her, Marilyn, or Lillith all day. His mother had mentioned seeing the women at tea earlier today, but no one had seen them since.

Had Aunt Lillith found out about the liaison in the study? Perhaps she had followed Katelyn? Or perhaps he was being paranoid.

Rory laughed at something the woman beside him said, and Betsy straightened, her sharp gaze moving to her youngest son.

As though sensing his mother's disapproval, Rory cleared his throat and turned his full attention to Miss Suzanne's performance.

Three performances later, Sinjin was ready to excuse himself when Marilyn and Katelyn approached the pianoforte. His heart nearly leapt from his chest. Katelyn was so pretty in an ice blue gown, her hair styled beautifully. She took a seat before the pianoforte, and Marilyn stood beside her.

Katelyn began to play, and immediately it became obvious she had a natural talent for the instrument. He realized then how very little he knew about her. What other interests did she have? What were her favorite foods, her favorite writers, her favorite colors? It dawned on him that he'd never been interested to know these things with his other lovers.

How nice to watch her and have a reason to stare without being obvious. Every move was one of grace, her hands light on the keys.

Marilyn sang the first verse with her sister and Sinjin smiled. What a talented duo. Any parent would be proud. Any husband would be proud of such a treasure.

Aunt Lillith had sat down near Sinjin, and she glanced at him. He nodded and she smiled softly, before returning her attention to her nieces. She could not be much older than himself, and yet in those lovely blue eyes he saw a lifetime of living.

Sinjin could feel his mother watching him, and he made sure not to stare at just Katelyn, but it was difficult, especially after doing everything in his power these past days to avoid looking at her in order not to cause undue suspicion.

Katelyn played the final note, and the entire room erupted into applause. The sisters stood and bowed, and it was then she finally looked up and met his gaze. She abruptly looked away, up at her sister, and smiled. They took a seat next to their aunt, and Lady Celeste sat down to perform next.

"Lady Celeste was a pupil of Jacque le Cue, one of the most sought-after musicians in Paris," his mother murmured.

To Sinjin's irritation, Thomas sat down beside Katelyn and whispered something in her ear.

Sinjin drew his hands into fists at his sides. He glanced in her direction, but she did not notice, too intent with whatever Thomas was saying.

"She plays beautifully, does she not?" his mother whispered behind her fan, and Sinjin returned his attention to Celeste, whose high voice was beautiful and befitting of any opera singer.

"Indeed, she does."

He felt Katelyn's gaze burning into him and he shifted. However, he could feel his mother watching him, and it took all the will he possessed to stay put, focus on Celeste, and stand to applaud her the second she finished.

His mother winked at him, and as Celeste returned to her seat, she had a triumphant look on her face that unsettled him.

In her mind, she was already celebrating and planning the wedding.

Katelyn shifted in her seat. Lady Celeste was doing everything in her power to win over Sinjin, and it was obvious to everyone that she had already succeeded in winning over Lady Rochester, because the woman positively beamed throughout Celeste's flawless performance, and now they sat on the settee looking like one happy family.

Marilyn squeezed Katelyn's hand in quiet commiseration.

Thomas leaned in. "I would be delighted if you would take a walk in the gardens with me, Lady Katelyn." His gaze flicked to Aunt Lillith. "With your lovely aunt's permission, of course."

Aunt Lillith glanced at Katelyn, then Thomas. "Of course, but only if I accompany you."

His smile slipped only a little, and he inclined his head. "Of course. I would consider it an honor to walk with the most beautiful women at Claymoore Hall."

Aunt Lillith's lips curved into an amused smile. "Very well, then. I shall go upstairs and get our wraps. Shall I meet you out on the verandah in—let's say—five minutes?"

"Are you coming, Marilyn?" Katelyn asked.

Marilyn shook her head, but Katelyn pinched her thigh. "Of course."

They were just leaving the house when Victor passed them. "There you are. I was hoping to catch up with you and see if perhaps I could interest you both in a walk about the grounds."

Marilyn smiled, looking happy to see him. "We are already going with Thomas, but you are welcome to come along."

"You do not mind?" he asked, already extending an arm for Katelyn to take.

"Not at all," Katelyn and Marilyn said in unison. "We are awaiting our aunt, though. She is getting our shawls."

"I have not had the honor of meeting your aunt yet. I look forward to it."

Thomas looked exceedingly disappointed that Victor had joined their little party, while Katelyn couldn't have been more relieved.

Aunt Lillith arrived shortly after and stepped onto the verandah. "Here you are, my dears." She handed a shawl to each, then finally noticed Victor. A blush touched her cheeks and she looked almost girlish.

Victor nodded. "Ah, you must be the lovely Aunt Lillith I have heard so much about. I am Victor."

"One of the Rayborne brothers, I presume?"

"Yes, I am smack in the middle."

One side of her mouth lifted the slightest bit. "I am a middle sibling also. It is nice to meet you, Lord Graston."

"Please, let there be no formality between us, Lily."

Lillith opened her mouth as though to reprimand him for using her Christian name, and a nickname at that, but pressed her lips together a second later.

"Shall we go, ladies?" Thomas asked, and Katelyn felt guilty because she had completely forgotten about the man.

Aunt Lillith slid her hand around Thomas's elbow, while Marilyn took the other; Victor and Katelyn followed behind.

"You look quite fetching tonight," Victor said, falling into step beside her.

Katelyn grinned. "As do you."

"You're too kind. I look like hell. Feel like it too. Damn the side effects of one too many brandies. I never could hold alcohol like my brothers can."

"You look just fine," Katelyn said, meaning it.

As the others walked ahead, Katelyn noticed Victor slowed his pace considerably.

"If I am not mistaken, you are trying to draw me away from the others, Lord Graston."

Victor laughed under his breath. "My brother wishes to meet with you at one in the morning."

"Meet me where?"

"In your chamber."

"My chamber?"

He lifted a brow. "It is far easier for him to come to your room than the other way around."

Katelyn's heart skipped a beat. There is no way she could entertain Sinjin in her chamber. "I don't know—"

"Your aunt is not sleeping in the same room with you, is she?"

"No, she is not—but Marilyn is."

"I shall speak with Marilyn myself, if you'd like."

"I will not ask my sister to leave the comfort of our room in the middle of the night so that I may steal a few moments alone with your brother."

"Nor does my brother intend to put her out," he said, though Katelyn had an idea he said it only for her benefit. "He merely wants to talk with you."

She sincerely doubted Sinjin wanted merely to talk.

He stared at Lillith's back, his gaze sliding slowly over her. Katelyn cleared her throat. "You are staring, my lord."

"Am I? I do apologize. I had not realized I was being so rude. Your aunt is quite young, is she not?"

"I would tell you her true age, but I feel she would not appreciate me doing so."

"Then let me guess. Nine and twenty."

Katelyn lifted her brows. "I will not tell, so you may as well stop guessing."

"Two and thirty."

Katelyn shook her head. "You are impossible."

"I must be getting warm. Five and thirty, and not a year older."

"You will have to ask my aunt herself, for I would never tell her secrets. She is not just an aunt, but a dear friend."

Victor patted her hand. "Then she is lucky, indeed."

16

Katelyn twisted and turned in the bedsheets, then finally tossed them aside when she realized sleep would be a long time in coming this night.

The candle flickered in the slight draft of the room, and she looked at the clock. One thirty-five in the morning and still no sign of Sinjin.

Perhaps he could not get away, after all.

Beside her, Marilyn snored softly, and Katelyn eased onto her side, hoping against hope he would come. It had been such a long day—exceedingly tedious and depressing, especially watching Lady Rochester and Lady Celeste bond.

Damn Lady Celeste! She was the perfect bride for any groom. She had so much more to offer Sinjin than herself.

The doorknob turned slightly, the door opened and closed just as quickly, and a tall figure emerged.

Her pulse skittered.

She'd recognize those broad shoulders anywhere. She sat up slowly and put her finger to her lips, signaling Sinjin to be quiet.

His long, dark hair fell past his shoulders in wild disarray, the tail of his shirt had been shoved into his pants, and he wore no shoes.

He had never looked so desirable. "You are barefoot, my lord."

"I did not want to make any noise," he said, leaning over her, kissing her to silence.

She rejoiced in the touch of his lips against her own, the musky smell of him. He pulled away, glancing toward Marilyn. "Well, good evening, Lady Marilyn."

"Do you not mean good morning?" Marilyn said, glancing toward the clock.

"Very well, then, it is good morning."

She yawned and slid her legs over the side of the bed.

"Where are you going?" Katelyn asked as her sister pulled on her wrap and tied it.

Marilyn picked a book off her nightstand. "There is a small sitting room just off the landing, and that is where I shall be for the next hour."

"You do not have . . ."

"The story I am reading is most engaging, so the time shall fly by. If anyone asks what I am doing, I will tell them I did not wish to wake my sister, who is a light sleeper." She crossed their room and donned her slippers. "Do not forget to lock the door, else our aunt comes calling in the middle of the night."

"Thank you, Marilyn," Sinjin said, following her to the door.

The door closed behind her, and Sinjin locked it. He walked back to the bed, reached behind his head, and removed his shirt. He tossed it over the back of a chair.

Excitement and anticipation rippled through Katelyn.

He had a knee on the bed; then his large body covered hers, and she welcomed the heat. Her thighs fell open and he groaned low in his throat as he settled between them.

Her hands moved down his strong back, savoring the feel of tight skin over muscle, the hard planes that contracted when she cupped his ass.

Pulling her chemise up and over her head, he tossed it aside and used his knees to spread her legs wider.

Sinjin had not intended to bed Katelyn tonight. He had merely wanted to see her, to talk to her, and let her know how important she had become to him in such a short period of time. Yet, when Marilyn had left and he saw Katelyn sitting up in the bed, the sleeve of her chemise falling off her shoulder, he could not help himself.

He loved her hair down as it was now, the thick curls framing her beautiful face. He threaded his fingers through the glorious locks, brought them to his face, and inhaled deeply. She smelled of vanilla and jasmine, an intoxicating combination.

Pulling the gown from her body, he went up on his knees to look down at her. The candlelight cast shadows on her amazing body. She was perfect in every way. He lowered his head and kissed her belly, his tongue circling around her navel.

The breath left her in a rush, and he smiled to himself as he kissed a trail to her mound and the hot flesh between her thighs.

He stroked her with his tongue and she nearly came off the bed, her fingers curling around the slats of the headboard.

He tasted her, delving inside her tight channel, licking her clit over and over until she was moaning and moving her hips against his mouth.

Long fingers slid into her weeping slit. She cried out with pleasure and her sex pulsed against him. He relented until the first tremors eased a little; then he started all over again.

Katelyn's entire body tightened again and again. She wanted to feel his long cock inside her, and yet she could not say the words.

So she reached for him, her hand sliding into the band of his pants. He stopped, then looked at her, his blue eyes burning with desire. "What do you want, Katelyn?" he asked, his voice low, silky smooth.

He knew damn well what she wanted, but he would hear it from her lips.

"I want you." She fumbled with the buttons of his pants and felt like she possessed nothing but thumbs, but soon she unleashed the solid length.

She took him into her hand and stroked his velvety cock.

His hand covered hers, squeezing her fingers. "I want you too badly."

Understanding his need all too well, her hand fell away.

He shoved his pants down and she helped him out of them, tossing them aside. He urged her onto her knees, and she instantly remembered how Rory had taken Lady Anna in a similar fashion.

Excitement licked her spine as Sinjin edged up against her, his cock probing her slick entrance.

With a deep-throated moan, he slid inside her slowly, and she gasped at how his thick cock stretched her. Her fingers dug into the blankets beneath her as he began to move in slow, steady thrusts.

Exquisite heat rushed through her body with each fluid stroke. He played with her breasts, pinching her nipples lightly. One hand slid down her belly, to the soft curls of her sex, and two fingers flicked over her clit, encircling the sensitive pearl, teasing it until her entire body felt as taut as a violin string.

He kissed her back, her neck, her ear, his tongue delving inside. The sensations were delicious.

His pace quickened, and she sensed he was very close to climax, too. She lowered her upper body to the mattress, arching her back, and he moaned with pleasure.

He cupped her hips, holding her firmly in place as he pumped against her in fast, shallow strokes.

She moaned as she came hard, and seconds later she felt hot semen showering her back.

Her sex still quivered from the intense orgasm. He fell over her, taking her with him to her side. She was shocked to see he was still semi-erect, and already her insides clenched with the promise of him filling her again.

Marilyn was completely absorbed in the chapter when she sensed herself being watched.

Lady Anna stood in the doorway of the sitting room, dressed much like Marilyn, in nothing save a wrapper and a chemise.

"May I join you?" she asked, nodding toward the settee across from Marilyn.

Marilyn nodded and set her book aside.

"You could not sleep either?"

"No," Marilyn replied.

The woman was even more beautiful up close, her skin like porcelain, her hair like golden spun silk, her eyes as dark as chocolate.

Such a strange combination, but lovely.

"Tonight was intensely boring, was it not?" Anna sighed heavily. "I much prefer the ball. I find it so much more entertaining. I am so looking forward to this weekend's festivities."

Lady Anna stretched her long legs out on the settee. Her wrapper fell open and Marilyn could see the shadows of her curvaceous body through the thin material.

Marilyn swallowed hard and quickly looked away.

"I watched you the other night. You dance very well."

"As do you," Marilyn said.

"I was not aware you had noticed me."

Marilyn nodded, slightly uncomfortable with where the discussion was leading.

"I have not seen you before this party." Anna bit her fuller lower lip, and Marilyn wondered what they would feel like pressed against her own.

"I spent very little time in London," Marilyn blurted, uncomfortable with the direction her thoughts had taken.

"I was in France for the better part of the year and just returned this past April."

"And you are here hoping to marry one of the Rayborne brothers?"

Anna laughed under her breath. "Actually, my grandmother, who is my guardian, is hoping I marry one of the Rayborne brothers. Myself, I would be content to be an old maid. I should hate to be told what to do by a husband."

Marilyn sat forward, intrigued. "As would I."

Anna wound a strand of hair that had come loose from her chignon, around her finger. "If I marry, I would think having an ugly husband would be to a greater advantage than having a husband as handsome as Sinjin, Victor, or Rory."

Marilyn could not help but smile. "True."

"Yet, there are benefits to marrying such a handsome man."

And wouldn't she know it, Marilyn thought to herself.

Anna looked around the room, her gaze shifting to the book on the nightstand. "A sweet story," she said, sounding amused. "I have a book you should read. It's by Lady Duke, and quite scandalous. Though it is fiction, it is rumored to be the biography of a certain courtesan."

"Truly?" Marilyn asked, intrigued.

"Yes."

No wonder the woman had a voracious appetite for sex . . .

given her preference of reading material. "You can borrow it if you wish."

"I am actually enjoying the current story."

"Oh, come, Marilyn, it won't harm you. Perhaps it shall even do you good."

It was a dare, and Marilyn had never backed down from a dare. "Very well, if you insist."

"Excellent," Anna said with a wink, her gaze shifting from Marilyn's downward.

Marilyn felt her cheeks grow hot as the other woman stared at her breasts.

"The book is in my room. I'm just down the hallway." Anna's gaze ripped back to Marilyn's. "I'm assuming you are on this floor as well?"

Marilyn nodded. She knew there was nothing wrong being alone in the company of another woman, but there had been something about the way Anna watched her that made her increasingly nervous.

"And what of you, Marilyn . . . Which Rayborne brother do you favor?"

Was this a trap? Was she trying to retrieve information in order to use it against her? "I think they are all nice."

Anna rolled her eyes, which made Marilyn feel childish.

"Yes, they are all *nice,* but which one do you like the most?"

"Sinjin," Marilyn blurted, since he was the obvious choice, and had been the only brother who had not been in Anna's bed. But what did she know—perhaps Anna had sampled all the Rayborne brothers.

Her eyes lit up. "A handsome devil."

"They all are very handsome, I think."

Anna's lips curved. "Indeed."

"And which one do you prefer?"

Anna lifted a brow. "If I had to pick one, I would say Rory. He is fun, that one."

Glancing at the clock, Marilyn sighed inwardly. It was only two o'clock, and she had told herself she would give Katelyn and Sinjin another thirty minutes alone. However, she couldn't stomach thirty minutes in Anna's company. She made her too nervous.

Rory appeared at the door as though thinking of him made him materialize. "There you are."

Marilyn's heart missed a beat, until she realized he was talking to Anna.

Of course.

Anna smiled at him and didn't move. "I couldn't sleep, so I went in search of company."

His brows furrowed. "And you overlooked my room?" he said teasingly.

Anna glanced at Marilyn, who reached for her book. She felt horribly awkward as she flipped to the page she had left off on.

"It was lovely talking to you, Marilyn. I hope to have the opportunity to converse with you again very soon. I would very much like to get to know you better." Anna slid from the couch and wrapped the belt tighter around her waist.

Marilyn could make out the outline of her nipples against the soft fabric, and she quickly looked away.

Anna reached out and brushed a stray strand of hair over Marilyn's ear. She was so close Marilyn could smell the scent of rose emanating from her. She brushed the backs of her long, slender fingers over Marilyn's cheek. "You have such lovely skin, Marilyn. You are so fortunate."

Marilyn glanced over at Rory, who seemed intrigued by the exchange. In fact, he looked ready to invite her to join them, so she quickly returned her attention to the book before her.

"Good night, Marilyn," Rory said, taking Anna by the hand.

"Good night," Marilyn murmured.

Anna glanced over her shoulder at Marilyn. "I shall see you at breakfast."

Marilyn nodded, confused and irritated by the sudden race of her pulse.

17

Katelyn woke to a hard body beside her.

Sinjin.

The sheet was draped across his lower body, just barely covering his groin. She stared at him in slumber, amazed at his beauty, that even in sleep, the intense man she knew him to be could look so boyish.

But there was nothing boyish about him, she thought with a smile, recalling the past hour in his arms. They had made love twice, and still she ached to be taken by him yet again.

How wanton she had become.

They had talked for a little while, and she discovered he had a weakness for dark chocolate, had an estate in Somerset, and he rather enjoyed hard labor. She had seen the excitement in his eyes when he talked about the mill he had just purchased in Rochester, but had sobered just as quickly when he spoke of his father, and then grew quiet altogether, save for asking her about her life, her favorite things. She was excited he wanted to know everything about her, seeming genuinely intrigued.

Glancing over at the clock, she sighed. She had to wake him, for Marilyn would be returning shortly. She sat up on her elbow and laid a hand against his bicep. "Sinjin."

He opened his eyes slowly and breathed in deeply, his eyes squinting as he stared at her. Suddenly, his mouth curved upward.

Her pulse skittered. "Come here, you," he said, pulling her on top of him.

He flipped quickly, so she was beneath him.

His cock was so hard.

"Marilyn will be here shortly."

Reaching between their bodies, he slid his cock inside her. "I won't be long," he promised.

Moving within her, he did not once look away. She loved the way he stared at her when he was inside her, the way his eyes turned dark, and the way his jaw clenched tighter with each thrust.

He pulled out of her slowly, the tip of his cock just teasing her opening. She lifted her hips, needing him to fill her. Her insides tightened as he kept it up, over and over again, teasing her mercilessly by almost withdrawing.

He would have her begging for it, and to her horror, she moaned in frustration when he did it again, her hips following him.

Pleased by her need, he smiled and gave her every inch of his cock, grinding his pelvis against her, giving her the friction she craved.

He gripped her waist, his fingers digging into her hips as he pumped against her, harder and harder with each long stroke.

Katelyn cried out her release, her honeyed walls clamping his cock tight, her hands squeezing his ass.

Sinjin froze, watching her reach orgasm, and with four more thrusts, he followed her over the edge.

* * *

Lillith craved a stiff drink, and she hadn't had liquor in ten years, after a binge that had dreadful repercussions. Thankfully, the only person who had witnessed that dreadful encounter was her husband . . . and his lover, a young French noble.

Lillith had walked in on the two making love in Winfred's library, right on the rug in front of the fire. Her husband had looked directly at her and continued pumping away into Jean Pierre. He nearly lifted the young man off the ground with each hard, steady thrust. He had never made love to her so fiercely.

Lillith had stood in open-mouthed horror until the two finished, and only when Jean Pierre looked up and saw her, did she run to her chamber and lock the door.

Winfred had followed her there, pounding on the door, demanding to be let in. Only when he threatened to break down the door did she let him in.

He had slapped her across the face with the back of his hand, not caring that his ring would leave an ugly welt for all to see. "How dare you embarrass me in front of my friends!" he screamed.

"You? I am the one who is embarrassed to have a husband such as you."

Jean Pierre had appeared at the door, a glass of wine hanging from his long fingers, a wide smile on his face. He was shorter than Lillith, slighter too, like a boy, although he had to be at least twenty.

Twenty, like dear, sweet Katelyn.

Lillith shook her head of the awful memories and pushed away from the desk, flexing her cramped hand. She had spent the past hour writing a letter to her sister, pleading with her to reconsider the betrothal between Katelyn and Lord Balliford. Lillith listed the reasons she felt the match was not a good one, her final point being that Katelyn had fallen in love with Sinjin Rayborne.

Somewhere in the manor the clock struck two.

She wasn't even tired. That was a lie—she was exhausted, both mentally and physically, but there was no way she could sleep.

A servant stuck her head into the drawing room that Lady Rochester had set up for guests to write correspondence. "Lady Nordland, could I get you another cup of tea?" the young woman asked.

"No, dear. Thank you, though."

"Should I stoke the fire?"

"No, I will be retiring soon."

The girl looked relieved. "Good night, then."

"Good night, and thank you for looking after me so diligently."

"It is my pleasure, Lady Nordland."

Pulling her shawl tight about her shoulders, Lillith stood and walked over to the fireplace. She held her hands to the heat, wondering what on earth she was going to do.

Katelyn loved Sinjin Rayborne, and if Lillith didn't do something to stop her upcoming marriage to Lord Balliford, then she would feel responsible for her niece's misery.

Memories of her own farce of a marriage flashed before her eyes, and Lillith hugged herself. She would not let Katelyn endure the same. It wouldn't be fair. What if she took her away to Bath? No, Loraine would find her there. What about Venice? Lillith adored the floating city and would be more than happy to spend a year there with her nieces until things blew over in England.

"Couldn't sleep?"

She gasped and turned to find Victor Rayborne standing in the doorway, his jacket tossed over his shoulder, looking like he had just stepped from a lover's bedchamber.

She managed a smile. "No."

His gaze shifted to the desk. "Late-night correspondence."

"Yes."

Having been married to a libertine of the first order, she knew men like Victor all too well . . . which made her exceedingly uncomfortable.

"No . . . yes. Not much for conversation, are you, Lady Nordland?"

Embarrassed, she forced a smile. "Forgive me. I just have a lot on my mind."

"Your nieces, perhaps?" he asked, stepping into the room. His shirt was completely rumpled and appeared to have been shoved into his wrinkled pants.

"For one."

"Your husband?"

"Is dead."

His brows lifted. "Yes, I know. I wondered if perhaps you were thinking about him . . . you seemed so lost in thought." He tossed his jacket over a chair and approached her. He was absolutely gorgeous—his hair so silky looking, she craved to touch the curly locks, just to see if they were as soft as she hoped them to be. His shirt had opened at the neck, and she could see the wide expanse of chest. He had an athletic build, broad at the shoulders, narrow at the hip.

She had not realized she'd been staring until a dark brow lifted, along with the corner of his lip.

How utterly humiliating. Being alone with him felt awkward, and she suddenly felt like a caged canary. "Well, I should be going." She passed by him, ready to snatch up the letter, when he reached out and grabbed her hand.

"Don't go."

How long had it been since a man had touched her? Certainly she had the occasional greeting, but always she had gloves on, and never skin-to-skin contact.

She looked back at him, her gaze searching his face. He was at least ten years younger than she was. Certainly he knew that. Why, when he had a house full of younger women, did he wish to be in her company?

"Lillith, stay." His thumb brushed over hers, and it was then she snapped out of it and pulled away.

"I must go," she said, reaching for the letter with trembling fingers.

He didn't say a word as she rushed to the door. She had always prided herself for being in control, of always leaving the very best impression. At the door she turned to him, and her heart literally missed a beat.

Hip resting against the desk, he watched her, head slightly tilted, long-fingered hand resting on the back of the chair she had just vacated. He was pure temptation, sin incarnate . . . and he had just left the arms of his lover, she reminded herself.

"Good night, Lily."

Lily.

She swallowed past the lump in her throat. "Good night, Lord Graston."

Lady Anna closed the door behind Rory and immediately began undressing.

Rory sat back on his bed, watching her with appreciation, his erection straining the fabric of his pants. She knew none of the brothers would dream of marrying her, and she had no intention of marrying any one of them either.

They were all too pretty, but she would have her fun while she could. She spent too many months in the York countryside, holed up in the mausoleum of a home, with little to do and even less companionship.

The only fun she had was with the servants, but she was becoming quickly bored with all of them.

From the time she'd turned eighteen, Anna had decided she would explore her sexual side . . . just as any man was expected to do. Women had so few opportunities in life—why should men have all the fun?

In fact, she could hardly wait to return to London and attend some of the sordid parties she'd been initiated into last summer. "What was that about in the sitting room?"

"What do you mean?" Anna asked innocently, sliding her chemise from her body, where it pooled at her ankles. She stepped over the slip of silk and walked toward him.

Rory's gaze raked over her, stopping at her bald mons. "Lady Marilyn."

"She's delightful, is she not?"

His gaze shifted back to hers. "Indeed, she is. I had thought you might ask her to join us."

"She would not be so inclined."

"How do you know?"

She laughed, then pushed him onto his back. "Because she is a virgin."

"How do you know?"

"I can tell." She brushed her hand over his wide chest. Rory was the most beautiful man she had ever met in her life, and he was her equal in bed in every way. Nothing was forbidden, and he never judged, which was rare. Even though her many lovers said they wouldn't judge her, she knew better. None would defend her, and none would marry her.

She fisted Rory's cock in her hand, her fingers sliding over the thick head. Licking her lips, she went down on him. His fingers gripped her shoulders tight, and she smiled inwardly. She knew she was skilled at oral pleasure, had been told so on a number of occasions.

His large cock reared up against his belly, and she felt her quim tighten as she swirled her tongue around the fat tip, while fondling his jewels. She loved the feel of balls in her hand, loved stroking the soft patch of skin that had him groaning and arching his hips.

Rory slipped his hand between her legs and he smiled. She was so wet for him already, hot and dripping.

Unable to wait another second, she straddled him and took him into her body, inch by delicious inch.

He fell back onto the bed with a sigh, his hands moving to her breasts, weighing the globes in his hands before plucking at her nipples. Rory had to be one of the most patient lovers she'd ever had. Whoever married him was a lucky woman, indeed. If ever he could be faithful.

Rory sat up and kissed her breasts, his tongue flicking over the tight peaks. He looked up at her and smiled.

She rolled her hips, already feeling the first round of climax begin. Her juices coated Rory's cock, and she sensed his need to prolong the ecstasy and increase hers. He carefully slipped a wet finger into her back passage, and she sighed when he added another.

She moved slowly up and down, savoring the multiple sensations as his fingers mirrored the movements of his cock. He increased his pace and pulled from her seconds before spilling himself, his thick come coating her belly.

"Tomorrow night, then?" she said when they had caught their breath.

18

Katelyn sat with her sister and aunt in the nearly empty parlor. Though it was early afternoon, many of the ladies present had already retired to their rooms to nap and prepare for the ball taking place that evening.

She couldn't sleep if she wanted to. Her heart still raced as she remembered waking up to Sinjin in her bed, the feel of his hard body beside her—the feel of his hard body *inside* her as he brought her to climax again and again.

She could hardly wait until tonight.

Lillith poured herself a cup of tea, adding two heaping teaspoonfuls of sugar to it and a spot of cream. "Katelyn, you should wear that lovely cream-colored gown this evening. It would look delightful."

"She is so right. It is so beautiful," Marilyn agreed.

Marilyn had been rather quiet throughout the day, and Katelyn wondered if perhaps she was angry with her for turning her out last night after she'd been sleeping so peacefully.

Sinjin had kissed Marilyn on the cheek on his way out the

door, and she had climbed into bed, saying very little except to comment on how soft the newly changed sheets were.

"What will you be wearing tonight?" Katelyn asked her sister, who sat back on the settee with a sigh.

"I do not know. Perhaps the rose silk."

"Or the royal blue." Lillith tapped her spoon on the side of the cup.

Marilyn shrugged. "Either one will do."

"What on earth is the matter with you, my dear? You have been quite somber all day," Lillith asked, concern in her hazel eyes.

Marilyn sat up and stretched. "Have I? I'm sorry, I did not realize. Perhaps it's from lack of sleep."

Katelyn's cheeks turned hot.

"Then perhaps you should retire for a nap?"

"Perhaps I shall, but only after I finish my hot chocolate. It's delicious."

Lillith brought the teacup to her lips, her glance shifting to the doorway. She nearly dropped the cup, spilling some of the contents onto the floor.

Katelyn followed her gaze . . . and felt her heart fall to her feet.

Lord Balliford stood just outside the parlor door, in the hallway. He was speaking to a servant, his voice firm and authoritative, and he was asking for her.

"Oh my God," Katelyn said under her breath.

Marilyn leaned forward to see what had caused both her and Lillith's reactions.

"Bloody hell, he's come hunting you down."

Lillith set her cup on the table. "I cannot believe he would be so bold as to come here. The nerve of him!"

"You do not know him very well, then," Katelyn said, wishing the floor would open up and swallow her. *Why now?* she wanted to scream.

The servant looked into the room and pointed at Katelyn.

Ronald entered, his gaze zeroing in on Katelyn. "There you are, my dear."

She bit the inside of her lip to keep from saying what she yearned to. She felt physically ill. He looked so much older than she recalled. His hair seemed thinner, his face softer, more weathered. He was tall and broad-shouldered, but his waist did not narrow or taper like Sinjin's. Indeed, his waist had the same, if not wider, dimensions than his shoulders, and his legs were so spindly they looked like they could barely hold up his larger upper body.

He was so different than Sinjin, who truly was sheer perfection. She loved every hair on his head, every inch of his body.

Her pulse skittered. She loved Sinjin Rayborne, loved him with a passion. And sadly, now with Ronald's arrival, she may never get another second alone with him.

"You look lovely, my dear."

Marilyn nudged her, and she realized she had yet to say anything. Ronald had apparently noticed her silence, for his expression was one of concern—and a touch of anger.

Katelyn cleared her throat. "Thank you, my lord."

"What a surprise," Lillith said, her voice casual but cool. "I was not told of your impending arrival."

Ronald actually looked somewhat embarrassed as his gaze shifted from Lillith to Katelyn. "I did not realize I needed your approval, madam."

His voice dripped of sarcasm, and Lillith straightened her spine.

"I fear I missed Lady Katelyn so much that I came to take her back home to Rose Alley. In fact, I have asked the valet to have a female servant ready your belongings." He looked straight at Katelyn. "We should be ready to leave within an hour's time."

"I do not understand," Lillith said, anger flashing in her eyes. "I arrived at Claymoore Hall to chaperone my nieces. I was never told that you would be arriving to take her away from the festivities."

Ronald lifted his chin high. "I am her intended. I will do as I wish."

Lillith cleared her throat loudly. "With all due respect, my lord, you are not her husband yet. Katelyn has come to Claymoore Hall to spend time with her sister. I do not see why her time should be cut short merely because you miss her. When you are married, you shall have the rest of your lives to spend together, and time with her sister will be rare indeed."

Licking his lips, Ronald merely shrugged. "I am sorry you are disappointed, but I did not come all this way to leave empty-handed."

"My lord, I wish to stay," Katelyn blurted, and Ronald flinched as though she'd struck him.

He abhorred when women spoke out of turn. Indeed, he had once commented that a woman should speak only when spoken to—and never, under any circumstance, should she start a conversation with a man. Katelyn had been appalled, while his sister had merely nodded in agreement.

Ronald watched Katelyn through narrowed eyes. "I see."

"The party will be over in a week, and at such time I will deliver my niece to you myself," Lillith remarked, looking cool as could be. The only sign that she was agitated was the bloom of color high on her cheeks.

Ronald forced a smile, completely ignoring Lillith. "Katelyn, we shall be leaving promptly."

Lillith cleared her throat loudly. "*Sir*, apparently you have not heard a word I've said." She managed to keep her voice calm, but with great effort. "Clearly we are in a quandary because I am afraid I will not budge on the matter. My niece has the rest of her life to spend with you. Can you not give her this final week with her sister?"

"Her place is at my side."

Lillith took a deep breath, then released it. "She is staying at Claymoore Hall, and that is my final word on the matter."

He took a step toward Lillith, and to her credit, she did not flinch. She merely lifted her chin in order to look him in the eye.

"Perhaps we should discuss this elsewhere."

"Why? I have nothing to hide from my nieces. I have told you my wishes and intention, and I would ask if you will comply."

A nerve ticked in Ronald's jaw. "Lady Katelyn's mother thinks it is wise to bring her back to Rose Alley."

"Yes, she would, wouldn't she?" Lillith whispered under her breath.

"I beg your pardon?" Ronald asked, his brows furrowing together.

"Lord Balliford," Lillith said, "my sister has not sent me word to that effect, and until she does, I must insist Katelyn stay on with me at Claymoore Hall."

Ronald licked his thin lips, and turned to Katelyn. "I will admit I am stunned. I imagined you would be most anxious to see me and return to your home."

"Rose Alley is not my home."

His eyes narrowed into slits. "But it will be."

Katelyn bit the inside of her lip to keep from saying exactly how she felt, which was probably a good thing since Sinjin chose that moment to walk into the room with Victor fast on his heels.

Katelyn's heart stuttered, and she resisted the urge to run

into his strong arms. He looked positively gorgeous in leather pants that hugged his muscled thighs. His black Hessians were spotted with dirt, his long hair ruffled.

He must have been out riding with his brother, who was dressed in a similar fashion.

"Lord Balliford, my valet tells me you have just arrived," Sinjin said in a cordial tone. "I am Sinjin Rayborne, Lord Mawbry, and this is my brother Victor, Lord Graston."

Ronald inclined his head and gave both Sinjin and Victor the once-over. "A pleasure to meet you both."

Victor glanced at his brother, who did not hide his surprise at seeing Ronald one bit.

"What do we owe the honor of this visit, Lord Balliford?" Sinjin asked, hands on narrow hips.

"I came to deliver my bride back to Rose Alley."

Sinjin's brows furrowed. "I am sorry to hear that, my lord, especially when the women were so looking forward to tonight's ball and the coming events that my mother has so painstakingly planned."

Ronald appeared uneasy. He had always had the highest regard for those who outranked him in title and wealth, and in this case, Lady Rochester and her family trumped him in every way. "You will be delighted to know that Lady Marilyn and Lady Nordland will still be staying on with you for the duration of the party."

Katelyn folded her trembling hands before her, desperate to say what she longed to.

"Lord Balliford, could I interest you in a brandy?" Victor said, nodding toward a footman who jumped to attention.

"I do not partake of alcohol. It is the devil's drink."

"What a surprise," Marilyn said. Victor laughed, but covered it with a cough.

"Tea, then?" Sinjin asked.

155

Ronald pulled out his pocket watch and checked the time. "I can spare half an hour, and then we really must be on our way."

"Did you bring your sister by any chance?" Lillith asked, lifting her chin a fraction.

"No . . . I did not." Ronald tugged at his waistcoat.

"A shame," she said stiffly, glancing at Victor, who smiled at her with obvious interest. She quickly looked away.

"Who is serving as chaperone on the return journey to Rose Alley, then?" Lillith asked, her voice coming out stronger than expected.

Ronald puffed out his chest. "Katelyn requires no chaperone. She is traveling with me, and I would never dream of compromising her virtue."

"That will not do at all, I am afraid. As my niece's chaperone, I must insist she stay on with me until I am able to deliver her to Rose Alley personally . . . at the end of the party."

Ronald's cheeks turned red and sweat dripped off his forehead, onto his jacket.

Lady Rochester walked into the room, her smile warm. "Lord Balliford, what a delightful surprise."

Suddenly, Ronald became all pomp and grace, nearly bowing to the floor. "Lady Rochester, it is an honor."

"Will you be joining us for the duration of the party?"

"No, I fear not, my lady."

Lady Rochester frowned. "No? Forgive me my ignorance, but why on earth would you come all the way to Claymoore Hall if not to join in on the festivities, my lord?"

"He is taking Lady Katelyn away, Mother," Victor murmured, taking a seat in the nearest chair, crossing his long legs at the ankle.

Aunt Lillith bit her lip. Katelyn could tell she ached to say something, but she did not dare in front of Lady Rochester.

"Oh, what a shame, for Lady Katelyn and Lady Marilyn have been favorites of mine since their arrival," Lady Rochester said, looking and sounding sincere.

Favorites? She had barely even looked at Katelyn.

"Lady Marilyn shall remain," Ronald blurted in an effort to appease Lady Rochester.

"But it will not be the same for her sister if she is to leave, will it, Lady Marilyn?"

Marilyn nodded. "Indeed, you are right, Lady Rochester. I would be devastated by Katelyn's departure."

"Well, there, you see we cannot have Lady Marilyn devastated. That will not do at all, so therefore, allow Katelyn to stay on." Lady Rochester tapped Ronald on the shoulder with a fan as though they were the best of friends. "Your future bride is meeting so many influential ladies—future brides of very powerful men like yourself."

Ronald said nothing, but Katelyn could see his agitation build by the second. He thrived on being in control of every situation. "Perhaps I shall stay on at Claymoore Hall as well."

Katelyn's stomach dropped to her toes.

Lady Rochester smiled. "We would be delighted to have you stay on, my lord, though I fear most of our rooms are full."

"I require no special treatment."

"I will speak to my valet and see what he can do." Lady Rochester smiled. "I shall see you all at dinner, then."

"Thank you, Lady Rochester," Lillith murmured.

Ronald managed a smile, and bowed as Lady Rochester nodded and exited the room.

"Gentlemen, if you will please excuse us, my nieces and I will retire to our chamber and prepare for dinner." Lillith didn't even look at Ronald as she motioned for Katelyn and Marilyn to follow her out of the room.

Katelyn could feel Sinjin's stare on her as she walked out. She wanted so desperately to go to him, to bury her face in his chest and tell him to take her far, far away.

"Wait," Ronald said, and Katelyn's stomach tightened as he came toward her. "I wanted to give you this." He pulled a box out of his coat pocket. "Perhaps you can wear it for me tonight."

Katelyn felt her cheeks turn hot, aware of piercing blue eyes watching her.

She forced a smile, when all the while she felt like crying. "Thank you, my lord."

"Well, open it."

She opened the box to find a dainty string of pearls staring back at her. "They're lovely."

"I'm so glad you like them, my dear," he said, his voice far too intimate.

Ronald extended his arm, and Katelyn turned back to look at Sinjin. Jealousy flared in his eyes.

19

Lillith ripped a leaf off the branch, crushing it in her fist. How dare Ronald arrive at Claymoore Hall demanding to take Katelyn back to Rose Alley with him! He was everything she despised in a man, and if she had anything to do with it, her niece would never become Lady Balliford.

And to think that just this morning she had crumpled up the letter she had written Loraine and tossed it in the fire. Damn!

The leaf dropped from her fingers, and she pressed her hands against her stomach, taking deep breaths to regain her composure.

In the years since Winfred's death, she had maintained her place in society, attending every event possible, acting the typical widow, saying little, staying to the background, and living day after endless day hoping that something in the future might change.

Men like Ronald and Winfred were the reason she would never give up her solitary lifestyle. She had earned it, after all.

Fifteen years of facing a husband and his many lovers across the dinner table had taught her to smile through the pain, even if it nearly killed her.

She had become a master at pretending.

"You look angry."

Lillith turned around, shocked to find she was no longer alone. Victor leaned against a tree, his arms folded across his wide chest, his head tilted at an angle as he watched her with piercing blue eyes. "Why do you keep doing that?"

"What?" he asked innocently.

"Sneaking up on me."

"I thought you heard me; and for the record, I did knock last night. You just didn't hear me."

"I'm sorry, Lord Graston." She released a frustrated breath. "I am just at the end of my rope."

"Do not apologize, Lily." His gaze slid slowly down her body in a way that made her very aware of being female.

She cleared her throat, and his lips curved, his gaze finding hers once more.

"You do not care for Lord Balliford."

It wasn't a question.

She pressed her lips together, weighing her words. "It is not a matter of caring for him or not. I think it inappropriate that he arrive at Claymoore Hall without first giving notice, and then to demand to take Katelyn with him—well, it's just too much."

"I agree," he said, pushing away from the tree.

What was she doing telling this man her innermost feelings? After all, he was a notorious rake who did what he wanted, when he wanted, with no thought of consequence. From the moment she had arrived at the party, Lillith had heard rumors about each of the Rayborne brothers, each more scandalous than the last. Knowing one of her nieces had fallen victim to such charm made her uneasy to say the least, and yet, she wanted Katelyn to be free to make her own choices.

Victor stopped inches from her, so close she had to bend her head back to look at him. He smelled incredible—a purely male scent that had her pulse tripping.

"How long have you been alone, Lady Nordland?" His voice was silky soft.

"What do you mean?"

"How long have you been a widow?"

"Three years."

"Three years—and you have been alone all that time?"

She swallowed past the tightness in her throat, stunned he was being so bold, though given his reputation, she shouldn't have been. "That is none of your business, Lord Graston."

"Victor."

Calling him by his Christian name was altogether too intimate. "I prefer Lord Graston."

His gorgeous lips quirked. "Have it your way, Lily."

Not liking the hooded look to his eyes, she stepped away. "You might speak to one of your young debutantes in such a way, but I would ask you not to use such a tone with me."

His gaze shifted over her face, making her increasingly uncomfortable. She knew the years were beginning to show.

"What are you afraid of?"

He was incredibly sexy, primal, beautiful, and young—at least a decade younger than she, perhaps more—and it had been ages since anyone had looked at her in such a way.

"I'm not afraid of anyone, or anything."

"Yes, you are."

He was so aggravating!

She took another step away, her gaze scanning the horizon, seeing if anyone was watching. Given she was a chaperone, she could get away with being in the company of a man, but not for long. Everyone would start talking.

"Don't worry, we are all alone."

She turned on him. "What exactly do you want from me, Lord Graston?"

He tried to look innocent but failed miserably. "Your friendship."

"Very well, then. We are friends."

"May I have a kiss?"

"You most certainly may not." She could feel heat rush up her neck to her cheeks. "I am no young miss you can charm with your wit and good looks."

"You think me good-looking?" he said, flashing a wolfish smile that made her thighs tighten.

She ran a hand down her face and counted to ten twice. "Yes, I do."

"I think you are beautiful."

The words shocked her. Winfred had told her she was beautiful when he had courted her, and by the time he had died she'd been convinced she was the most undesirable being in all of England. "Thank you, my lord. You are too kind."

She stared at him, taking in the high cheekbones, the square jaw, the full-lipped mouth. He watched her in return, and Lillith shook her head, wondering what on earth was wrong with her to be so rude and gawk at him. "I really must be going," she managed to say.

"I shall see you this evening."

She nodded, and as she walked away, she felt his gaze follow her.

Sinjin swallowed the last of his brandy, enjoying the slow burn as it worked its way to his knotted stomach. Since Balliford had arrived, his thoughts were in chaos.

"You could take him in a duel."

Sinjin turned to Rory, who leaned against the four-poster bed in Sinjin's room. Both his brothers had come to console him before the ball, and though he was thankful for their thoughtfulness, it still did not help the dilemma he found himself in.

Katelyn's betrothed would be underfoot the entire weekend, and given his luck, he might even stay for the rest of the party. Damn the man! Why had he not just stayed away?

It had been bad enough with Aunt Lillith's arrival, but they had found a way around that. How could they possibly find their way around an insecure fiancé?

"She looked bloody miserable," Victor said, finishing off a cup of tea. "Did you see the look on her face when we walked into the drawing room? You would have thought she had seen a ghost."

She had looked pale, until Balliford had given her the pearls. Then she had flushed to the roots of her hair.

Sinjin grit his teeth, angry at the circumstance he now found himself in. *He* wanted to be the one to give Katelyn jewels and pretty things. Did the man not recognize that she did not want him? She had barely been able to keep eye contact with him, for God's sake!

"Her aunt was quite determined about her staying, wasn't she?" Victor said, lifting his brows. "She's quite a delightful creature, I must say."

Lillith's reaction to Balliford had actually surprised Sinjin.

"I'm sorry I missed it," Rory said, straightening his jacket. "I can hardly wait to see how it all plays out tonight."

"I will do my best to keep Balliford occupied so that you may entertain Lady Katelyn," Victor said.

Jeffries walked in. "It is time for the ball, my lords."

* * *

Sinjin dreaded the hours to come. He was in a horrible mood. The entire house was alive with laughter and chatter. Any other time Sinjin would have looked forward to hosting such an event, but he couldn't help shake the sensation of loss he felt. He'd been living in a fantasy these past days since taking Katelyn's virginity, and now with Lord Balliford's arrival, reality had hit him straight between the eyes.

Taking his place at the receiving line with his brothers and mother, Sinjin resolved to keep his cool.

Betsy smiled at each of them, her gaze falling on Sinjin and lingering. "All will be well, my dear. You shall see."

He didn't have time to ask her what she meant by that comment when the doors opened and the guests filed through.

Thirty-five minutes passed by the time he finally saw Katelyn. She stood in line with Lord Balliford, her aunt, and her sister, looking like a rose amongst daisies. The cream-colored gown hugged her lithe body, the low bodice showing a huge expanse of skin. She wore her hair up in a high chignon, which emphasized her long, delicate neck and the pearls her betrothed had given her.

"You're staring," Victor said under his breath, and Sinjin looked away, diverting his attention back to the guests.

Endless minutes passed; then she stood before him, more ravishing than ever. Her green eyes were guarded, and he remembered not to hold her hand too long or to pay her too much attention, especially since her future husband stood not a foot away, watching every single gesture with an eagle eye.

Sinjin had cavorted with married women before, so he knew how to fake it with the best of them, but he found it especially hard to pretend indifference when he wanted nothing more than to sweep Katelyn up into his arms, whisk her away, and never return.

"Enjoy your evening," Sinjin said, dropping her hand and coming face-to-face with his nemesis.

Balliford dressed in an unflattering suit that fit too tight at his waist, the bottom button threatening to break loose at any second. His face was flushed and shiny, the light gleaming off his forehead. "Good evening," he said with a curt nod, then walked off.

Sinjin watched from a distance as Katelyn and Balliford took to the dance floor. The man was graceful, aware of every step and every touch. He was proud of Katelyn, too, his chin lifted high, a smug smile on his thin lips, looking around to see who watched them. Sinjin had already heard one group of young ladies snicker that Lady Katelyn's old fiancé had come to the ball because he was so possessive and jealous.

Across the room, Sinjin caught Lillith's gaze. She flashed a sympathetic smile in his direction before going back to watching her nieces.

After receiving their final guest, Sinjin made an effort to dance with a myriad of women, and to make conversation with each, but his mind continued to be with Katelyn. He had not yet asked her to dance, and he feared doing so, sure that anyone watching the two would be able to tell that they were more than just friends.

It was shortly after midnight when he saw Katelyn and Balliford walking toward the double doors that led out to the verandah, along with an older gentleman who Sinjin did not recognize.

Katelyn glanced Sinjin's way and he motioned for her to come to him. She said something to Balliford, who looked aggravated but nodded, and the older man stepped out onto the verandah with his companion.

Sinjin made his way into his father's study, making sure to keep the door slightly ajar.

Katelyn appeared a second later, closing the door behind her. "Sinjin, I can't be long. He's waiting for me."

He crossed the room and took her into his arms.

"He wants to leave tomorrow."

Sinjin's stomach fell to his feet. "Tell me he is the only one leaving."

"*Both* of us are leaving, Sinjin."

"Tell him no."

"You don't understand. I have no choice in the matter. He won't listen to anyone, not even Aunt Lillith. I have talked about my desire to stay with my sister, but, as always, my pleas fall on deaf ears."

He felt physically sick at the prospect of never seeing her again.

She stiffened in his arms. "Oh my God, I can see him from here." She took a step away from the window and ran her hands down her face. "I am in hell."

Sinjin came up from behind her, and sure enough, from where she stood, he could see Ronald and his companion smoking cigars on the verandah.

Katelyn slinked away from the window and from Sinjin. "I don't know what to do, Sinjin," she whispered, terrified of discovery. "If he insists on leaving, I should go with him."

"You are not married to him, Katelyn." His irritation was obvious. "He has no right to take you from your chaperone."

"I feel so helpless."

He pulled her up against him and kissed the top of her head. "Don't leave, Katelyn. Please don't leave."

"I don't want to. I want to stay with you." She hugged him tight, her hands moving down his strong back, over the curve of his high buttocks.

Every hair on Katelyn's body stood on end as tendrils of desire rushed through her. She lifted her face to his and kissed him with all the desperation she'd been feeling since Ronald had arrived.

What if this was the last time they would be together?

He kissed a trail to her shoulder, his hands moving up to her breasts, where he slid his fingers into her bodice, his thumb and finger playing with her nipples, pulling them into tight nubs.

He lifted her skirts with a hand and found her hot, moist center. His cock was against her belly, so hard and throbbing.

Sinjin lifted her in his arms, set her on the edge of the side table, and stepped between her spread thighs.

He went to his knees, then licked her folds.

She bit her bottom lip as he continued to pleasure her, all the while she could see Ronald's shoulder from the corner of her eye. If he were to turn slightly to his right and look their way, he could see everything.

Sinjin had loosened her gown enough so he had full access to her breasts, and her skirts were bunched up to her waist. He licked and sucked until she was moaning and writhing.

When he stood, his cock swelled against his navel; he unbuttoned his pants and pushed them to his knees. He stepped between her spread thighs and slid the thick head of his shaft inside her welcoming heat.

He lowered his head and suckled on a nipple, using his teeth with infinite skill. She bit her lip to keep from crying out in ecstasy, and glanced toward the window. Sinjin followed her gaze. Balliford was so close.

Sinjin's thrusts became harder and bolder.

Her breasts bounced with each deep thrust, and he reveled in the feel of her nails digging into his back as he pumped into her in long, steady strokes.

Sinjin kissed Katelyn, and she deepened the kiss, her hips arching against him as she started the steady climb to a powerful orgasm.

He tilted his pelvis against her, grinding against her sensitive nub, over and over again. It was the perfect amount of pressure and she swallowed a moan.

"Do you like that?" he whispered against her lips.

She nodded.

Her eyes were so heavy-lidded, so intense and passionate that he couldn't look away.

Ronald moved closer to the window. He stood in profile, his back slightly to the window.

Sinjin nearly pulled out, but she whispered, "No." Her legs clamped around his waist, her hips arching.

He barely moved and she came hard, rolling her hips against him. He followed close behind, his hot semen filling her hot channel.

Katelyn fought to catch her breath. Sinjin rested between her spread thighs, his clothing in wild disarray, as was her own. They were so dynamic together, the chemistry so intense that, if they did marry, they would never be able to keep their hands off each other.

"Come, Katelyn, we must get back."

"I don't want to go."

"I don't want to either." He kissed her softly, his hands framing her face. "Just promise me you won't leave."

"I promise."

20

Marilyn sat on the top rail of the fence, just outside the stables, waiting for Aunt Lillith to appear.

Although she had slept for seven hours, she felt like she had slept for two. Poor Katelyn had been in agony since Ronald's unexpected arrival and had finally cried herself to sleep. She had refused breakfast and told Marilyn that she was staying in bed all day so she did not have to see Lord Balliford.

Aunt Lillith had gone to check on her thirty minutes ago and said she'd meet Marilyn in the stables in an hour. Perhaps they should all leave Claymoore Hall. What had started as an exciting trip, away from the restrictions of an overbearing mother and fiancé, had turned into something altogether disturbing.

Truth be told, Marilyn had been having a grand time until Balliford's visit, and if Katelyn left, there really was no reason for her to stay.

Restless, Marilyn slipped from the fence and walked into the stables. The groomsman had her mount ready. "Will you tell my aunt that I'll be in the north meadow? She is tall and slender, with golden blond hair and hazel eyes."

"Aye, I know of her," he said, a kind smile in place. "I shall tell her, but I do wish you would not go alone, my lady. What if something happened—"

"Thank you for your concern, but I am quite comfortable when it comes to riding."

He didn't look convinced, but he did not argue with her. "Very well, my lady, I shall relay your message."

Marilyn mounted with no help and rode off toward the north meadow, enjoying the feel of the cool air against her cheeks. Dark clouds lingered on the horizon, so she would take full advantage of the nice weather now.

She leaned low over the horse's neck, her blood pumping in her veins. One day she hoped to marry a man who had vast lands and an impressive stable full of the best horseflesh England had to offer.

Any of the Rayborne brothers would have been a fine match, but she did not feel anything for them save for brotherly affection, especially Victor. Marilyn wondered if she, like her sister, would end up in a loveless marriage. Poor, poor Katelyn.

Yesterday, after Ronald's arrival, Katelyn had mentioned leaving. Indeed, she had asked Marilyn to leave with her, and in front of Aunt Lillith, no less.

Perhaps they should have left in the middle of the night? Perhaps they should leave tonight? In fact, maybe Marilyn would say something to Aunt Lillith. Would she go with them, or would it be folly to bring it up in front of her aunt, who might very well try to stop them?

Remembering the exchange between Aunt Lillith and Lord Balliford, Marilyn smiled. Apparently Aunt Lillith was not fond of the match either.

She raced across the meadow, deep in thought, when she saw

two women in the distance, both on horseback, both watching her. One of them waved.

Slowing her mount, Marilyn smiled in return and waved at Anna and a young lady she had never before met but had noticed. The woman had chestnut hair, was quite plain, and had an unfortunate figure, but she had a true talent for singing.

"Good afternoon, Lady Marilyn," Anna called.

"Good afternoon."

Lady Anna wore a snug riding habit made of navy velvet. Her hat sat at a jaunty angle on her head, and her smile was wide as she stared at Marilyn. "Why, Lady Marilyn, you looked like the devil was on your heels just then, did she not, Miss Jameson?"

Miss Jameson nodded. "Indeed, you did, Lady Marilyn. I was terrified you might fall."

"I decided to go for a ride while waiting for my aunt."

Anna's hand tightened on the whip. "We shall wait with you, then."

"I would not dream of keeping you from your ride," Marilyn blurted. "It might be a while before she arrives."

Miss Jameson looked toward the manor. "I should be returning to the hall. My mother is expecting me."

"I shall see you this evening, then," Anna said, sounding relieved the other woman was leaving.

Miss Jameson left without so much as saying good-bye.

"I wanted to talk to you last night, but I could not get you away from your aunt or sister to save my life."

"It was quite an eventful evening."

"I did not know your sister's betrothed would be coming."

"Nor did we," Marilyn said before she could stop herself. She needed to be careful. She didn't know Anna well enough to trust her with personal information.

Anna frowned. "I hear that your sister might be leaving today. I hope you are not leaving, too."

She wanted to ask why it would matter, but she refrained. "My sister is not leaving, nor am I."

"Well, that is an immense relief."

Marilyn's confusion must have shown on her face, because Lady Anna smiled. "I wished we would not have been interrupted the other night." Her gaze shifted to Marilyn's chest. "You have lovely breasts, Lady Marilyn. Has anyone ever told you that?"

Marilyn's heart started to race, and she felt a blush rush to her cheeks. She cleared her throat. "No."

Anna brought her mount close—so close their legs touched. She leaned toward Marilyn and brushed a hand across her jaw. "You have the softest skin. As smooth as cream."

Marilyn could feel the pulse beating wildly at her throat. Her hands tightened around the reins.

"What is wrong, Marilyn?"

"I saw you with Rory and Victor."

Anna frowned, as though she did not understand.

"You were alone with the two of them."

Her eyes widened. "You do not mean—oh dear, I can see by the change in your complexion that is exactly what you mean. You saw us."

"Yes . . ."

"Do you judge me, Lady Marilyn?"

Marilyn shook her head.

"I do not pretend to be innocent. I never have."

Marilyn heard hoofbeats coming toward them and looked up to see Aunt Lillith just over the rise. She pulled away from Anna. "My aunt is here."

Anna glanced in Lillith's direction. "Will you meet me in the sitting room tonight?"

"Why do you wish to meet me?" Marilyn asked, trying not to sound skeptical.

"I want to talk to you and get to know you better." She straightened her shoulders. "I feel like we got off on the wrong foot."

"I do not know. I have to—"

"Please try. I'll be there between midnight and one, and I'll be waiting for you."

Ronald had a horrible feeling deep in his gut that he could not get rid of.

From the moment he'd stepped foot in Claymoore Hall, he knew something had changed between Katelyn and him, and he feared she had fallen in love with another man.

It hadn't taken long to realize who the other man was, either. Whenever Sinjin Rayborne came around, Katelyn became nervous, shifting on her feet, her cheeks flushing pink.

Sinjin was handsome, to be sure, and a womanizing rakehell who had a reputation as a renowned lover, or at least such was the reports Ronald had received since arriving at Claymoore Hall.

Just how far the relationship had progressed, he was not sure. He wanted to believe Katelyn's bitch of an aunt had taken some responsibility and played her part as chaperone, but she had only just arrived a few nights before. What had happened before her arrival is what he'd like to know.

And how on earth could he take her away without causing further speculation, for the last thing he wanted was the *ton* thinking he had no control over his betrothed, or that she had given herself to another man.

Most, if not all, of the men he knew would call off the wedding. Katelyn would be ruined, destroyed, destined to become a spinster, or most likely, a mistress or courtesan. She would be in high demand, to be sure. Most men did not have a fiancée like Katelyn. She was too beautiful to give up. His nails bit into his palms.

What to do . . .

He could handle things one of two ways—remove her from Claymoore Hall and push up the wedding; or stay on the remainder of the party, and act the besotted suitor and riddle her with praise. At least that way everyone would believe they were happy. Once he took her home to Rose Alley, she would never again see Sinjin or her family. He'd keep her on a very tight leash.

His gut told him to take her home, but his pride screamed to stay on and prove to Sinjin Rayborne that he had won her. That he would marry her.

He met Katelyn at her chamber door. She looked amazing in an emerald-colored gown that hugged her firm breasts. He was surprised she did not wear a modesty piece as he had requested in his home. No doubt another display of independence. Well, he would squash that stubborn streak soon enough.

They walked to the dining room in silence. Only when they were seated did he engage in conversation. "You look a bit pale, my dear."

"Am I?" she asked, not even looking at him.

Ronald cleared his throat, demanding her attention. "Are you well rested after your nap this afternoon, my dear?"

"Yes, my lord," she replied, her voice barely above a whisper.

At Rose Alley, she had tried to engage him in conversation, but it had been awkward in his sister's presence. Meredith had always been mistress of his home, and she did not like the idea of sharing those duties with Katelyn.

"Did you enjoy your ride this afternoon, my lord?"

"I did not ride, but instead wrote to my sister."

She nodded. "I am sure she misses you."

He felt his cheeks turn hot. "I understand staying with your sister is important to you, and therefore, I have written my steward and asked him to clear my calendar so that I can remain here at Claymoore Hall with you."

Her eyes instantly lit up, and he was not fool enough to think her happiness had anything to do with him.

He glanced down the table at his nemesis, who was talking to a handsome young woman who seemed to monopolize his attention. It must be tearing Katelyn apart to watch the bastard woo another woman, he thought with an inward smile.

"Are you pleased?"

"Yes, thank you, my lord."

"I am glad. I had hoped you would be."

"Very much so, my lord."

Ronald had brought along one of his most faithful servants, and he would have Katelyn watched around the clock from here on out.

After the final course had been served, Sinjin stood and tapped his knife against a wineglass. "Gentlemen, please join me for brandy and cigars in the parlor. Ladies, follow my mother into the drawing room for tea."

"I shall see you to your room after I have a cigar with the men," Ronald said.

"Yes, my lord."

He helped her to her feet and placed a hand on her slender hip.

Sinjin glanced at them, his gaze slipping to where Ronald's hand rested at her waist.

Ronald walked her toward the drawing room where he kissed her hand, lingering over it while Sinjin watched. "I do believe Sinjin Rayborne is smitten with you. I would not think it wise for you to do or say anything that might encourage him."

As expected, she looked alarmed. Her throat convulsed as she swallowed hard. "You are mistaken, my lord. Lord Mawbry has no interest in me."

He leaned toward her, his fingers tightening on her arm. "I do not like being laughed at or made a fool of, Katelyn, is that understood?"

She glanced down at where he held her. "You are hurting me, my lord."

He loosened his grip slightly. "Do you understand?"

"Everyone knows I am engaged to you, my lord."

"Do they, now?"

"Yes, especially since your unexpected arrival."

He dropped his hold on her. She barely inclined her head before walking off in the opposite direction.

"Katelyn," he said before she could get too far.

She stopped but did not turn to look at him. Soon enough he would sever that willful streak.

"I shall walk you to your chamber at a quarter past nine. Be ready."

She continued on her way.

Katelyn trembled as she made her way toward the drawing room. Her worst fears had been realized. Ronald knew about Sinjin. Just how much he knew was uncertain, but that did not matter now. He knew, and he would stop at nothing to end it. No doubt he had sent word to her mother. What next—would she too arrive at Claymoore Hall?

Tears burned the backs of her eyes as she rushed down the hallway and up the steps, anxious to be in her room, far away from prying eyes. Far away from Lord Balliford, and most of all, far away from her dismal future.

Marilyn glanced at the clock yet again. It was nearly one in the morning, and she was trying to read the same page as when she'd entered the room over an hour ago, but her mind would not settle.

Why had she come to the study? What was she hoping

would happen when Lady Anna arrived? She was a beautiful creature, yes, but with a deviousness that put Marilyn on edge.

"You are a fool," Marilyn said to herself, heading for the door.

"Where are you going?"

Lady Anna met her at the doorway, and Marilyn wondered how long she had been standing there, watching.

"To my room."

Anna's gaze shifted to Marilyn's lips for a moment. "I could not get away until now. My chaperone kept checking in on me."

Marilyn didn't have to wonder why the chaperone kept her on a short leash.

"It is late, and I must return to my room."

"Why?"

"Because my aunt might check on me."

"Your aunt might also be sound asleep."

Lady Anna's long golden blond hair fell in fat curls to her slender waist. She lifted a graceful hand to Marilyn's face, the backs of her fingers brushing along her jaw.

Marilyn's heart thudded against her breastbone.

"You have the most delicate features I have ever seen, Lady Marilyn."

She had never had her looks called delicate before. Beautiful, handsome even, but never delicate. More than anything, Marilyn wondered why she seemed so interested in her.

"You and your sister are similar in some ways, and yet so different in others."

"Yes, but so are a lot of siblings. Do you not have a sibling?"

"I am an only child. A pity, too. I would have enjoyed having a sister. I imagine the two of you share everything."

"Most things, yes." Marilyn gripped the book tighter in her hand.

"Will you stay with me for a little while, Lady Marilyn? Please." She sounded almost desperate.

"It's quite late. I should—"

"I would forever be in your debt. I need a friend to talk to."

Ignoring the warning bells clanging in her head, Marilyn stepped back into the room and sat down on the settee. Anna closed the door and sat right beside her. They did not touch, but Marilyn could feel the heat from Anna's body through the thin material of her wrap.

"Why did you wish to meet with me?" Marilyn asked, her heart pumping in double time.

"I think you know." Anna's smile was coy. She reached for a lock of Marilyn's hair, brought it to her nose, and inhaled. "Rosemary," she whispered, before leaning forward and kissing Marilyn.

Marilyn did not pull away from the soft kiss. In fact, she found herself wanting more. Anna's lips were so gentle, full, and tasted like strawberries.

Anna pulled back the slightest bit, as though gauging Marilyn's reaction. A smile touched the corners of her mouth, and she leaned in again. Anna's tongue slid along the seam of Marilyn's lips, coaxing her to open.

Marilyn opened her mouth the slightest bit and Anna took advantage.

The breath left Marilyn as Anna deepened the kiss and pushed her back upon the settee.

Marilyn could scarcely breathe as the blood coursed through her veins. Her heart pumped nearly out of her chest, and excitement rippled along her spine. Anna's hand was suddenly covering her breast, her fingers brushing the outline of a nipple.

A shiver spiked through Marilyn and she swallowed a groan.

She was so caught up in the moment she didn't hear the door open. Not until it was too late.

Anna looked up and smiled.

"Do not stop on my account," Victor said, a lazy smile on his handsome face.

Marilyn was horrified. What must he be thinking? Her cheeks flushed with color, and she wished more than anything to disappear.

Oh dear God, how much had he seen?

Enough to tell them not to stop.

Feeling sick to her stomach, Marilyn stood quickly, but her gown was caught beneath Anna, and the material made a loud ripping noise.

Anna stood, freeing Marilyn, who rushed for the door. She did not make eye contact with Victor. She couldn't.

"Marilyn," he said, his voice soft, apologetic even.

She rushed past him, but she didn't stop. In fact, she started running.

21

Katelyn wished she had stayed in bed like her sister had, rather than venture out with Ronald this morning. He had said he had a surprise for her. Little did she realize that surprise was watching an archery match between himself and a few male acquaintances, including the Rayborne brothers.

Sinjin barely glanced at her. Apparently, he had read her letter. Last night she had told him in little words that they could no longer be, that Ronald knew the truth, and to continue on as they had been would be foolhardy.

"You look upset, my dear."

Aunt Lillith, who sat down beside Katelyn, kept her voice low so that the few other guests did not overhear her.

"I barely slept last night."

"I am so sorry, Katie." Lillith squeezed her hand. "I want you to know that you can confide in me, my dear. You can tell me anything, and I swear I will not utter a word to anyone."

"Ronald knows about Sinjin."

Her eyes widened in alarm. "How on earth?"

"I must have been obvious. He told me that he would not

give me up, and so I sent Sinjin a letter telling him that Ronald knew about us, and that we must end our relationship."

"And you regret sending the letter."

"More than anything, even though I know it is for the best. Sinjin must find a woman to marry, and I will have to marry Ronald."

"Is that really what you want, Katelyn?"

Katelyn glanced over at Sinjin, who looked incredibly handsome and relaxed in navy pants tucked into black Hessians, and a plain linen shirt that opened at the neck. "No."

Lillith smiled softly. "Perhaps you should speak to Sinjin. Tell him how you feel, that you don't wish to marry Ronald. That you wish to marry him."

"I don't know if he wants to marry me."

"Then perhaps now is the time to be honest with each other. Time is of the essence."

"I'm afraid of what his answer might be. I mean, what if he is relieved?"

"Look at him, Katelyn," Lillith whispered. "He's furious. You can sense it in him, from his stance to the way he's gritting his teeth. I'm surprised they don't snap."

Hope flared within Katelyn. "Do you think so?"

"Yes, you might be surprised how much he wants you."

"I would be so happy . . . But as you said before, my mother would never stand for it."

"Your mother might *have* to stand for it," Lillith replied, not hiding her agitation.

With her mind made up, Katelyn said, "I'll speak to him."

Lillith's gaze shifted to something beyond Katelyn's shoulder. "You might want to talk to him sooner versus later."

"What are you ladies talking about?"

Katelyn gasped, surprised she had not heard Ronald approach.

Ronald smiled, exposing crooked, slightly yellowed teeth, and Katelyn cringed. His jacket was ill-fitting, and his white pants fit obscenely tight, showing the dimples in his buttocks.

She would talk to Sinjin as soon as she could get him alone.

"Wish me luck, my dear," he said, taking her hand, bringing it to his lips for a kiss.

"Good luck, my lord."

She felt Sinjin's gaze on her and very nearly ripped her hand away from Ronald's. Sensing her reaction, Ronald's fingers tightened around hers.

Ronald glanced at Lillith. "And might I say you are looking quite fetching this morning, Lady Nordland."

Lillith smiled tightly. "Thank you, Lord Balliford."

"Well, I must return or lose my place in the contest." When he turned his back, Aunt Lillith rolled her eyes. They remained silent as Sinjin and Victor stepped forward. Both men drew back on their bows, and at the signal from the footman, released the arrows.

Both men hit their targets, but Sinjin came closest.

"He's quite good," Lillith said, and Katelyn could not help but smile.

Ronald was Sinjin's next competitor. Katelyn's heart raced and her palms began to sweat. Standing side by side, Sinjin's attributes contrasted greatly with Ronald's obvious imperfections. They were close in height, but that is where all similarity ended. A shiver rushed through her as she stared at Sinjin's broad shoulders and his high, tight buttocks. She recalled those muscular legs entwined with her own—his long, hard sex buried deep within her.

The footman gave the signal, and both men pulled back on the bows and released. The arrows struck their targets.

"Damn," Aunt Lillith said beneath her breath, as the servant on the far end of the lawn pointed to Ronald's target.

Ronald turned to look at Katelyn and beamed. She forced a smile and nodded at him. When he turned his back on her, she glanced at Sinjin, who was shaking Ronald's hand.

"Good morning, ladies," Victor said, a warm smile in place.

"Good morning," they said in unison.

"Would you like to join us?" Katelyn asked, noting the pleased expression on her aunt's face.

He nodded. "Don't mind if I do." He took the seat closest to Lillith. "Where is your niece this morning?"

"I fear she's not feeling well."

"I am sorry to hear that. Please tell her that I hope she is feeling better very soon."

Lillith sat up straighter. "I shall be happy to relay the message."

"Thank you, Lily," he said.

Lillith's eyes widened.

"Oh, this should be good," Victor said, motioning toward the men.

Rory and Ronald drew back on the bows. The youngest Rayborne brother laughed at something the footman said, and at the count, released.

Both men hit dead center.

Ronald wiped his sweaty forehead with a kerchief from his waistcoat pocket, while Rory seemed cool as could be.

"I do believe I was not as blessed as my brothers when it comes to certain things, archery included."

"I think you are all blessed," Katelyn said before she could stop herself.

"Thank you, Lady Katelyn," Victor said in a voice that had her remembering the liaison he'd had with his brother and Lady Anna.

Good God, he did not think she was referring to him being blessed in terms of—

"Sinjin is giving Rory pointers . . . as though he needs it."

Katelyn kept hoping Sinjin would talk to her, but he kept his distance, instead talking to his valet and Rory. He put his hand on his little brother's shoulder, leaned in, whispered something in his ear, and then stepped back, crossing his arms over his wide chest.

This time Ronald hit off target, and Rory once again hit center.

Rory grinned at Sinjin.

"My hand slipped," Ronald said, his voice clipped, his agitation obvious.

"There is not a man here who can beat Rory," Victor said, pride in his voice.

Katelyn and Lillith shared a smile, but the smile faded when Lady Celeste and a few friends came around the corner and crossed the lawns toward them. "Do you mind if we join you?" she asked prettily, twirling her parasol.

"Please," Aunt Lillith said, motioning to the empty chairs nearby, which Victor pulled closer.

Celeste looked incredible in a blue-and-white print walking dress, her shoes of the finest silk. Katelyn hid her own well-worn shoes beneath her chair.

"Why do you not participate, Lord Graston?" Celeste asked.

"I fear I am already out this round—as is Sinjin."

Celeste looked alarmed. "Oh dear. Well, I am certain you will both fare well next round now that I am here to cheer you on."

Lillith gave Katelyn a pained expression that she hid with a soft smile when Celeste glanced at her.

Sinjin looked their way and Celeste waved exuberantly. He nodded in return and flashed a wolfish grin.

Jealousy ate at Katelyn's insides.

"I was so delighted when Lord Mawbry asked me to join him for the walk today," Celeste said in a too-sweet voice.

Katelyn's heart fell to her feet.

"How nice for you," Lillith said, sounding sincere.

Both men shot again, and once again, Rory ended up being the victor. This time Ronald did not argue the point.

"Lady Katelyn, I had the honor of meeting your intended last night," Celeste said, nicer than she'd ever been before. "He's such a nice man. How excited you must be for your up-coming wedding."

Katelyn schooled her features. "I am."

"I can hardly wait until the day I am a bride. I have already picked out my dress." Her gaze shifted to Sinjin.

"That day will be very soon," her companion murmured, watching Katelyn closely.

Katelyn bit the inside of her cheek. What a handsome couple the two would make. Indeed, they would be the toast of the *ton.*

Sinjin walked toward them in long strides, and Katelyn's heart pounded in time with each step that brought him closer.

"Good morning, ladies," he said, a pleasant smile in place. He barely glanced at Katelyn.

"I look forward to our walk, my lord," Lady Celeste blurted.

"As do I, Lady Celeste."

"You are quite accomplished with bow and arrow, my lord," Aunt Lillith said, and Sinjin smiled genuinely.

"Thank you, Lady Nordland . . . though I fear Lady Kate-lyn's betrothed has bested me today." His gaze slid to Katelyn for a second. His eyes lacked the warmth that had always been there before.

Katelyn's stomach twisted. She wanted a private moment alone, to tell him she didn't mean a word she'd written in that letter. That she yearned to feel his hands on hers once more . . . to lay in bed with him and relish the sensation of skin against skin, of making love and losing herself in the moment.

By damned she would not let Ronald ruin her last chance at happiness.

Sinjin strolled with Lady Celeste, all the while watching the couple ahead of him, walking arm in arm, looking the very picture of pre-wedded bliss.

We can no longer see one another, the letter began, written in Katelyn's elegant script.

He should be grateful, he told himself, that Lord Balliford had arrived when he had, and, in turn, made him realize how foolhardy he had been in getting involved with a woman engaged to another man.

Indeed, after coming to terms with the end of his liaison with Katelyn, he had lain in bed last night thinking of all the reasons he should pursue Lady Celeste. After all, she had an impressive lineage and would bring to the marriage a dowry that no other debutante could touch.

She was the prize of the Season.

And yet he could scarcely tolerate her presence. Plain and simple, she was not the woman he wanted.

For the tenth time in as many minutes, Lady Celeste mentioned her figure, and how expensive her gown was, saying she had bought it in Paris when she had been visiting with her family some months before.

"My mother constantly tells me that I must eat numerous times throughout the day in order to keep the weight on my bones."

She went on to tell him that she conditioned her hair with special oils in order to get a silky sheen, and that her maid insisted she take a parasol with her at all times in order to keep her creamy skin pale and freckle free.

He quite liked freckles.

Katelyn wore a bonnet, and the parasol that hung from her hand had not seen any use thus far.

Lord Balliford's hand slid to Katelyn's waist, and she glanced up at her intended, a forced smile on her lips.

Let her go, Sinjin! his mind all but screamed, and yet his heart said something altogether different.

"I shall play the pianoforte for you this evening," Lady Celeste said, tearing Sinjin out of his thoughts. "Your mother keeps saying how impressed you are by my playing. Perhaps I shall play a song for you . . . and only you."

He nodded. "Of course."

"Tonight before dinner?"

"Certainly."

"My chaperone has agreed to let me have a few minutes alone with you. I have assured her that nothing shall happen." She laughed playfully. "I told her she is welcome to stay next to the parlor door during the entire performance."

"I would expect nothing less," Sinjin said, relieved when the abbey, their destination, came into view. He had grown weary of conversing long before and now wanted nothing but a few quiet minutes to himself.

After touring the abbey and its grounds, the carriages with luncheon arrived, and the guests took their places on the abbey's lawn.

Lord Balliford stood outside the abbey with Lady Anna's chaperone, looking up at the ancient building. Seizing the opportunity, Sinjin walked into the abbey and found Katelyn and her aunt near the back, looking at a stained glass window depicting the third crusade.

"Ladies," he said when he was close enough to Katelyn and Lillith.

Katelyn's expression was difficult to gauge, while Lillith smiled softly. "Good afternoon, my lord."

"Good afternoon, Lady Nordland." He glanced at Katelyn and nodded. "Lady Katelyn." The dark circles beneath her green eyes made her seem fragile, and he ached to take her in his arms and away to a place they could be alone together.

"The abbey and grounds are breathtaking," Lillith said brightly.

"I confess that I have not been here since I was a boy."

"Claymoore Hall sits on some of the most beautiful land I have ever seen," Aunt Lillith said. "I told Katelyn on our walk here that the woman who marries you and inherits such an amazing estate is a lucky woman indeed."

Katelyn shifted on her feet.

"You are far too kind, Lady Nordland."

"Lord Mawbry, your mother is waiting." Lady Celeste's voice came from behind him. "She told me she would like for us to sit with her."

He felt like a young boy being scolded by his mother, and he did not like it one bit. He counted to ten twice. "Please excuse me, ladies."

Katelyn opened her mouth as though to say something but closed it as quickly, her gaze shifting just past his shoulder to where Celeste awaited him.

22

Lady Anna took Thomas's hand and allowed him to walk her toward the small clearing hidden behind a thick grove of trees. She smiled inwardly, knowing full well what he had in mind.

It was what every man had in mind. She knew her reputation. Knew that men talked, and those rumors used to bother her . . . but no longer. She enjoyed sex, and she would make no apologies for her healthy escapades.

Thomas had intentionally fallen behind the others, walking slowly, keeping her by his side, asking her question after endless question.

The time for talking was over.

She hated senseless chatter. She wanted merely to get down to business and be done with it. Time was of the essence, especially since her chaperone had found someone who loved conversation as much as she. However, she would shortly discover Anna's disappearance and come looking for her.

Her gaze shifted to the erection that strained Thomas's pants and excitement rippled along her spine. He didn't have a long cock, but it was thick, and it would do.

"What do you have in mind, Thomas?" she asked, immediately going in for a kiss. She didn't particularly like kissing, but she didn't pull away as his moustache tickled her lip and he opened his mouth wide. Her hand slid to his erect cock. "We must hurry if we don't want our absence noted," she whispered against his lips, walking toward a large tree.

He nodded, flipped her skirts over her buttocks, and sucked in a deep breath.

She hadn't bothered with drawers, and she knew how going naked beneath her gown excited all her lovers. Thomas was no exception.

He brushed his hands over her buttocks, his fingers slipping to the crack, over her back passage, to her soaked slit. He slid a finger inside, added another, and she gasped with pleasure.

She held on to the tree for support, arching her back, anxious for him to fuck her. She heard him fumble with his pants, felt his cock nudge her opening.

She leaned back against him, urging him to get on with it. They were not so far off the beaten bath that someone looking for a place to relieve themselves or like-minded lovers would not stumble upon them.

He slid within her on a moan, his hands cupping her breasts. He touched her nipples, his fingers barely brushing over them. "Harder," she said, and he pinched the peaks hard. She preferred her lovers to be a bit rough and aggressive. Her hand covered one of his, and she showed him just how she liked to be touched.

The sensation was effective, making the flesh between her legs wetter.

He trembled as he thrust, and she knew he struggled to keep from coming.

Thomas swelled within her and he slowed his pace, his nails

digging into her hips as he gained control. Anna excited him in ways no other woman had. He had heard of her sexual exploits from a number of men but had never had the good fortune to meet her until last night. All day she'd been throwing him seductive glances. His efforts had certainly been rewarded.

She had met all of his heated stares, and now as his balls tightened against his body, he was grateful he had stayed on. To think he had almost left, thinking the entire party had been a waste of time, especially after Lady Katelyn's fiancé had arrived.

Anna moved against him and cried out, her inner muscles squeezing him tight. She looked back at him, her dark eyes wide and full of passion. Her nails bit into his ass, and his thrusts increased. With a massive groan, he pulled out, ropes of sperm covering the ground beneath them.

During the picnic, Katelyn sat with Ronald, Aunt Lillith, Lady Anna, and her chaperone, trying not to watch Celeste and Sinjin. He had sought her out earlier, so maybe he wanted to talk with her.

"Lady Katelyn, where has your sister been?" Anna asked, popping a strawberry into her mouth.

Katelyn hated to admit it, but she was actually enjoying the other woman's company. Anna had an amazing ability to carry a conversation all on her own, and she annoyed Ronald to no end. He looked ruffled every single time Anna opened her mouth. "Marilyn is not feeling well, I'm afraid."

"I am so sorry to hear that," she murmured, looking sincere in her apology. "Please send along my well-wishes to her, and tell her I look forward to seeing her again very soon."

"Thank you, I shall do that."

Lady Celeste's laughter interrupted the conversation. Sinjin and the duke's daughter sat directly to Katelyn's right, so it wasn't difficult to miss them.

"Lord Balliford, I understand you know my uncle well," Lady Anna said.

"And who would your uncle be, Lady Anna?" Ronald forced joviality into his voice.

"Cornelius MacKalveroy."

Ronald's brows lifted high. "Indeed, I know Mr. MacKalveroy well. He owns land just east of Rose Alley."

"Indeed, he does. I remember meeting you and your sister many years ago when I visited with him for a few weeks."

His brows furrowed. "I'm sorry I do not recall the meeting."

Anna's lips curved into a smile. "Let me refresh your memory then. You and your sister were out riding, and you passed by a giant oak tree. I was playing in said oak tree, and needless to say, you were not pleased."

"Not pleased?" Aunt Lillith asked, looking intrigued by the conversation.

"Not at all—isn't that right, my lord?"

His lips quirked and he looked a bit flushed.

"Well, as I remember it, I was playing on a tree that was on Lord Balliford's property and not my uncle's."

"Surely you jest?" Lillith said, her brows furrowing.

"I assure you, she does not *jest*, madam," Balliford said, lifting his chin and looking down his nose at Lillith. "I do remember the occasion, and I was acting in Lady Anna's best interest and mine."

"Oh dear, I did not mean to embarrass you, Lord Balliford," Anna said, though it appeared she definitely had.

Katelyn was not at all surprised by the story. He had so little tolerance for women or children. She could only imagine what Ronald would be like as a father. No doubt a strict disciplinarian, and God forbid they have a daughter. He would make life unbearable for both mother and child.

Anna cleared her throat. "I was shocked you had even seen me, you were so occupied."

"Does something amuse you, my dear?" Ronald said abruptly, directing his gaze on Katelyn.

Katelyn, who had been enjoying Ronald's discomfort, felt her cheeks flush. "I am merely recalling a time in my youth when I visited my grandmother's country estate."

"I so enjoyed growing up in the country," Lady Anna said, effectively redirecting the attention back to her, and Katelyn could have hugged her.

By the time lunch was over, Katelyn was ready to return to Claymoore Hall and see how Marilyn was faring. Lady Anna kept Aunt Lillith and Ronald engaged in conversation about a summer she spent in the Scottish highlands.

Celeste hung on Sinjin's arm the entire way back. Katelyn had no business being angry with him, but she was. She didn't want to share him with anyone.

"I shall see you this evening, my dear," Ronald said to Katelyn the second they stepped into the manor. "I have business to attend to."

"I think I shall rest."

"Very well," he said, leaving her with Lillith and Anna, who promptly went in search of tea.

Katelyn walked up the stairs to her room . . . and kept on going up the next flight. She remembered Sinjin showing her from the gardens where his room was. If she recalled, he was on the third floor, corner chamber.

She would be horrified if someone caught her sneaking around the host's chambers, but she could not stop herself from going.

Laughter coming from the landing stopped her in her tracks, and she quickly hid behind a thick drapery panel. Her heart pounded in her ears as she heard two women conversing, and the topic of conversation made her pause.

"I do not know why I am even staying on any longer. Lady Celeste has surely won his heart."

"There are two other brothers, dearest," an older woman's voice said.

"Yes, but Sinjin is the heir. He is extremely wealthy in his own right. My cousin said he has an incredible business sense."

"I think it is because you do not care for Lady Celeste that it hurts as it does."

"Shhh, lest someone hear us." The woman lowered her voice. "All my life I have had to live in that miserable woman's shadow. True, the younger Raybornes are a considerable catch as well, but it is just this once I wanted to win."

"The ring is not on her finger yet, my dear."

"No, it is not. We have three more nights before the party ends."

"And anything can happen in three nights."

"I have even heard the rumor some women are being invited to the family estate in Rochester." They continued down the hallway and their voices faded.

Was it true that certain women were being invited to the family's main estate?

How very sobering.

Taking a steadying breath, Katelyn slipped from behind the curtain. Twice she nearly turned back, but when she reached the top floor, she forced herself to take the steps that lead to the last room at the end of the long hallway. By the time she reached the door, she thought of a million reasons why she should abort the plan.

She stood poised at the door, hand fisted, ready to knock, when the door whipped open and Sinjin appeared.

Her heart gave a sharp jolt, and it was all she could do not to throw herself into his arms.

He looked shocked to see her.

"I—um." She shifted on her feet.

A slow smile spread across his lips. "Lady Katelyn, what a wonderful surprise."

"I—wanted to see you."

He glanced past her shoulder. "Please, come in."

Not wanting to be caught standing at Sinjin's door, Katelyn didn't hesitate and stepped into the room.

Everything about the space screamed masculinity, from the large, dark furniture, to the imposing, canopied bed with dark panels that took up the far end of the room.

She could feel him watch her intently, and she struggled to find the exact words she wanted to say.

He took a seat on the edge of his bed, leaning back on his elbows, looking as in control as could be, and so incredibly sexy she wanted to rip his clothes off, push him onto his back, and have her way with him.

"You wished to speak with me?" he prompted.

She chewed her bottom lip. "I—"

He lifted a brow.

"This was probably a mistake." Katelyn had a hand on the door handle when she felt him behind her. He placed his hand over hers, urging her fingers away from the handle.

"Don't go," he whispered, his breath hot against the back of her neck.

She closed her eyes and leaned her forehead against the door. *I want to be with you.* How she ached to say the words, and yet, she could not get them past her lips to save her life.

He turned her in his arms, then cupped her face with his hands. "Break off your engagement, Katelyn. End it now."

They were the words she most wanted to hear from him all day. "You don't want to marry Lady Celeste?"

"Lord, no. I've been paying attention to her only because my mother has asked me to. Who I want is standing before me. I want you, Kate, and only you. I have from the first minute we met, and I want you to be my wife."

Joy, unlike any she had ever known, rushed through her. Sinjin wanted to marry her. "But what of your mother? She would not approve."

"My mother will come around. Just tell me that you will break off your engagement."

"I'll break off my engagement."

His eyes searched hers, and a smile curved his lips. He lowered his head and kissed her.

Her arms slid around his shoulders and she clung to him as he kissed her, his tongue velvety soft against her own.

Locking the door, he kissed her again, slowly, no urgency at all.

He reached behind her, pulled at the lacings at her back, and seconds later the gown sagged at her waist. He helped her out of it, following with her chemise.

She kicked off her shoes but left on her stockings.

Sinjin took a step back and looked at the beauty who had appeared on his doorstep. And to think minutes before he'd been frustrated beyond belief. In fact, he'd been ready to come out of his skin and was heading out of his room in order to take a long ride to clear his head, when there she was, the very woman he'd been trying not to think of, standing before him.

And she wanted him. She would call of her engagement to Balliford.

He would go to his mother and tell her that he had found his bride, and that he would marry Katelyn Davenport.

He pulled Katelyn to him, savoring the feel of her soft, naked body against him. She reached out and ripped the shirt from his pants, her hands smoothing over his flat belly, the muscles contracting beneath her fingers.

He reached back behind his neck and pulled off his shirt. Katelyn smiled. She kissed his chest and went slowly to her knees.

Katelyn worked the buttons of his pants with a skill that surprised her, and pushed them down to his knees. His long, thick cock stood at attention; she grabbed the length firmly at the base and licked the purple, plum-sized head.

He watched as she took her time kissing him, licking him, sucking him. Her hands moved to his thighs, her fingers splaying there.

He reached down, cupped her breasts in his hands and played with her nipples. Liquid fire rushed through her veins, straight between her thighs.

She became more aggressive, and finally when he could take no more foreplay, he kicked off his pants, picked her up, and strode toward the bed.

Setting her on the bed, he urged her legs apart using his thighs and slid into her welcoming heat.

Katelyn moaned low in her throat and he smiled, knowing he would never forget the sound. He took his time, slowly moving in and out of her.

She explored the planes of his back, the thick, rigid muscles moving beneath olive skin. She kissed him, for once being the aggressor, her tongue sliding along his, matching the rhythm he had set with their bodies.

He stared down at her, his eyes so intense and full of desire that she knew she'd never forget this moment. Her insides contracted as his cock slid in and out of her honeyed walls.

He came with a loud moan, not caring who heard them, rejoicing in the fact he had the woman he loved, and she truly belonged to him.

23

The following morning, Katelyn sat beside Ronald, who was at the moment placing a heaping teaspoon of sugar into his cup. They were one of seven people in the parlor, drinking tea and conversing quietly. Aunt Lillith had left to check on Marilyn, and already Katelyn was counting the minutes until her return.

"I have been thinking that perhaps we can go to London for the Season. After our wedding everyone will want to meet you and be your friend," he said, before taking a bite of a scone.

Ronald had always made it clear that he detested town and had always talked negatively about London in particular. It dawned on her that he was trying to make her happy. Nothing he could do would ever make her happy, and now it didn't matter because she would marry Sinjin, not Ronald.

Oh, happy day! She felt as light as air and wanted to shout her good fortune from the rooftops.

He wiped his thin lips with a napkin. "What do you think, sweet Kate?"

Sweet Kate? Since when did he use such endearments? She did not like this one bit.

"That sounds lovely," she said, her mind a million miles away.

She once again recalled Sinjin's words last night when he had made love to her and told her he wanted to marry her.

She had barely been able to sleep for all her excitement. When Aunt Lillith arrived at her door this morning, she had intended to tell her about her plans to call off her engagement and wed Sinjin, the man she desired with all her heart, but Ronald arrived minutes later to escort her to breakfast.

Ronald inched closer toward her, his gaze shifting to her décolletage. "I am very excited to make you my wife, my dearest heart." He brought her hand to his lips and kissed her fingers. "I hope you know that."

She swallowed hard, uncomfortable with the direction the conversation was headed and the touch of his dry lips on her skin.

Ronald cleared his throat loudly.

Sitting up straighter, she forced a smile and murmured, "I am glad."

He frowned, no doubt disappointed she did not return the sentiment.

I do not want to marry you. I am in love with someone else. How tempted she was to blurt out those words, to finally get them off her chest once and for all.

Treading in dangerous waters, she managed a smile. "I am sure you are anxious to return to Rose Alley."

He nodded and slid his arm across the back of her chair. "I always yearn for Rose Alley when I am away. I will be especially anxious to return this time, and with you on my arm."

Oh dear. She really must talk to Aunt Lillith as soon as possible.

"I'm rather tired and have a slight headache. Would you mind terribly if I returned to my chamber?"

He seemed genuinely concerned. "You are no doubt worn down from the constant stimulation."

If he only knew . . . "I'm sure you are right."

"Shall I walk you to your room, then?" he asked, and she nodded.

She slid her hand around his elbow and fell into step beside him, nearly tripping over her feet when she noticed Sinjin talking to Lady Celeste and her chaperone. He stood with his back to Katelyn, an arm on the balustrade. Snug black pants cupped his high, tight ass; the light-colored shirt only emphasized the width of his shoulders, and the silver and black waistcoat defined the leanness of his waist.

At their approach, Celeste saw her and smiled, her gaze moving to Ronald.

Katelyn's stomach coiled. Sinjin smiled, then glanced at her and then Ronald. "How are you this fine morning?" he asked, his voice cordial, his grin welcoming, and she was instantly reminded of the night before in his arms, of all the times he had brought her to climax.

"Quite well, Lord Mawbry," Ronald said, his hold on her tightening.

"And how are you, Lady Katelyn?" Sinjin asked, his voice as smooth as silk.

"I am well." Their eyes caught and held, and it was all she could do not to turn to Ronald and tell him the marriage was off. How she would love to see the look on Celeste's face when she learned that Katelyn would marry Sinjin.

"I would stay and linger, but I fear my fiancée is feeling a bit peaked."

"I am sorry to hear that," Sinjin replied. "I hope you feel better very soon, Lady Katelyn."

"Thank you, my lord. I'm sure it is nothing a nap will not cure."

As they walked away, Katelyn felt Sinjin's gaze on her. Ronald said nothing at all.

When she came to her chamber door, she turned the handle, hoping Marilyn would be on the other side.

Unfortunately, the room was empty.

Ronald licked his thin lips. "May I have a kiss?" he inquired, and she impulsively took a step back, into the room.

"My lord, I am not comfortable doing so before the wedding—"

But he did not listen to her, and instead lowered his head.

Sinjin walked slowly behind the couple and lingered near the stairs as Ronald spoke with Katelyn outside her room.

The blood roared in his ears when the older man lowered his head for a kiss. It was not a long, lingering kiss, more like a peck, but Sinjin was not prepared for the emotions rushing through him at seeing the woman he loved share any intimacy with another man.

Even if that man was her intended.

As least for now. He had been stunned to see the two having tea together. He had nearly joined their little party but assumed Katelyn might be taking advantage of the time alone with Balliford to break things off.

Apparently, that hadn't happened.

Sinjin waited patiently until the door to Katelyn's chamber closed and Balliford started back down the hallway.

When the coast was clear, Sinjin started for Katelyn's room and knocked.

Silence.

He tried again, and this time Katelyn opened the door. "Thank God it's you."

"I saw the kiss. I assume you had no time to talk to him."

She pulled him into the room. "No, not yet. It is difficult to find the right time, Sinjin. I must speak with my aunt. What of you?"

"I have a meeting with my mother in an hour."

Her green eyes widened. "What do you think she will say?"

"I'm assuming she will be pleased that I have found a bride, especially a woman I love."

"I love you, too." She slid her arms around his neck and kissed him ravenously.

Sinjin was surprised at the intensity of the kiss, the way she tugged his shirt from his pants and reached for his cock, her fingers sliding over him.

"You are like a fire in my blood that can't be quenched," he said, the words sending a delicious shiver up her spine.

He lifted her in his arms and she let out a delighted yelp. Crossing the room, he flung her onto the bed and lifted her skirts. He bent down and licked her sweet slit from back passage to clit, his tongue swirling around the tiny, sensitive bundle of nerves.

Her fingers threaded through his hair, holding him there. Tendrils of fire slid through her veins, swooping low into her stomach and sex.

His hands moved beneath her body, cupping her buttocks, bringing her closer to his face. He took infinite care, tasting her, licking her relentlessly.

"Sinjin," she whispered on a moan, as climax claimed her.

She looked down at him, felt his large shaft pressing against her leg.

"I want you inside me," she whispered.

She didn't have to ask twice.

He crawled up her body and slid into her slick heat with a moan.

"When we marry I may never want to leave our bedchamber," she said on a sigh.

He smiled against her lips; then the time for talking was over as she reached for the stars, her body climbing toward the ultimate finish.

He went up on his knees, brought her legs up, and hooked them over his shoulders. She watched each thrust, his huge member sliding in and out of her, her honeyed juices coating him. His gaze followed, too, and when their gazes caught and held, the heat in his eyes made her heart skip a beat.

They climaxed together, their cries loud, ringing out for any and all to hear.

Sinjin walked into his mother's sitting room where they were sure to remain undisturbed.

Betsy turned to him and motioned to a high-backed chair. "Have a seat, my dear." She removed her earrings, set them aside, and rubbed her lobes before taking a seat.

"I wish to marry Katelyn Davenport."

Her blue eyes widened and she pressed her lips into a thin line. She wiped the corners of her mouth with her fingers. "Lady Katelyn is engaged and her betrothed is here . . . as well you know."

"I am in love with her."

"For the moment you might feel some—affection for her, and she is lovely, to be sure, but my love, you can do better."

The words infuriated him, and he fought to keep his cool. "You are mistaken, Mother. I could not do better."

Betsy stood so fast the chair nearly upended itself. She smoothed her hair back with a trembling hand. "I thought you had put this passing fancy behind you. Lady Celeste is—"

"I do not want Lady Celeste, Mother."

"She is everything a man could want—"

"Perhaps, but I do not want her. I want Katelyn Davenport, and I will have her—with or without your approval."

She stared at Sinjin for an uncomfortable minute that had him shifting in his seat.

"Let me ask you this, my dear. When you close your eyes and see your life ten years from now—do you see yourself with Lady Katelyn, or is this merely a passing fancy like all of your previous liaisons?"

"I see myself with Katelyn forever," he said, never so sure of anything.

She paced before him, cracking her knuckles. "I can see that you will not relent in this matter, and so therefore I have little choice but to give you my blessing."

He steadied himself for her next words.

"I will support you, but I am here to tell you that Balliford will not take this affront on his pride lightly, particularly in front of so many well-known lords and ladies. Perhaps Lady Katelyn can wait until the end of the party to break the news to him."

Sinjin nodded. "As you wish, Mother. We will be very happy together, Mother. Katelyn will be a wonderful wife and mother . . . just as you are."

"Do not think to flatter me, boy," she said, with the hint of a smile playing at her lips.

"Thank you, Mother—for your understanding."

She made Sinjin nervous when she remained quiet.

She took a deep breath. "Well, then I suppose there is only one thing for me to do."

His stomach tightened as he waited for her next words. "Which is?"

"Invite Lady Nordland to tea."

Lillith took a seat at the small table by the window. She had been escorted from her room to the opulent suite of her hostess, and now the Lady of Rochester waited patiently as a servant walked slowly toward the door and shut it behind her.

"My son tells me that he wishes to marry your niece."

Lillith did her best to hide her surprise. She knew Katelyn had fallen hard for the rake, but Lillith had only dreamed the man would ultimately marry her. In this case, she was glad to be proved wrong. "I am delighted to hear the news, Lady Rochester."

"So you approve?"

"Very much, my lady." Lillith cleared her throat. "I want my niece's happiness, and I know she cares deeply for your son."

Lady Rochester nodded. "And yet she is still engaged."

"That can be rectified."

"Indeed, and tell me, Lady Nordland, how do you think Lord Balliford will take the news?"

Lillith cleared her throat. "Badly."

A dark brow lifted. "I feared you might say that."

"He has paid my sister handsomely for Katelyn's hand already."

"I will pay him double," Lady Rochester said, her tone matter-of-fact.

"It is not a matter of money in this case, Lady Rochester. I've watched Lord Balliford with Katelyn. He desires her, and already considers her his possession. He is an odd man, and I do not trust him."

"He will call Sinjin out." It wasn't a question.

Lillith nodded. "I am afraid so."

For the first time since Lillith had met Betsy, the other woman showed weakness. Lillith could see fear in the other woman's eyes before she quickly looked away, but only for an instant. "Perhaps Katelyn should wait to break off the engagement until Sunday, right before they are set to leave."

"I think that is wise. I shall speak with Katelyn, plan the time and place of such a meeting, and I will let you know."

Betsy nodded. "I will tell you, Lady Nordland, that I have fought the idea of this marriage from the very beginning. But my son assures me that his happiness depends on this marriage, and far be it for me to deny my son anything, particularly his future. Please, for both our sakes, try to convince Lord Balliford that I will be very generous if he will go away quietly. No one need know the circumstances."

She did not want a duel to take place, and Lillith did not blame her. It was impossible to know the outcome of such an event, and Lord help all of them if Balliford won.

"I shall do my best, Lady Rochester."

Betsy nodded. "I am counting on you, Lady Nordland."

24

Marilyn, who had been sitting in the labyrinth, trying her best to read with little success, looked up to find Victor standing before her. "I do believe you've been avoiding me, young lady."

She had been staying to herself for days now, complaining of a headache when, in essence, she had been avoiding Lady Anna. The other woman had even slipped a note under her door that said to meet her in the study again, and Marilyn had immediately tossed it into the fire. "I haven't been avoiding you, Victor."

"Yes, you have."

She set her book down on the bench and met his gaze. "Very well, I have been avoiding everyone."

"At least you do not deny it." He picked a piece of lint from her skirts and flicked it away. "Now I understand why you are not interested in me . . . at least in that way," he said, his voice teasing.

"You are insufferable," she said with a laugh, grateful for his company. Being alone and keeping her thoughts to herself had been excruciating. She had wanted to talk to Katelyn about her feelings but could not be sure on how her sister would react. "Please, have a seat."

Victor sat down beside her, stretching his long legs before him. "You know that you deserve better than Anna."

"And here I thought you were *fond* of her."

"I *am* fond of Anna. I just don't trust her."

Marilyn didn't trust her either, and that's what concerned her about spending any more time alone with her. She had never felt about another woman the way she did about Lady Anna. "What do you mean?"

"Lady Anna has a certain reputation. It is not uncommon for people to . . . experiment with sex, meaning they like both sexes."

"Lady Anna being one."

He nodded. "Apparently."

"I think she kissed me to shock me and for no other reason."

"I don't know about that." He cleared his throat. "If I tell you something, do you promise not to tell a soul?"

She swallowed hard, wondering if she wanted to hear what he had to say.

"You cannot utter a word of this to anyone. You are sworn to silence," he said looking very intense all of a sudden.

Marilyn's heart pounded against her breastbone. "I swear."

"About a year ago, I attended an exclusive party in the heart of London. Everyone was required to wear masks. At no time were you able to remove said mask, and therefore your identity would be kept a secret. Well, at this party there were five men to every one woman. As you can imagine, this caused quite a dilemma for the men. Sure, you had some men who did mind being with other men, but there were those of us who also didn't mind sharing a woman."

"How scandalous," Marilyn said, not at all surprised to learn of such parties.

"I was intrigued by a particular blonde with dark eyes who wore a turquoise mask, and she enjoyed making love to an audience. One by one her lovers would take her, and she moaned and sighed for each. I have been with enough women to know this was no act. Anyway, many parties followed that one, and each time I found my way to her. For a while, I became infatuated with her but realized she felt no such attachment. Many dubbed her the Ice Princess, and she did not care. She merely laughs it off."

Marilyn could not imagine any young lady behaving in such a way. Did she have only the women and her chaperones fooled?

"Mark my words, that one is destined to become a courtesan."

"No doubt she would be successful."

"No doubt."

Marilyn shifted on the bench. "Was she ever with other women at these parties?"

"Yes, but only when another man was with them. That doesn't mean it never happened. It just means I never saw her with just a woman." He smiled softly. "I do not wish to hurt you, my friend, but rather to inform you of the danger behind the smile."

"I appreciate your concern, but I wouldn't worry. I am merely besotted because she was my first kiss."

His eyes widened. "First kiss? Do you mean you have never kissed a man?"

She shook her head. "Never."

"Then let me be the first."

"I do not think—"

He kissed her before she could say another word, just the lightest of kisses. His lips were soft and supple, and not at all unpleasant. However, the kiss lacked that certain spark she'd felt with Anna.

She pulled away for a moment, her brows furrowing; then

she leaned in again. He teased the seam of her lips with this tongue and she opened to him.

"Oh good lord."

Marilyn pulled away from Victor and looked at her Aunt Lillith, who stood watching them with hand over heart, a shocked expression on her face.

"I . . . I apologize. I did not. I—just wished . . ." Lillith closed her eyes, took a deep breath, and turned.

"Wait, Aunt Lillith!"

Lillith straightened her shoulders and turned back to face them. "Marilyn, would you please be so kind as to join me?"

"I must go, Victor."

Victor nodded, his gaze skipping past her to Lillith, his expression impossible to read.

Lillith didn't even hide her agitation. "If you will excuse us, Lord Graston," she managed, her voice a bit higher than usual.

"Of course, Lady Nordland," Victor replied, his tone bordering on seductive.

Lillith took Marilyn by the hand. "Come, my dear."

Ronald felt his cheeks turn hot as his footman stood before him, staring down at his boots.

"I am sorry, my lord. If—"

"That will be enough. You shall be compensated for your trouble. As always, do not repeat what you have seen or heard to anyone, is that understood?"

"Of course, my lord."

"Thank you, George. That will be all."

"Yes, my lord." The man bobbed his head, and opened and closed the door behind him.

Ronald took a deep breath. All morning Katelyn had been acting strangely, refusing to make eye contact, and when he'd kissed her, she'd barely been able to hide her revulsion.

Now he knew the truth. She had been fucking that scoundrel all along. How dare she humiliate him in such a way!

Well, in two days' time, they would be heading for Rose Alley, far away from the threat the other man presented. The moment the marriage vows had been read, he would get Katelyn with child, and she would be content to live a quiet life with just him and his sister in the country.

Katelyn would no longer visit her sister or aunt, or her bitch of a neglectful mother for that matter. Her mother should have never allowed Katelyn to act as chaperone to Marilyn to begin with.

He shook with fury.

She would have to settle into the docile life of a married woman. Indeed, she would play the perfect hostess to his friends and associates. She would be seen and not heard.

Ronald looked in the mirror and fussed with what little hair remained. He was not a handsome man, but he was extremely wealthy and titled, and never at a loss for female attention, much to his sister's dismay. Meredith hated the interest other women paid him.

Ronald started down the hall toward Katelyn's chamber, and he nearly missed his step when the door opened and Sinjin Rayborne appeared. He looked disheveled, his shirt haphazardly pushed into his pants, his hair ruffled—as though someone had ran her fingers through it.

A feminine hand pulled him back in, and Sinjin's laughter was like a knife in Ronald's heart.

He backtracked to his room, stepped out onto a balcony, and caught his breath. To learn by way of his servant that his fiancée was being unfaithful was bad enough, but to see it was even more gutting.

His trembling hands gripped the iron balcony. How tempted he was to have a drink in order to calm his nerves.

Once he had his emotions under control, he started back toward Katelyn's room, avoiding eye contact with a plain young woman and her escort. Perhaps he should have married someone plain, someone whom other men would not desire the way they desired Katelyn?

Someone who resembled Meredith, his faithful, loyal Meredith. He would hate to hear what she had to say about the circumstances he now found himself in.

He came to Katelyn's door and opened it without knocking.

Katelyn sat at the vanity, brushing out her hair. She whipped around, her eyes wide. "Ronald, what are you doing?" she asked, alarm in her voice.

He glanced at the rumpled bedding, at the thin chemise, at the red, swollen lips. "I've come to see what you are up to, Katelyn."

She stood slowly, setting the brush aside. "I just woke from a nap."

"A nap?" He pursed his lips. She didn't even blink an eye, but he sensed her nervousness, noted the way her throat convulsed as she swallowed hard. His gaze shifted from her innocent face, the beautiful features, to her long, statuesque body. The curve of her breasts and rose-colored nipples was evident through the thin material of the chemise, and he could even see the shadow of auburn hair that covered her sex.

He walked toward her, and the closer he came, the angrier he became. How dare she make a fool of him—he, the man who had paid a small fortune for her hand?

"Yes, a nap." She must have sensed his fury because she took a quick step back, knocking the vanity against the wall and causing a bottle of perfume to fall off the ledge and onto the floor.

Stopping inches from her, he noted she had to bend her head back to look up at him. When their gazes met and held, he recognized fear in those green depths.

Good, let her fear him. She should fear him!

He reached for her, pulled her close, and lifted her chemise with one hand, while his fingers found her sex. "You are still wet from him, aren't you, you whore?"

She wrenched away from him, pulling her chemise down. "How dare you!"

Katelyn's heart hammered in her chest. She saw the rage in Ronald's eyes and knew she was in trouble.

"Do you deny it?" he asked, a nerve pulsing in his jaw.

"No," she said, shocked by her bravery. She was tired of pretending. She was in love with Sinjin and she didn't care who knew it, especially the man before her.

He slapped her so hard she tasted blood, but she refused to cry out.

"You slut! Did you think I wouldn't find out?" His fingers slid around her arm and he dragged her toward the bed. Alarm rushed through her, and she was ready to scream when he pulled her against him and clamped his hand over her mouth.

She fought against him, and stopped only when she felt the hard length of his arousal against her back.

He pushed her facedown on the bed, and keeping her hands pinned down, he kicked her legs apart and positioned himself behind her.

"Stop it, Ronald," she screamed, every little movement exciting him more.

His hand moved to her throat. She tried to scream, but his fingers squeezed tight and she started choking. "Do you like that?" he asked, his cock brushing her buttocks.

"Stop it, Ronald. You don't want to do this!"

"Oh, I have every intention of sampling my fiancée, especially since you have already given yourself to another man." She sensed his excitement as he unleashed his erection.

"I should have done this long ago—before you gave your virginity to that scoundrel."

The door flew open and Aunt Lillith stood on the threshold, her eyes wide.

25

"**M**ove away from Katelyn this instant, or so help me God, I shall bring this entire household down around us," Aunt Lillith said, reaching for the door she had just closed. "And if I do— you will have a lot of explaining to do, my lord."

Ronald looked over his shoulder at her, the crazed look that had been there moments before replaced with shock that this was actually happening. He stuffed his prick back into his pants and moved to stand between Katelyn and her aunt.

"If you do, be sure to tell everyone the truth of what she has done."

"Which is?" Lillith asked, taking a step closer.

"Your niece has been fucking Sinjin Rayborne."

Lillith's expression didn't change at all. "My niece has fallen in love with another man, which does not give you the right to abuse her."

"She has admitted to sleeping with him. My footman heard them as well, so there is no denying it."

"You've had your man watching her?" Lillith's voice rose with every syllable.

"Yes, and with good reason. I suspected the affair."

"So therefore you believe it is your right to rape Katelyn?"

"She is my betrothed."

Aunt Lillith's eyes widened. "You offend me on every level, my lord. Get out of this room this instant before I throw you out myself."

Katelyn took the opportunity to slide away from Ronald. She took her robe off the back of the chair and wrapped it tight about her waist.

Ronald straightened his jacket, his erection now withered. "We are leaving immediately. My footman is already en route to Rose Alley to see that all the arrangements are made, and that the priest will be available to marry us."

"I will not marry you," Katelyn said. "I don't love you, and I never have."

Aunt Lillith took Katelyn's hand and squeezed it tight. "There, you have it—Katelyn no longer wishes to marry you."

"The marriage contract has been signed, and monies exchanged."

"I will return the funds you gave to my sister, with interest, of course," Lillith said, matter-of-factly.

"I don't want your money."

Lillith cleared her throat. "I shall double what you paid for your trouble. Certainly that is more than fair."

"Are you deaf? I do not want your money, Lady Nordland," he said with a snarl. "I will have Katelyn, and that is the end of the matter."

"My hearing is perfect, my lord." Lillith took a step closer to Ronald. "The wedding is off. I shall see that the funds my sister took from you are repaid in full. Do not try and contact my niece in any way." She turned on her heel and opened the door wide. "Good day, my lord."

Ronald didn't budge. "If Katelyn does not marry me . . . I shall let everyone know of Marilyn's true parentage."

Lillith swallowed hard and slowly closed the door.

"My sister's true parentage—whatever do you mean?" Katelyn asked, not liking the expression on her aunt's face one bit.

"Your sister is only your half-sister," Ronald said, looking pleased. "You see, during your parents' marriage, your whore of a mother slept with a servant, a lowly groomsman, who just so happens to be Marilyn's father."

"That is a lie," Katelyn said, but she could tell by her aunt's expression that it must be true.

"Ask your mother if you don't take my word for it," Ronald murmured. "In fact, ask your aunt."

Katelyn's stomach tightened. She didn't have to ask Lillith. Her silence said everything. "You cannot prove it."

Ronald laughed, a taunting sound that grated Katelyn's nerves. "Your mother confirmed the information herself not two months ago when the marriage contract was signed. She does have a weakness for wine, does she not?"

Katelyn felt the blood drain from her face. Her mother was loud and unusually talkative when she had more than a drink or two.

"When your father was alive, he told me the story, and I never repeated it to anyone or brought it up, because I knew from the moment I saw you that I wanted you as my bride. That is why I have kept the information quiet for all this time. When I saw you again after all these years, after your father's passing, I wanted to know what skeletons might be lurking in your family's closet, so I asked your mother—assuring her all along that it would make no difference in my decision to marry you." He pulled a kerchief from his waistcoat pocket and wiped the sweat off his brow. "So, you see, I must insist you become my wife, or I will tell the world what a whore your mother is, and that your sister is not a lord's daughter at all, but the by-blow of a lowly servant. A bastard!"

"You would want me even though I have given myself to another man?" Katelyn asked, incredulous.

He flinched as though she'd slapped him. His jaw tightened. "And I can forgive you that atrocity ... this one time, but never again, my dear. You will wear a chastity belt if need be, but no one will touch you, save me."

Katelyn could only imagine the hell he would put her through if she was forced to marry him.

"And what will you do if she does not marry you, aside from telling the world the secret?" Aunt Lillith asked.

"I will tell everyone who will listen that Marilyn is a bastard and that Katelyn is Sinjin Rayborne's mistress. A whore like her mother—and her sister—and the family name will be forever ruined. Even you with your titles, status, and great wealth will have to fight to save your position in Society, and I know how highly you regard your reputation."

Lillith lifted her chin and straightened her shoulders. "I do not take kindly to threats, my lord."

His lips thinned. "This is no threat. It is a promise. Either Katelyn marries me, or I shall tell the world about your family."

"Every family has secrets," Lillith said, a strange tone to her voice.

Katelyn's legs suddenly felt too weak to hold her. As much as she detested Lord Balliford, she knew she would marry him rather than ruin Marilyn and the rest of her family.

Aunt Lillith opened the door. "Lord Balliford, I would ask that you leave so that my niece may have time to consider her options."

His gaze shifted between them. "I would think there would be nothing to consider."

"You have already abused her. I see the bruises forming near her eye and the marks around her neck. I am not opposed to telling everyone what *you* have done."

His lips quirked. "Do you threaten me, Lady Nordland?"

"I have dealt with men like you before, my lord. Do not think to bully me, for I will not have it."

His gaze shifted to Katelyn. "I suggest you think long and hard about your answer, my dear. Your family's future is at stake. I shall return to my chamber and give you the opportunity to consider your options—or lack thereof." His gaze shifted over Katelyn. "And for God's sake, freshen up. You reek of his cologne."

"I shall meet you downstairs in one hour with my niece's answer," Aunt Lillith remarked.

"You truly are a bitch. I can see why your husband preferred others to you."

Aunt Lillith opened her mouth but closed it just as quickly.

He walked out of the chamber and Lillith shut the door firmly behind him.

"Aunt Lillith—I am so sorry."

"Do not apologize. None of this is your fault."

"What will I do? I cannot have him telling everyone about Marilyn's true parentage."

"Nor can you marry that monster."

"But if I don't marry him, he will try and destroy us. I know him, and what he's capable of."

Aunt Lillith sat down in the nearest chair and ran a hand down her face. "I am so angry with your mother, forever shirking her duty to you and Marilyn. Had she only been honest with us from the very beginning, none of this would have happened. I would have gladly paid off your father's debts, and given you and your sister the coming out you both deserved. We would have never found ourselves in such a position."

"But you heard Ronald. He said Father told him the truth years ago."

"Yes, and he filed the information away to use against us at a later date." She shook her head. "Of all the nerve!"

"Poor, poor Marilyn. She will be devastated if she discovers the truth."

"But you cannot make it right by marrying Ronald, because knowing him, he will hold the information and use it against you every chance he gets. Life as his wife would be intolerable, Katie. You would be in purgatory forever. Why should you be held accountable for the sins of your parents?" She took a deep breath, released it. "We will be honest with Marilyn and tell her the truth before someone else does. Also, tell your mother you know what she has done, and that she must be the one to pay the price. If the tables were turned, I would rather be a social pariah than know my niece is married to an intolerable man who beats her—because heed my words, he will beat and rape you if you were to marry him."

Katelyn glanced at her reflection in the mirror. A red mark in the shape of a handprint already showed on her pale skin, and her eye had started to swell. By this evening, a bruise will have formed, and everyone will know that something grim had transpired.

"You love someone else, Katelyn, and you have given yourself to that man. You need not apologize for it."

"I could not help myself, Aunt Lillith. Sinjin makes me so happy."

"Which is exactly why we must find Marilyn and speak with her before Ronald does."

"Speak with me about what?"

Aunt Lillith jumped at the sound of Marilyn's voice.

Marilyn shut the door behind her and glanced from Katelyn to Aunt Lillith and back again. "What is wrong?"

Katelyn and Lillith shared a look, and Katelyn nodded. "Go ahead, tell her."

Lillith cleared her throat. "My dear, there is no easy way for me to say this, so I shall just come out with it. You and Katelyn have different fathers."

Marilyn's eyes widened and she folded her hands in front of her and was silent for a full minute. "Well . . . that explains a lot, doesn't it?"

Katelyn had expected a completely different response.

"Father always treated us differently. I never sensed any affection from him, and didn't you ever wonder why he had little patience with me?"

"I am sorry, Marilyn." Katelyn walked toward her and gave her a hug.

"So who is my father?"

Lillith cleared her throat. "He was a servant who worked for your family many years ago. Understandingly, he was sent away shortly after the truth was discovered."

"A servant?" Marilyn stepped away from Katelyn, went to the window, and looked out. "Why tell me now?"

"Because your sister has fallen in love with Sinjin Rayborne and wishes to call off her wedding, and Lord Balliford knows the truth of your parentage and is threatening to use the information if Katelyn does not marry him."

Marilyn shook her head and turned to Katelyn. "And you would marry Balliford so he will remain quiet."

Katelyn nodded. "Yes, I would."

The sides of Marilyn's mouth lifted, but the smile did not reach her eyes. "You are very kind, Kate—but I honestly don't care what anyone thinks of me. Indeed, perhaps now I will not have to worry about Mother pushing me into a marriage with the likes of Lord Balliford, because no titled man will want me." For the first time in days she laughed, and Aunt Lillith smiled.

"There you have it, Katelyn. I will speak with Lord Balliford and tell him that the marriage is off for good. I want the two of you to prepare for tonight's festivities. No matter what happens, you will hold your heads high."

26

Katelyn had never been so happy in all her life. Ronald had left Claymoore Hall, and Sinjin's mother had given him her approval to marry her.

She could not believe her good fortune. Thank God she had come to the party, and had met the man who had changed her life so completely. Sinjin Rayborne, thirteenth viscount of Mawbry, was going to be her husband. They would have a houseful of children, and life as she knew it would be heaven on earth.

Oh happy day!

If only Marilyn could find such happiness. Her poor sister had taken the news that she was not their father's legitimate daughter surprisingly well. She had made mention to Katelyn before they came downstairs that she had always wondered, given the fact that their father had red hair, their mother blond, and Marilyn's hair was so dark.

Marilyn came up from behind Katelyn and hugged her tight. "You are positively glowing, dear sister."

"I am happy."

"I can tell." Marilyn's blue eyes sparkled.

"How are you?"

"Wonderful, now that I know you will no longer be marrying that old sod. Instead, you shall be Lady Mawbry." She gave a shiver. "What a difference a few days can make."

"I hope that you will find someone you truly love, Marilyn."

"Perhaps I shall find such a person in London."

"London?"

"Yes, Aunt Lillith says I can stay with her this summer."

"And will you?"

"Yes, most definitely. I hadn't realized how very much I missed her until she arrived at Claymoore Hall."

Lillith extracted herself from one of the other chaperones and handed them each a glass of punch. "That woman can talk your ear off if you allow her to." Her eyes widened. "I thought I would never get away."

Marilyn giggled and took a sip of punch, her assessing gaze taking in Lillith's gown. Made of pale blue silk, it was of the latest fashion and hugged her slender form, showcasing her tiny waist. "You look different, Aunt Lillith."

Lillith frowned. "Whatever do you mean?"

"You look younger, more radiant."

"You are too kind, my dear, but I assure you I look the same as I did yesterday."

"Perhaps being in a house full of gorgeous young men has brought back some of your spirit," Marilyn said with a grin.

"I bet you are right." Katelyn kissed Aunt Lillith's cheek. "You look beautiful, Aunt Lillith. Truly."

"As do you. I cannot tell you how proud I am of both of you. I have had the time of my life these past few days—well, aside from a few horrific moments—and I wouldn't trade this time for anything."

"We have enjoyed our time with you, too, and I was just

telling Katelyn that I do believe I will be staying in London for the summer."

Aunt Lillith clapped her hands together. "I am so happy to hear it." She beamed, and making sure no one nearby could hear, said, "Katelyn, I do hope that you will stay as well."

"Absolutely. I am already looking forward to it."

"Oh, look at who is coming our way," Marilyn said, glancing past Lillith and Katelyn.

Aunt Lillith followed her gaze and her eyes widened. Marilyn and Katelyn shared a smile.

Victor looked extremely handsome in a dark suit with a contrasting pale gray waistcoat. His unruly hair had been brushed back and held with a band, showing his fine bone structure in a new light.

"Ladies," he said with a formal bow. "You all look enchanting this evening."

"And you look very handsome, Victor," Katelyn said.

"Indeed," Marilyn added. "I didn't realize you could get your hair to actually lay flat."

Victor winked. "Jeffries is a master with a brush and comb, and a mystery ingredient."

"Mystery ingredient?"

He shrugged. "We quit asking years ago."

Katelyn noticed that her aunt had gone unusually quiet.

"Lady Katelyn, may I be the first to offer my congratulations. My brother just told me the news, and we are all delighted to have you as part of the family."

"You are too kind," Katelyn said, pleased to hear the family was happy by the news. "Speaking of your brother, where is he?"

"He is momentarily detained."

"Nothing serious, I hope?" Katelyn asked.

"Not at all. Rory needed his assistance. They'll be down momentarily."

Victor turned to Lillith. "Lady Nordland, could I have the next dance?"

"I do not dance, Lord Graston. I am a chaperone, after all."

"Come, Aunt Lillith, there are other chaperones who dance," Marilyn urged. "Go, have fun for once."

"Yes, have fun for once," Victor said, a challenging grin on his lips.

Katelyn nudged her toward Victor, who extended his arm.

"Oh, very well," she said, slipping her hand around his elbow. "I will be right back, girls."

Both Katelyn and Marilyn watched as Victor and Lillith approached the dance floor and the music began. Lillith looked like a radiant girl as she went through the steps, smiling and laughing.

"It's lovely to see her so happy," Katelyn said.

Marilyn hugged Katelyn. "Yes, it is. She deserves to be happy. We *all* deserve to be happy."

"Here, here."

Lady Anna motioned for them to join her from across the room. "Should we?" Marilyn asked.

"I'll be right there. I'm just going to get a breath of fresh air."

"I'll go with you."

"No, go ahead. I'll be right there," Katelyn said. "I just want a moment alone, count my lucky stars and all that."

Marilyn nodded in understanding. "Very well. Hurry up now."

Katelyn stepped out onto the verandah and took a deep breath. It was a perfect night, the stars were out in force, the moon large and bright. She could hardly wait until they could tell everyone the news of their upcoming wedding. Then they would no longer have to hide their love.

A brisk wind blew, and after saying a quick thank you to the heavens, she started back inside, when from the corner of her eye she saw a black figure approach from out of the darkness.

Before she could scream, a cloak was thrown over her head.

Katelyn was tossed unceremoniously into a waiting carriage. Her hands had been tied, and she struggled to push the cloak off of her. When she looked up, a chill raced up her spine.

Ronald sat across from her, fury in his eyes.

Katelyn screamed at the top of her lungs.

He slapped her hard and she screamed again.

He grabbed her roughly by the back of the neck and brought her face close to his. "Scream one more time and I'll kill you. Your lover will find your cold, lifeless body in a ditch."

"Will you at least untie my hands?" she asked, trembling with fear and anger.

"I will only untie you when we are a safe distance from Claymoore Hall and your lover."

Katelyn dug her nails into her palms and panicked as the lights from Claymoore Hall disappeared. She should have known that Ronald wouldn't give up without a fight.

A lump formed in her throat as she thought about the three people she loved most in this world—all oblivious to the fact she had been kidnapped right from under their noses. "They will come after me."

"And it will be too late."

"Too late?" Her pulse skittered. "What do you mean?"

"You will be married to me. By the time we reach Rose Alley, the priest will be there and the vows read. You will never see your family again."

"I will not marry you. I am in love with Sinjin Rayborne."

Ronald reached out and grabbed her chin with cold fingers. "I want you to understand that from this moment on you shall never again speak of Sinjin Rayborne. Is that clear?"

Giving any response proved difficult since his fingers continued to tighten on her chin.

When she remained silent, he released her and sat back in his seat. She closed her eyes, not wanting him to see her tears.

The rest of the trip was made in silence, and thankfully Katelyn fell asleep, awaking the following morning just as they pulled into Rose Alley.

Ronald's sister met them at the door, looking elated to see her brother. Her gaze settled on Katelyn for a moment, lingering on the bruises on her face, before she blinked a couple of times and looked at her brother with a bright smile. "Welcome home, my lord. How was your journey?"

"Long."

"You traveled all night?" she asked, her brows furrowing.

"Yes, we traveled all night," Ronald said with increasing irritation.

His sister recognized his foul mood and glanced nervously at Katelyn. "You both must be tired."

Ronald removed his coat and tossed it at his valet. The poor man barely had time to catch it, the buttons hitting him full in the face. "Did the priest arrive yet?"

"The priest?" Meredith asked, brows furrowed.

"Yes, Meredith, the priest. I sent George ahead for that very reason."

"George arrived in the early morning hours, but I knew nothing about a priest. I do not understand. Your marriage is set for later in the summer. Why—"

Ronald backtracked toward her. "It is not your affair, do you understand?"

She swallowed hard. "Yes, Ronald. I mean, my lord."

Ronald's face turned bright red. He removed his hat and gloves, and set them on the sideboard as they entered the house. "Meredith, please see that Katelyn is taken to her room, and she is not to leave there."

Meredith nodded, her expression turning concerned. Katelyn hoped she would be helpful to her. "Very well." She motioned for Katelyn to lead up the stairs.

"I shall see you both at dinner this evening, five o'clock sharp." Ronald's study door slammed shut behind him and Meredith flinched as though she'd been struck.

She looked confused and upset, nearly on the verge of tears.

As they entered Katelyn's chamber, Meredith watched Katelyn closely. She closed the door behind them. "How did you come by the bruises, Katelyn?"

"Your brother. He kidnapped me from Claymoore Hall."

"He would not do anything of the sort," Meredith said in disbelief.

"Where are my bags, then? Why am I dressed this way to travel?"

Clearing her throat, Meredith shook her head. "Ronald's anger sometimes gets the better of him."

"Do not try to make amends for his behavior."

"I wasn't. I merely—" She clamped her mouth shut and quickly looked away, toward the window.

"I told him I didn't want to marry him, and he kidnapped me and brought me back here. My aunt will come with the authorities."

Meredith's eyes widened. "Why did you break the engagement? I thought you loved Ronald. Your mother told him as much. In fact, she said you cared very deeply for him and were anxious to wed."

"My mother lied."

Meredith licked her thin lips. "So you will not marry."

"No, I am in love with another man, and I told Ronald as much."

"But the contract has been signed, and he paid your mother a fortune."

"My aunt will repay him every shilling and interest, too." Katelyn reached out and took Meredith's hand. "Meredith, I was at the ball with my sister and aunt, and left for only a second, and the next thing I know, I'm being shoved into a carriage and taken away from my family and the man I love. Help me."

She pulled away from Katelyn. "I am sorry, I can't."

"Meredith, please, I need your help," Katelyn pleaded.

"Ronald is stubborn. When he wants something, he will stop at nothing to have it." She lifted her chin. "And he wants you, Katelyn."

"Meredith!" Ronald bellowed from downstairs, and she jumped.

"I must go and see what he wants."

"Help me, Meredith," Katelyn said one more time before the other woman shut the door.

Sinjin made another pass of the ballroom and the nearby rooms. His brothers were each taking a floor, Jeffries and a few footmen were checking the grounds, and Lillith and Marilyn were searching their chambers in the hope Katelyn would surface.

His heart sank to his toes when he saw Lillith and Marilyn without Katelyn. "I checked both our chambers and she's not there."

"What about her belongings?"

"Everything is how we left it," Marilyn said, her worried expression mirroring her aunt's.

"He took her. I know it," Lillith said, tears welling in her eyes. "She told Marilyn she was going outside for just an instant, and that is the last she saw of her." She put her hands together in prayer and pressed them to her lips. "I should have stayed with her."

"We'll find her, Lillith," Sinjin said with conviction. "Victor is speaking with Jeffries and the other servants to see who has left the manor this evening."

Marilyn shook her head. "I should have known that bastard would do something like this."

27

Someone was pounding on the front door.

Katelyn's heart slammed against her ribs. She couldn't get out of the room. She'd already searched every drawer for the key, to no avail.

Please God, let it be Sinjin or the police, and not a priest.

The knocking stopped and she heard voices, but she couldn't make them out.

She pounded on the door, shouting for someone to open it.

Silence met her plea.

Rushing toward the window, she tried to open it. The ledge was not very deep—one wrong move and she would slip and fall, and perhaps even kill herself.

From her bedchamber she could see only into the back garden, so she had no idea who was visiting. Perhaps it was only a neighbor come to visit now that Lord Balliford had returned.

She seriously doubted Ronald would allow anyone past the front door, though.

Please let it be, she silently pleaded as she tried the window again.

She stopped when she heard Ronald's voice raised in anger, and then another man's voice, calling out her name, demanding to see her.

Sinjin!

Sinjin stared down the barrel of Ronald's pistol and did his best to not flinch or show fear. Not the easiest task when the man holding the pistol had a wild look in his eyes.

"Lord Balliford, please," Lillith said, keeping her voice level as she stepped in front of Sinjin.

"Lady Nordland, if you think for one moment your presence will stop me from blowing Lord Mawbry's head off, then you are sadly mistaken. I will take this shot, with you in the way or not."

Sinjin gently pushed Lillith aside. "Thank you, Lillith, but I do not need your protection."

"Ronald, are you okay?" came the woman's voice from the other side of the study door.

It was the same middle-aged woman who had answered the front door. Sinjin had walked straight past her into the hallway, asking for Lord Balliford, and he had found him in the small study. Ronald's fingers were stained black, and there were ink smudges on his face.

And now they all stood in the small study where Balliford had been writing a letter.

No doubt to Katelyn's mother.

"Will you please tell Katelyn that Sinjin is here to take her home?" he said to the woman standing in the doorway.

Ronald's eyes narrowed. "She will most certainly not. You are not welcome on my property, and I would ask you kindly to leave. If you do not, I shall remove you with force."

"Do you think I fear you?" Sinjin asked, fury of what Balliford might have done to Katelyn nearly choking him.

Ronald's smile thinned. "I doubt you fear anyone." He lifted the bell and rang it. A tall, bald-headed, barrel-chested man about a decade older than Sinjin arrived at the study door. "Yes, my lord."

"Please escort my guests out and see that they leave the property."

The servant moved toward Sinjin, but Lillith stopped him by grabbing his arm. "We will leave . . . once I have my niece, and not before."

The servant did not take another step, and surprisingly walked out of the room a second later. "Your niece is not leaving here, Lady Nordland. She is to be my bride . . . by the end of the day. Indeed, the priest will be here at any moment."

"She does not want to marry you, Balliford," Sinjin said, trying to ignore the fact that a pistol was trained on him. "She is going to marry me."

The sound of knocking came from a distance, and the faintest sound of a woman's voice could be heard. White-hot anger raced through Sinjin. "What have you done with her?"

"That *is* Katelyn," Lillith said, rushing for the door, but she was met on the other side by Ronald's sister, who blocked her.

"Move out of my way," Lillith said, pushing the woman with force, but she didn't budge. "Katelyn! Where are you?"

"Here!" came the cry from directly above.

Sinjin was following after Lillith when he heard the distinct clicking sound.

"Do not move another step." Balliford had another pistol, this one trained on Lillith's back.

Lillith turned, her eyes wide. "Do not do something you will surely regret."

"I already regret allowing Katelyn to attend a party with her sister where she was seduced by a scoundrel. Clearly, she needed a chaperone herself. I shall regret letting her attend that party for the rest of my life."

"Ronald, perhaps you should listen to them," Meredith said, trembling. "Katelyn is not happy, and she told me that she loves Sinjin. She is going to marry him. You are not in your right—"

"Be quiet!" Ronald yelled, and Meredith jumped.

"My niece is in love with Sinjin, and she is going to marry him," Lillith said. "Let her go, Lord Balliford."

"If you wish, we can finish this outside, away from the ladies," Sinjin said with a calm he didn't feel.

"Why don't you leave and never return. What is the name they call you and your brothers—the Rakehells of Rochester," he said, a lascivious smile on his face. "Soon you shall grow tired of her . . . just as you have grown tired of every other woman you've possessed. Why do you not just walk away, and count your blessings that you will no longer have to worry about her? You fucked her and got what you wanted. Be grateful no more is required of you."

Infuriated by his words, Sinjin said, "I want to marry Katelyn. She could very well be carrying my child."

Ronald's face turned bright red. "You seduced her. Soon she will forget about you, and I will make her happy. If there is a child, I shall raise it as my own."

Meredith had moved slightly, giving just enough room for Lillith to slide past her.

Seeing the movement, Ronald fired the gun.

Lillith felt the swoosh of air pass by and then heard the other woman gasp.

When she turned Meredith had fallen to her knees, a bright red circle of blood growing on her chest.

"Oh my God," Ronald yelled. "What have I done?"

Katelyn heard the gun blast and immediately after, the sound of footsteps coming her way.

A chill rushed up her spine.

"I don't have a key," Sinjin said from the other side, and she nearly fainted with relief, so happy to hear his voice. "Stand back. I'll kick the door in."

Katelyn did as he asked. "I'm clear!"

The door burst open and Sinjin appeared. Katelyn rushed into his arms. "I heard a shot. What happened?"

"Ronald shot Meredith."

"Oh my God."

"Are you okay? Did he hurt you?" He touched her cheek tenderly, his blue eyes full of fury upon seeing the bruises. "That son of a bitch. I'll kill him."

"Let's just go, Sinjin. Please. Let's get out of here."

They started down the staircase, and Katelyn looked over the banister to see Meredith laying in the hallway, her face white as a sheet, her gown stained red, and at her side Ronald wept, holding on to her hand, bringing it to his lips.

Aunt Lillith stood at the foot of the stairs, near the front door, motioning for them to hurry.

"Do not leave me, Meredith," Ronald pleaded, kissing each of her hands. "Please." His voice was full of anguish.

Meredith opened her eyes. "I love you, Ronald. I always have. You and only you."

Ronald looked up and, seeing the three of them, screamed, "Leave us! This is all your fault. If you hadn't of—"

Meredith lifted her hand and caressed her brother's cheek. "Shh, my dearest. Tell me how much you love me."

It was obvious to all of them in that moment that the two shared a different relationship than that of siblings.

"Don't leave me," Ronald said, his cheek against her chest. "Please, you are my life . . . my love . . . my everything."

"Let's go," Sinjin said, rushing for the door.

"Did you send for the surgeon?" Ronald yelled at his valet, who nodded and looked on helplessly.

Katelyn glanced back at the man who had caused her such grief, and for the first time ever, she felt sorry for him. He had stood in judgment of others all his life. How ironic given his own family's secret.

Sinjin helped Lillith and then Katelyn into the carriage before joining them. He sat beside Katelyn, put his arm around her, and held her close.

Blood splatters stained Lillith's gown, and she turned to look at Rose Alley as they pulled away. She pressed her lips together and shook her head.

The sound of a gunshot blast pierced the quiet, and Sinjin shouted out the window. "Stop the carriage."

"Don't go in there alone, Sinjin. Please," Katelyn begged.

He kissed her forehead. "I'll be right back. I promise."

"He'll be all right, Katelyn," Aunt Lillith added, hoping to ease her fears.

Sinjin walked right into the house.

"How utterly horrifying," Lillith said, shaking her head.

"I just want to get out of here," Katelyn said, watching the front door.

Sinjin walked out a second later, his expression intense. "Ronald has killed himself."

Katelyn and Lillith both gasped.

"I'm staying until the coroner arrives. I need to give a full statement. The driver will take you to King's Crossing. I'll meet you at the inn by the bridge as soon as I am able."

"We can wait with you," Aunt Lillith said. "I'm sure it won't take long."

"This is no place for you, ladies. Go ahead, and I shall be along shortly." He leaned in and kissed Katelyn. "I shall see you soon."

"Please hurry," Katelyn urged, hating the thought of leaving him behind.

He nodded at the driver and stood on the stone pathway as the carriage pulled away.

Both Katelyn and Lillith watched him until they pulled onto the main road; then Sinjin walked in long strides toward the manor and disappeared inside.

"He'll be fine, my dear," Lillith said with a reassuring smile. "Do not worry. Plus, King's Crossing is not so far. We shall make it there by suppertime, and before you know it, Sinjin will be joining us."

Katelyn nodded, so happy her aunt was with her now. "What if something—"

"Ronald is dead, Kate. He cannot hurt him."

"Of course. I'm being silly."

They sat in silence for a few minutes. "Poor Meredith," Lillith murmured. "Such a sad creature she was."

"Did you know about Ronald and Meredith?" Katelyn asked, still reeling from the truth.

"I confess that I suspected something was amiss when my husband made a strange comment about the relationship Ronald had with his sister. I never thought much of it until your mother told me the news of your engagement. My fears were always there, and I spoke to your mother about my concerns, but of course, she said it was hogwash. But the moment I saw Ronald and Meredith together, and saw the way they looked at each other, I realized it was the truth."

Ironically, now that Katelyn knew the truth, she thought back on the odd behavior she had seen on occasion between the two siblings. And yet he had seemed so prim and proper. "The secrets one keeps behind closed doors."

"Indeed," Lillith said absently. "We must put this all behind us, my dear. The future is bright, and you have everything to look forward to. Just think, soon you shall be Lady Mawbry."

"What of you, Aunt Lillith? Do you think you will ever remarry?"

"No," she blurted, as though the very idea was preposterous. "I have enjoyed my freedom far too much to ever be tied down by a man."

"But perhaps one day you shall find a man who changes your way of thinking. A man who is worthy of you."

Lillith smiled a little. "Perhaps. I am more concerned about Marilyn finding a husband now."

"I just hope Mother does not arrange a marriage for her."

Lillith's eyes widened. "I would not allow it. Plus, it seems that Marilyn has feelings for Sinjin's brother."

"You mean Victor?" Katelyn asked, unable to keep the surprise from her voice.

"Yes, the two of them have grown quite close."

"Yes, they are friends."

Lillith lifted her brows. "I think they are more than just friends, Katelyn."

"Whatever gives you that idea?"

She shrugged. "Call it intuition."

"They get along very well, but I assure you that they are friends. Marilyn has told me so herself."

Lillith frowned "When was this?"

"A few days ago . . ."

"Well, anything can change in a matter of days," Lillith said, glancing out the window.

28

Katelyn and her aunt arrived at the small inn on the outskirts of King's Crossing just as the sun set.

Lillith went to her room and ordered a bath and a cup of tea, while Katelyn paced the floor in her rented room.

She had hoped Sinjin would catch up to the carriage before they arrived at King's Crossing, and every second that passed she feared they had made a huge mistake in leaving Rose Alley without him.

What if the servants had accused him of killing Ronald and Meredith, and they had taken him to prison? They should have left at least the footman behind to make sure everything would be okay. Perhaps she should send a courier to Claymoore Hall and let Lady Rochester, Victor, and Rory know what had occurred. Better to be safe than sorry.

Someone rapped lightly at the door. She rushed toward it and opened it, biting back disappointment when it was only the innkeeper's wife with tea. The woman set the tray on the small side table. "Are you sure I can't interest you in a bath, my lady?"

"No, thank you, though."

"Actually, do bring us up a bath," Sinjin said, stepping into the room.

Elated, Katelyn rushed into his arms.

"Right away, sir." The innkeeper's wife brushed past them and closed the door behind her.

Katelyn squeezed him tight, so relieved to see him. "I was getting so worried."

"I'm sorry, it could not be helped," Sinjin said, kissing her forehead, her nose, and her lips. "Nothing or no one will ever come between us again."

She rested her cheek against his wide chest, hugging him tight to her.

His hand moved up and down her back in a soothing gesture. "I cannot wait to marry you." He lifted her skirts, his hands cupping her bottom. "Do you think we have time before the bath arrives?"

"Scandalous man," she said, even as desire rushed through her veins. He stepped away, pulled off his shirt, and began unbuttoning his pants. She watched him, taking in every glorious inch of his body. He was perfection, and she was thrilled knowing he would be her husband.

His hands were at the back of her gown, unlacing the binds. Soon her undergarments joined the dress and she stood before him with nothing on save her stockings.

Smiling wolfishly, he lifted her in his arms and walked to the bed, where he followed her down onto the surprisingly soft mattress.

She sat up, her hands bracing his hips, and kissed the head of his thick cock.

His breath came out in a hiss, his hips flexing against her. Growing more daring, she opened her mouth wider, sliding her tongue over the head, down the ridge, and back up again.

Long fingers rested on her shoulders and tightened there. She glanced up at him and felt a surge of pleasure ripple through her at the heat in those brilliant blue eyes.

After a few more licks, she took him into her mouth, as far as she could without choking. He grasped the base of his cock with one hand, and her fingers covered his, following his instruction. He smiled down at her, obviously pleased.

She concentrated fully on what she was doing, and soon he was pumping against her mouth, the next second bracing her, and the next pulling away. "I want to be inside you."

He touched her between her legs, to the hot core that even now pulsed with the desire to be filled by his long cock.

He slid into her, his thick rod filling her in one quick stroke. Her inner muscles clenched him tight, and he moaned low in his throat as heat surrounded him. She watched him, his heavy-lidded gaze, as he watched her in turn. His gaze left hers to shift down her body slowly to her breasts. He leaned forward, took a nipple into his mouth, played with it, tugged it with his teeth, sucking, laving.

The sensation went from her breasts straight to her cunny where he filled her so completely. Her fingers wove through his long, dark hair, and a joy so intense rushed over her that tears clogged her throat.

She would enjoy this for the rest of her life. It was just the two of them, together forever.

Her nails dug into his scalp and she pulled him closer to her breast. His strokes slowed and she lifted her hips to meet each thrust.

Sinjin gloried in the fact he would have Katelyn forever. That no one would ever take her from him again. She watched him now, her beautiful green eyes dark and full of passion.

Her inner muscles tightened around him and she cried out his name. The headboard hit the wall with each thrust, and not wanting to alert all the patrons to what was happening behind closed doors, Sinjin lifted Katelyn and took her down to the floor.

Katelyn's back came into contact with the soft rug, and as Sinjin settled between her thighs, she sighed. She had been seconds from orgasm again, and with each long stroke, she drew that much closer.

Sinjin swelled within her, his balls drawing closer to his body. Katelyn bit her lip, her soft moans and the throbbing of her channel around his cock, sending him over the edge to his own climax.

Sinjin cleared his throat and the guests at Claymoore Hall fell silent.

He motioned for Katelyn to come forward, and Lillith nudged her. "This is your moment, my dear."

Whispers followed her as she made her way up the pathway to the head of the table where Sinjin sat, his mother to his right.

She stopped a foot away from him, and he took her hand, brought it to his lips, and kissed it lightly. Stunned gasps filled the room.

"I would like to present my fiancée, Lady Katelyn."

The surprised guests slowly broke into loud applause, which grew louder by the second, thanks in kind to Rory and Victor, who clapped heartily.

They had arrived at Claymoore Hall to find many of the guests had left, and none seemed the wiser that Sinjin, Katelyn, and Lillith had even been gone. Marilyn had stayed in her room, save for attending tea, at which time she said both her sister and aunt were not feeling well. A head cold, she had muttered.

Sinjin's absence would have been more duly noted than her own, yet his brothers had managed to divert all the attention.

Until now.

There were a lot of disappointed women in the room, most of all Lady Celeste, who stood in open-mouthed astonishment, her gaze shifting from Sinjin to Katelyn and back again. Her chaperone made her way to her side. Her effort to comfort her charge met with resistance, and Celeste rushed from the room.

Thomas stood in the back of the room with Lady Anna, looking awfully cozy, and both Marilyn and Lillith beamed.

Sinjin motioned to the servants, and they brought in trays of champagne. Once everyone had been served, Sinjin said, "I would like to make a toast to the two most important women in my life—Lady Katelyn and my mother, who without her assistance, I would not have met my beautiful fiancée."

Lady Rochester's face lit up and she embraced Katelyn. She had been delightful from the moment they had stepped out of the carriage. She seemed genuinely happy, and Katelyn was relieved she did not disapprove of Sinjin's choice in any way.

"Welcome to the family," Victor said, hugging her tight.

"Thank you, Victor. I can hardly wait to be your sister-in-law."

Rory kissed her on the mouth, and Sinjin pulled him away. "Careful, brother," Sinjin said teasingly, though his voice held an edge to it.

The rest of the evening was spent celebrating, and both Sinjin and Katelyn called it an early night, exhausted from all they'd been through these past days.

Sinjin lifted her in his arms and took her to his chamber overlooking the gardens. She walked out onto the balcony and he stepped behind her.

"It's so beautiful."

"You are beautiful."

She turned in his arms. "Are you happy?"

"Happier than I've ever been." He hugged her tight, kissing the top of her head.

"As am I."

"I am glad to hear it. I admit that when at first I couldn't find you, I wondered if you had changed your mind about me."

"I would never leave you."

His gaze searched hers. "Promise."

"Promise," she said with a grin.

His lips curved in a smile. "I hope we have a child soon, and I hope he or she favors you."

Her heart leapt. "I love you, Sinjin Rayborne."

He kissed her softly, and whispered against her lips, "And I love you, my soon-to-be Lady Mawbry."

Please turn the page for an exciting sneak peek at
VICTOR, the second novel in
the Rakehells of Rochester series,
coming in April 2010!

1

Victor Rayborne looked out over the grounds of his family's country manor. It had been a fortnight since his mother had made the announcement that he and his brothers must find brides or lose everything. His eldest sibling Sinjin had succeeded in winning the hand of the beautiful Katelyn Davenport, a woman who at the beginning of said party had been engaged to another man.

A man who now lay dead by his own hand.

Releasing a sigh, he scrubbed a hand over his face. Unlike his brother, who had fallen in love so quickly, Victor had not found a woman who caught his fancy among the young debutantes that his mother had brought to Claymoore Hall. However, he had found a chaperone that intrigued him.

Lillith Winthrop, Lady Nordland, widow and aunt to Katelyn and her sister Marilyn, was a beautiful blonde with striking hazel eyes and a body built for pleasure. The attraction had been instantaneous, and yet everything he'd heard about Lily revolved around her virtuous reputation for being the very picture of decorum and an example of what every young lady should aspire to be.

In short, she was the opposite of what kind of woman he was usually attracted to. Actresses and dancers had always been his type, much like his last mistress, the beautiful twenty-five-year-old Selene.

The door to his chamber opened, and his brother Rory appeared, his messy dark hair and rumpled appearance saying he'd just come from a liaison. Rory had been gifted with striking good looks that women found irresistible. When he entered a room, men held tight to their wives, daughters, and mistresses.

"You look like hell. Where have you been?"

Rory flashed a wolfish smile. "With the incomparable Lady Anna."

Lady Anna had entertained both Victor and Rory in her chamber just days into the party. Since that event, Victor had steered clear of the woman, but apparently Rory could not get enough of the sexual Anna. "I'm surprised her chaperone has not caught on yet."

"Yes, well, there is something to be said about having a chaperone that is both hard of hearing and has weak eyesight." Rory fell into a chair beside the fireplace.

"Perhaps you should ask Lady Anna to marry you?"

Rory snorted. "She is an excellent lover, but I cannot imagine having Anna as a wife. I could never trust her."

"Isn't that a bit like the pot calling the kettle black?"

"Yes, well . . ." Rory brushed his hands through his hair and yawned loudly. "What of you? I noticed you dancing with a certain widow last night. Do I sense interest on your part?"

His brothers knew him better than anyone, so it was no use denying it. "Yes, I find Lillith intriguing."

"She's lovely. Hard to believe she's the aunt. I would have

taken her more as the sister. Oh, and you'll love this; Lady Anna says that Lillith is unattainable."

Unattainable? Ironically, the news fascinated him even more. A woman as beautiful as Lillith, and a wealthy, titled widow at that, should have men beating down her door. Chances were she wasn't interested. Little wonder given what he now knew of her husband.

Every time he approached Lily she looked ready to bolt— until last night. Last night he had sensed a change in her when they had danced. She had laughed and smiled the entire time. He did take into account that said happiness could have been due to the fact her niece had become engaged, and less about her dancing partner, but he'd felt elated, nonetheless.

"Oh my God, you really like her." Rory sat up straight now, his lips curved into a knowing smile. "I'll wager you one hundred pounds that you can't get her into bed."

A part of Victor rebelled at making such a wager, and yet the rake in him couldn't resist the challenge. He and Rory had always had a strange rivalry. "Make it your gold pocket watch and we have a deal."

Rory frowned. "The one Grandfather gave me?"

Victor nodded. "Yes, the very one, which you never use." He had secretly coveted the piece for years. When Rory had received the treasured antique after their grandfather's passing, Victor had been crushed. Worse still, his brother rarely used it.

Rory's brows furrowed as he contemplated the wager. Then he stood and extended his hand. "Very well, you shall have the pocket watch, but only if you seduce Lady Nordland. And you will not just bed her and be done with it, but rather captivate her completely and make her your mistress."

Victor wasn't sure about his ability to "captivate her completely," but bedding her he could do, despite the fact her reputation suggested otherwise.

He shook Rory's hand. "Done," he said, with more confidence than he felt.

Lillith lifted her face to the sun. It was a glorious day, and she felt extremely gratified as she watched her niece Katelyn and Katelyn's fiancé Sinjin walk hand in hand along the grounds under the watchful eye of Sinjin's proud mother, Lady Rochester.

Any misgivings the countess might have had about her eldest son marrying Katelyn had apparently been put aside, for she positively beamed as she took tea with her friends.

If only Marilyn had found love with one of the Rayborne brothers or their male guests, then the party would have been an even bigger success. For a short while Lillith had thought her niece had fallen in love with Victor, especially when she had happened upon them kissing in the labyrinth.

However, Marilyn had assured her that Victor was nothing more than a friend. Lillith didn't push for more answers, as a part of her honestly didn't want to know. Admittedly, she'd been more than a little jealous when she'd witnessed the kiss.

Victor was a decade younger than Lillith, in his prime, and he made her feel small and feminine, and yes, even desired—something she had not felt for many, many years. True, she had been pursued by older gentlemen, content on taking a well-respected widow as their wife, but none of those men thrilled her the way Victor Rayborne did.

No, Victor brought out something in her that made her feel like a girl again. Indeed, he made her wonder what it would be like to behave badly. A new concept, given that she had spent the past two decades playing the elegant, loyal, ever-virtuous wife to a detestable man who paraded his many male lovers before her.

She had hoped to have children of her own, but her fifteen-year marriage had yielded no such blessing. Little wonder, given her husband had rarely visited her bed. The night of her wedding had been the stuff of nightmares, and she had come to hate Winfred's drunken visits. What a fantastic actor he had been during their courtship. If she could have only guessed that behind the sheep's clothing lay a malicious wolf.

But there was no use in crying over what had happened. Those days were long behind her. She could only move on to what could be.

"Lady Nordland," a deep voice said from behind her, and she turned slowly, her heart missing a beat.

Victor's brilliant blue eyes slid down her body and up again. His dark, wavy hair fell to his broad shoulders in wild disarray, and he had the most arresting features—square jaw, jutting cheekbones, and lovely, full lips. He was dressed in black from his shirt and snug pants, which hugged muscular thighs, to the slightly worn Hessians. His dark attire made his light eyes even more vivid, she realized.

"Lord Graston, good afternoon." She managed to keep her tone casual, a difficult feat when exhilaration rushed through her veins.

"May I?" he asked, motioning to the chair beside her.

She nodded. "Of course."

He sat in the chair, his long legs stretching out before him. He made her thoughts turn positively scandalous, and she wondered if the rumors she had heard this past week were true. Lord Graston was a gracious, well-endowed lover with incredible stamina. Lillith shifted in her seat. Truth be told, he excited her like no other man had.

Nearby, someone laughed out loud. Lillith glanced at the nearby table to see a young woman and her chaperone watching her closely. Were they laughing at her because Victor was showing interest?

"Lily, when will you stop worrying about what others think?" he whispered, his voice far too intimate.

"I am a chaperone, Lord Graston. And people talk if a young man spends too much time in the company of a widow."

He sighed heavily. "Who cares what anyone else thinks? Let them speculate."

If only it were that easy. She didn't want to destroy her hard-earned reputation in a few days time. And yet, he was right. Why did she always care what others thought of her? Why should she not savor the fact a young man found her desirable?

"You are leaving today?" he asked, his voice hinting at disappointment.

"We had planned to, but my nieces have talked me into another day."

His face lit up. "I am glad to hear it. Perhaps they will persuade you into staying another week."

"I'm afraid a week is out of the question," she said, feeling a blush work its way up her neck. "I have obligations I must attend to in London."

"Can I visit you in London?" he asked, so nonchalantly he might have been talking about the weather.

It was not unusual for her to welcome friends and new acquaintances to her home, but usually those "friends" were women, not men.

"We will be family soon, Lily," he said, as though reading her thoughts. "You need not worry what others would think."

Yes, they would be family soon, but given his reputation, no one would misconstrue what his visits meant. "Of course you can visit, but I thought you were returning to Rochester."

"I am returning to Rochester, but not for long. I suddenly have a strong desire to see London again."

Her stomach tightened. She understood innuendos well enough, the heated glint in his gaze, the way his stare burned into her, over her, taking everything in with a glance. The question was why, when he had a bevy of beautiful young women at his disposal, all aching for the chance to get to know him better in the hopes of marrying him, did he want her? A widow. *A barren widow*, she thought with growing dismay.

"Will you not ask me why I have such a strong desire to see London again?"

He could be so very exasperating! "Very well, Lord Graston, *why* do you yearn to see London again so soon after leaving?"

He reached for her hand, his long fingers sliding between hers. "Because I want to be near you, Lily. I would follow you to the ends of the earth if need be."

She knew rakes and scoundrels well—all the charming phrases they used to try and get what they wanted. Did women actually fall for this drivel?

His piercing, long-lashed eyes held her pinned to the spot and she found it very difficult to breathe. Apparently, she was no different than other women.

"You have grown quiet, Lily."

"Have I?" she asked, her voice coming out harsher than intended. "I suppose I do not know what you want me to say. It is well known your mother would like you to marry, and I am obviously not the best choice."

His brows rose. "Why would that be?"

She cleared her throat. "I am widowed, and I am—a good deal older than you."

"I have had many lovers older than yourself," he said, his eyes intense as he stared at her.

The admission made her strangely excited. She had not planned on getting into such an intimate discussion with him, but it was intriguing and comforting to know that he'd had lovers older than she was.

She pulled her hand from beneath his and reached for her fan. Flicking it open, she waved it rapidly to cool her heated cheeks. Good lord, she was beginning to perspire, and the more he stared, the hotter she became.

He leaned near and whispered in her ear, "Perhaps I can visit your bedchamber this evening?"

The breath lodged in her throat. Clearly she had not heard him correctly. "I do believe you are trying to unnerve me, Lord Graston."

His grin was devastating, and for a breathless moment she envisioned him naked, making love to her with expert skill, bringing her to climax for the first time. Heat swept through her body, making her nipples pebble against her bodice and the flesh between her thighs tingle.

It seemed he could read her every wicked thought, for his eyes took on a sensual quality, and as he watched her watch him, his smile deepened. "And am I succeeding?"

He leaned toward her and she sat up straighter, squaring her shoulders. "Lord Graston, certainly there is another woman here who you could flirt with who might be more receptive to your charms."

"I think you are receptive, Lily. You just need to let yourself go. Have you not wondered what it would be like to have a lover—a younger lover who would appreciate you, and per-haps, even surprise you in the bedchamber?"

The blood in her veins positively simmered. She waved her fan faster.

His gaze wandered over her face. "I wonder what you would look like with your hair down, falling about my pillow in wild disarray, your luscious body wrapped in my sheets."

The visual images and his sensual tone were too much. She stood so fast, she nearly upended the chair. Though no one sat close enough to hear their discussion, she was aware that they were being watched.

Always the lady, rather than storm off, she forced a smile. "Lord Graston, it was a pleasure."

"I have upset you." It wasn't a question. The smile had left his handsome face.

"I am unused to being talked to in such a manner, Lord Graston. I am no whore."

Oh, dear. Victor had hit a nerve.

"Forgive me, Lady Nordland. I only know what others have said, and I understand your husband was not—the most gracious of husbands." Victor regretted the words the moment they left his mouth, and even more so when Lillith turned on her heel and left.

He sat there for a moment, pondering his choices. Aware that others had been watching them, he stood slowly and walked in the opposite direction.

Avoiding eye contact at all costs, he continued at a leisurely pace until he rounded the manor and raced to the servants' entrance. Taking the stairs two at a time, he made it to the second floor in record time and smiled to himself upon seeing Lillith just ahead, chin lifted high, shoulders straight, her steps rushed.

She was furious.

"Lily," he said, stopping a few feet from her.

She stopped abruptly, took a deep breath, and turned.

His stomach tightened. Her expression was as cold as ice.

"I wanted to apologize to you. I didn't mean to come across so—"

"Arrogant? Callous? Rude?" she said through clenched teeth.

He opened his mouth, and then closed it just as quickly.

Her beautiful hazel eyes widened as she waited for his explanation.

"Yes, all of those things and more," he said, choosing his words carefully. "I meant no disrespect. I feel comfortable with you, Lily. Perhaps more comfortable than I should, and I oftentimes speak my mind without thought of consequence."

Her cheeks were flushed, her eyes sparkling with anger. He wanted desperately to throw her over his shoulder, take her to his room, and make love to her until she couldn't stand.

"Well, I accept your apology," she said, her tongue sliding over her bottom lip.

Oh, she shouldn't have done that. He wanted to taste those soft rose pink lips, to nibble at them, and do innumerable things to that mouth. He could already anticipate sliding his cock past—

"Is that all, Lord Graston?" she asked, a tawny brow lifting as she awaited his response.

"No," he said, and unable to resist, he took a step closer and pulled her against him.

Her fan fell to the ground and she gasped, looking up at him with a mixture of shock and something that resembled horror.

"I've wanted to kiss you from the moment I met you," he whispered against her lips, before kissing her softly.

Their breath mingled, and he could feel her heart racing against his own. Tentatively, he kissed her again. When she didn't pull away, he deepened the kiss, his tongue teasing the seam of her lips.

To his surprise, Lillith's hands moved to his chest, and her hands tightened into fists, catching the material of his shirt. She leaned into him, her mouth opening wider, her tongue sweeping against his.

Sweet acceptance.

She moaned, and the sound was like music to his ears.

He held her tight to him, one hand at the small of her back, the other weaving through the curls at the nape of her neck. As the kiss became more heated, his hand moved over her firm buttocks.

She abruptly wrenched away from him, her eyes wide with alarm.

A slender hand covered her mouth and she blinked in disbelief.

"Lily," he said, reaching out for her, wanting to rekindle the fire, but she shook her head.

"I'm sorry, I can't do this," she said, taking a step away from him, and then she turned and ran.